Searchin
by Ka

'Would you like to dance?'

Instead of answering, Amira just stepped closer
to Marcus. He took her into his embrace. He'd
been waiting all day to do this, waiting all day to
lean his cheek against hers, breathe in her
wonderful perfume and feel her body close to his.
They danced together as if they'd been doing it for
years. As minutes ticked by, they were hardly
aware of one song passing into the next.

Slowly Amira lifted her head and gazed into his
eyes. 'You gave me a wonderful day today. I'll
remember it always.'

She was talking as if she'd never see him again.
That was what he'd planned. In fact, in the back
of his mind, he'd decided he would take her to
bed tonight if she was willing and say goodbye
in the morning. But now he knew she was too
innocent for a one-night-stand, and he couldn't
do that to her. He also knew that one day of being
with her wasn't enough. She'd brought light and
sunshine into his life again, and he wasn't ready to
give that up...

The Royal Treatment
by Maureen Child

ᕭ ᖆᐷᕬᕤ

'You might as well go, Jade. You're not getting in.'

'You know,' she said, giving him a thoughtful, up-and-down look, 'you really should work on your people skills, JT. They were never your strong point.'

'Oh, that's good, coming from you.'

She flicked him a warning look, but Jeremy knew the palace gates were strong enough to hold off a tank, so they'd probably be able to protect him from a single reporter.

Even Jade.

'Besides, my people skills are fine, babe,' he assured her. 'It's my 'reporter' skills you seem to be having trouble with. And frankly, if you don't like 'em, then I must be doing something right.'

'As charming as ever, I see,' Jade retorted.

'You used to think I was pretty damn charming.'

'I used to believe in Santa Claus, too.'

Available in September 2003 from Silhouette Desire

Searching for Her Prince
by Karen Rose Smith
(Crown and Glory)
and
The Royal Treatment
by Maureen Child
(Crown and Glory)

All in the Game
by Barbara Boswell
and
Do You Take This Enemy?
by Sara Orwig
(Stallion Pass)

The Sheriff & the Amnesiac
by Ryanne Corey
and
Comanche Vow
by Sheri WhiteFeather

Searching for Her Prince
KAREN ROSE SMITH

The Royal Treatment
MAUREEN CHILD

SILHOUETTE®
DESIRE™

*Silhouette, Silhouette Desire and Colophon
are registered trademarks of Harlequin Books S.A.,
used under licence.*

*First published in Great Britain 2003
Silhouette Books, Eton House, 18-24 Paradise Road,
Richmond, Surrey TW9 1SR*

The publisher acknowledges the copyright holders of the
individual works as follows:

Searching for Her Prince © Harlequin Books S.A. 2002
The Royal Treatment © Harlequin Books S.A. 2002

*Special thanks and acknowledgement are given to Karen Rose Smith and
Maureen Child for their contributions to the Crown and Glory series.*

ISBN 0 373 04876 9

51-0903

*Printed and bound in Spain
by Litografia Rosés S.A., Barcelona*

SILHOUETTE®

DESIRE™

*proudly presents
a brand-new series*

CROWN AND GLORY

*Where royalty and romance
go hand in hand...*

July 2003 - Silhouette Desire 2-in-1
Her Royal Husband by Cara Colter
The Princess Has Amnesia! by Patricia Thayer

September 2003 - Silhouette Desire 2-in-1
Searching for Her Prince by Karen Rose Smith
The Royal Treatment by Maureen Child

November 2003 - Silhouette Desire 2-in-1
Taming the Prince by Elizabeth Bevarly
Royally Pregnant by Barbara McCauley

SEARCHING FOR HER PRINCE

by

Karen Rose Smith

KAREN ROSE SMITH

is a former teacher and home decorator. Now spinning stories and creating characters keeps her busy. But she also loves listening to music, shopping and sharing with friends, as well as spending time with her son and her husband. Married for thirty years, she and her husband have always called Pennsylvania home. Karen Rose likes to hear from readers. Visit her website at www.karenrosesmith.com.

To my editor, Tina Colombo, for her encouragement,
patience and valuable time she so willingly gives.
Thank you.

Chapter One

She couldn't fail the queen. She just couldn't.

As the high-speed elevator dropped ten floors in a matter of seconds, Lady Amira Sierra Corbin felt a bit dizzy. She'd considered this mission from the queen an honor as she'd flown to Chicago from Penwyck. She'd been excited, eager and never entertained a doubt for one moment that she wouldn't be able to meet Marcus Cordello. But for the past three days she'd been thwarted by his secretary.

Monday, she'd been told he was unavailable for two weeks. *No one* could be that busy.

On Tuesday, deciding to be assertive, Amira had confronted his "keeper of the gate" and maintained she would sit in the waiting room until Mr. Cordello had a spare moment.

Apparently, he'd never had a spare moment.

Today Amira had appeared at his secretary's desk early in the morning and hinted that the matter she wanted to discuss with Mr. Cordello was extremely confidential and could change the course of several people's futures. Still the secretary wouldn't budge. But her expression had softened a little as she'd explained that Mr. Cordello had meetings out of the office until Friday, and then he would be leaving the city for a week.

Now Amira glanced around at her fellow passengers on the elevator. She fitted right in, in her violet tailored but feminine suit that was the same color as her eyes. Her shoulder-length, wavy, blond hair was pulled back and arranged at the nape of her neck in a sedate chignon, and her patent leather, high-heeled pumps and handbag were suitable for an early October day in Chicago.

Even thinking about the "windy" city in which she'd landed couldn't distract her from her mission. Where was Marcus Cordello at this moment? Still closeted behind the steel doors to the rear of the secretary's desk? In meetings that would last through the evening and night? Somewhere else in the city where he was making deals and adding to his fortune? All she knew about him was that at twenty-three, he was a multi-millionaire. He owned this hotel and, as she'd so frustratingly discovered in the past few days, he was surrounded by a staff who catered to and protected him.

She had to see him. He might be a prince and the next heir to the throne of Penwyck!

The elevator doors swished open and Amira stepped into the sumptuous hotel lobby with its marble floor, Persian carpets, asymmetrical flower arrangements and groupings of love seats and chairs arranged for tête-á-têtes. It was dinnertime and the reception desk was busy with businessmen checking in for the night.

Her stomach grumbled and she felt a bit woozy as the aroma of steak and garlic drifted from the restaurant in the corner of the lobby. How long had it been since she'd eaten? Not that she couldn't order room service anytime she wanted, but she'd been so nervous about this meeting and frustrated by the waiting that she'd done no more than nibble the past few days. This morning she'd had a pack of crackers and a cup of tea before setting out for Marcus Cordello's office suite on the twentieth floor. Afraid she'd miss her chance to see the man if she went for lunch, she'd sat in the reception area all day, reading the paperback in her purse.

As she approached Interludes, the hotel's finest restaurant, she realized she was starved. Pulling open the heavy glass door seemed to tax her, but it was the crowd of people there that made her realize how extremely tired she was. There were at least ten people milling about, and the bar area was crowded.

As the maître d' looked at her expectantly, her ears began to ring.

"I'd like a table for one." She hoped he could slide her into an empty spot someplace.

"And your name, please?" he asked, picking up his clipboard.

"Amira Corbin. Can you tell me how long a wait I'll have?"

"At least a half hour, maybe forty-five minutes."

Amira didn't think she'd ever felt so hungry or tired in her entire life. Tears pricked in her eyes as she felt a bit woozy again.

She was aware of footsteps and a tall man coming

up behind her, but all she could think about was the wait, or a ride up in that elevator to her room and another wait. Her three days of waiting. Her failure as an emissary of the queen.

The room began to spin as the maître d' gave his attention to the man behind her. "You're early, sir. Your dinner will be ready in a few minutes."

She could barely hear the man's deep voice order, "Don't worry about me. Take care of this lady."

Amira's knees began to buckle as the fuzziness engulfed her.

She felt as if she were floating, then she realized strong arms had lifted her and she was being held against a man's chest—a very broad chest. She heard him say, "I'm taking her to my dining room. Make an announcement and see if there's a doctor in the restaurant."

Being held in his arms and feeling his strength, hers seemed to return. Looking up into very green, mesmerizing eyes, she insisted, "I'm fine. Please don't call a doctor."

"You're *so* fine, you collapsed," he noted wryly. His dark brown hair had a rakishly styled look. His charcoal suit sported a red-and-gray silk tie settled intimately against his gray silk shirt. She didn't think she'd ever seen anyone more handsome.

"I didn't have very much to eat today," she hurried to tell him, not wanting to cause a fuss.

"Then we're going to remedy that." He was already moving with her in his arms. As he strode through the dining room past deep forest-green leather booths, black lacquered tables, and lithographs on the wall, Amira only quickly glimpsed it all.

"Put me down," she murmured, totally embarrassed. "You can't just carry me off."

"I'm not abducting you. I'm taking you to a private dining room. Believe me, you'll get something to eat a lot quicker in there than waiting your turn out front."

"But..." she started. How could she explain about her very proper upbringing and the chaperone who usually accompanied her whenever she was with a man, even though she was twenty years old.

"No buts about it. I've got a porterhouse steak big enough for two on order. You can have my salad to get started. I'm sure there are rolls already on the table."

The idea of immediately having food in front of her made her *but* a thing of the past. This chivalrous gentleman looked totally civilized. Since she'd landed in Chicago, her Penwyck world seemed very far away.

"Well?" he asked, not slowing down one wit. "Are you going to let me treat you to dinner?"

She'd always wanted an adventure. Instinctively she knew sharing dinner with this man could be that. Forgetting propriety for the moment, putting aside everything her mother, the queen's lady-in-waiting, had taught her over the years, she gazed into his eyes and smiled. "Yes. I'll let you treat me to dinner. Are all the men in Chicago as chivalrous as you?"

He gave her an irresistible smile. "Not even close."

Captivated by the beauty of the young woman in his arms, Marcus Cordello could hardly keep his gaze from hers. Her eyes were a rare shade of violet, her hair golden-blond. It looked natural, and from the rich shade of her finely arched brows, he suspected it was. Her oval face was enhanced by the severity of her hair style and softened by her fluffy bangs. As he carried her to the supple green couch in his private dining room, he decided her skin was as flawless as the rest of her, though she did look a bit pale. That concerned him as much as her fainting had.

He asked a question he should have asked three years ago of another woman, a woman who had died because he hadn't been observant...because he'd been too selfishly absorbed in the empire he'd been building. "Do you have a medical condition I should know about?" he asked huskily. "Are you sure I shouldn't call a doctor?"

"No medical condition," she assured him. "I've been a bit anxious the past few days and haven't eaten properly. I only had two crackers and tea this morning."

Gently he lowered her to the couch. "What could a beautiful young woman like you be anxious about?"

"It's a long story," she said with a sigh.

He could see she really was anxious about something, but a good meal would go a long way to making her feel better. "You'll have plenty of time to tell me all about it over dinner."

"Oh, I don't know if I should..."

Just then a waiter came through the door bearing a huge tray. "Goodness, sir. I didn't know you were having company for dinner."

Marcus smiled. "I didn't know I was having company, either, but I am." He glanced at the tray. "That steak's large enough to share, but I'd appreciate it if you could bring an extra helping of the garlic potatoes and the broccoli. More rolls, too.''

As the waiter arranged the food on the table, Marcus took the woman's hand. ''Are you still dizzy?''

''Not dizzy. Just a little…airy.''

He helped her to her feet. ''Come on, let's get some of that food into you. If you aren't feeling better by the time we're finished, I *will* call a doctor.''

Marcus seated the elegant young woman at the table and watched, amused, as she quickly cut her steak and ate half of it along with the potatoes and a roll. By then her cheeks had taken on a healthier pink tint, and he found himself intrigued by *her* as well as her accent. ''Now about that long story you were going to tell me,'' he reminded her after the waiter returned with the extra portions and exited again.

He saw her debate with herself. Then she delicately wiped her lips with her napkin and gave him a smile. ''This is going to sound far-fetched and not something you Americans are at all used to.''

''I take it you're not an American?'' Her accent sounded English, yet not quite English.

''No, I'm not. This is my first trip-here. I'm from Penwyck, an island off the coast of Wales.'' She smiled shyly. ''I'm Lady Amira Sierra Corbin. My mother is lady-in-waiting to the Queen of Penwyck.''

If Marcus hadn't already been entranced by this young woman, he might have laughed out loud. She had to be pulling his leg.

His thoughts must have shown in the arch of his brows or the quirk of his mouth because she squared her shoulders and sat up straighter. ''I suppose royalty isn't something Americans understand very well.''

"You're right about that. But I'm intrigued. Continue with your story."

After a few moments hesitation, she leaned back in her chair and relaxed again. "As I said, my mother is lady-in-waiting to the queen. She would do anything for Queen Marissa and so would I. That's why I'm here. Actually my mother might have come herself, but she's on her honeymoon in the Greek Isles and this is a matter that had to be taken care of immediately."

Marcus's amusement faded because of the expression on Lady Amira's face. She was completely serious. Either she was totally deluded or she did have a story to tell. "And what is this serious matter?"

"The queen sent me to meet with Marcus Cordello, the man who owns this hotel and goodness knows how many other businesses. I have something to tell him that could change his life. He might be a prince."

Marcus practically choked on his steak. Finally he set down his fork and managed, "A prince?" How could he not know he might be a prince?

"It's quite complicated. Everything has to do with twins. King Morgan is a twin, you see. But he's taken ill and is in a coma. For now, his twin, Broderick, is running Penwyck. He's always envied his brother, and he did something terrible that he just admitted recently. Long ago he conspired against King Morgan and Queen Marissa and switched the newborn royal twins for a set of American fraternal twins who were going to be adopted by a couple in Illinois. King Morgan and Queen Marissa raised them as their own. At least that's what Broderick says. I'm here to speak to Marcus Cordello because he and his twin might be the true heirs to the throne!"

"You were right about the story sounding far-fetched." Marcus tried to keep his tone even.

"Oh, it's even *more* complicated than that. The queen found out about Broderick's plans before he was able to execute them—at least that's what she believes—and she thinks Dylan and Owen, the sons she raised, are truly the royal heirs. But she also knows that she and the king have been betrayed by enemies more than once, and her plan to foil Broderick might have gone awry. The head of the Royal Intelligence Institute is investigating all of it, but the bottom line is—Owen and Dylan, who have been raised to be the true heirs of Penwyck, might *not* be the true heirs. I need to speak with Mr. Cordello and convince him to tell me where his brother is. DNA tests could settle this whole matter."

Shocked by Amira's story—it sounded like an implausible plot from a soap opera—Marcus took a few moments to think about it while he continued eating. Was Miss Corbin truly acting as an emissary for a royal family? Or was this whole story some ploy to get to him and his money or connections? Was Lady Amira Sierra Corbin for real? And if she was...

The *last* thing in this world he wanted was to be a prince! He liked his life just the way it was. He didn't want to be involved in some royal family's intrigue. Besides, although he and his brother Shane *were* twins, they weren't adopted. His parents might have had their problems, but they never would have kept something like that a secret.

He studied Amira once more. She was beautiful and entertaining, and he hadn't been truly interested in a woman since Rhonda had died. Every time he looked at Amira, his whole body quickened. For the first time in a long while, he was interested in more than the Dow Jones Industrial Average or whether a company was ripe for a takeover. He wanted to check into this woman's background, get to know her a little better, possibly even take her to bed. But he couldn't do any of that if she knew he was Marcus Cordello.

"How long do you intend to stay in the United States?" he asked.

"Until I can meet with this man." She bit her lower lip and said almost to herself, "I *can't* fail the queen." Meeting his gaze again, she went on, "Mr. Cordello's secretary tells me he has meetings out of his office until this weekend and then he'll be gone for a week. I might have to wait until he returns. I have to figure out if it's worthwhile sitting outside his office door any longer, hoping I might catch him. I must think of a better way to get to him."

After taking a sip of water, she set down her glass. "Thank you so much for sharing your dinner with me. I don't even know your name."

The wheels in Marcus's head spun. When he was a boy away at school, he used his middle name, Brent, since there was another boy in his class named Marcus. "My name is Brent," he responded now. Then choosing a last name from thin air, he added, "It's Brent Carpenter."

She held out her hand to him. "It's good to meet you, Brent."

When he enfolded her hand in his, it felt delicate and fragile. Yet he sensed a strength about Amira that intrigued him as much as everything else. The softness of her skin under his made his blood rush faster, and he told himself to slow down. He told himself this was a woman like none he'd ever met. He had the urge to bring her hand to his lips…to do much more than that.

Before he could analyze his attraction to her, the waiter came in, carrying two apple tarts topped with whipped cream. Amira pulled her gaze from his, glanced at the tart and smiled. "Oh, that looks good."

He laughed.

The waiter left as unobtrusively as he'd come in and Marcus breathed a sigh of relief. The staff usually addressed him as "sir" and when he had a guest, they didn't converse with him at all. But there was always a chance someone would call him by name. He found himself liking the idea of becoming Brent Carpenter more and more. He needed a vacation, not only from the city, but from who he was and what he did and everyone's expectations of him. From now on when he was with Amira, he would think of himself as Brent.

As they both sampled their tarts, he asked her, "Have you seen anything of the city?"

"Nothing but the airport," she said with a sigh. "During the taxi ride from the airport to the hotel, I had to hold on to the seat in fear for my life, so I haven't dared take another one. After the warnings the queen gave me about big American cities, I didn't think it was a good idea to go out alone at night."

"Chicago's a wonderful city, Amira. You should see some of it."

"I'm not really here for a vacation."

She'd eaten her tart as delicately as any lady, but her beautifully curved upper lip was smudged with a dot of whipped cream. He couldn't help leaning toward her and sliding his thumb over the spot. Her deep-violet eyes became wider, and her intake of breath at his touch told him she was affected by it. He was, too.

His voice was husky as he explained, "Whipped cream," and brought his thumb to his own lips and licked the sweet topping.

They gazed at each other, lost in the moment. The thrum of sexual awareness between them practically filled the room.

Her cheeks became flushed and her lashes fluttered down as she demurely cast her eyes at what was left of her tart.

"Amira?" he asked.

She looked up at him once more.

"How old are you?"

"I'm twenty."

That's what he'd suspected. But he'd also guessed she was a very innocent twenty. Not at all like Rhonda. The familiar pain, guilt and blame rushed in with the remembrance of his fiancée. For two years he'd hardly looked at women. For two years he hadn't wanted the responsibility of a relationship…and he wasn't contemplating a relationship now, he told himself. Amira would be going back to her island. After next week's vacation, he'd be returning to mergers and interest rates and building a new hotel in St. Louis. But for the next few days…

Amira sipped the coffee the waiter had brought with dessert. He'd noticed her load it down with cream and sugar.

As she returned her cup to the saucer, she couldn't stifle a yawn. "I'm so sorry," she said embarrassed. "I think I'm still adjusting to the time change."

"Nothing to be sorry for. How are you feeling?"

"Wonderfully satisfied. Everything was delicious." She took her purse from the table where she'd laid it. "You must let me pay for this."

"Nope. It's my treat. You saved me from another dinner alone."

"Do you have dinner alone a lot? Never mind," she said with a flutter of her hand. "That's none of my business."

Her chagrin was enchanting. She was definitely a proper lady. "For a long while now, I've had lots of dinners alone. By choice. I put in a long day and just want peace and quiet in the evening."

"What do you do?"

He didn't want to lie to her, but he didn't know what she knew about Marcus Cordello, either. He answered vaguely, "I work in finance." To forestall her asking any more questions about his work, he laid down his napkin and stood. "I have a meeting in half an hour, but before I leave the hotel, I want to see you safely to your room."

"That's not necessary."

"It's very necessary." He wanted to make sure her lack of food had been her only problem, and she wasn't hiding a more serious condition as Rhonda had.

Amira gave him a smile that made him feel ten feet tall as she acquiesced. "All right. An escort will make me feel as if I'm back home."

"You have a bodyguard?"

"Not as the queen and king do. But when I go out at night I have a chauffeur, and when I attend public functions I have an escort from the Royal Guard."

"Do you feel as if you're always being watched?" he asked, knowing he could never give up his freedom like that.

"I'm used to it, so it doesn't seem out of the ordinary."

A few minutes later Amira was following Brent from the room, feeling as if this dinner had been a milestone in her life. She'd never had dinner alone with a man before. She'd never felt the sizzling attraction she felt toward this man. When his finger had touched her lip...heat had seemed to fill her and she'd been unable to look away from his green eyes. Fantasies had crowded her head and she'd known she shouldn't entertain them.

Yet as the dining room door closed behind them, Brent took her hand and secured it in the crook of his arm. "To keep you steady," he said with a wink.

The fine material of his suit was smooth under her fingers, and she could feel his muscled strength underneath.

When they stepped into the elevator and the doors swooshed shut, intimacy seemed to surround them. She peeked up at Brent and saw he was gazing down at her.

"What floor?" he asked, his voice deep and low.

"Twelve," she answered. Her mouth was suddenly dry, and her heart was beating much too fast.

When the elevator stopped on the twelfth floor, they stepped out onto plush wine carpeting. They passed marble-topped mahogany credenzas, Victorian-style velvet-covered chairs and arrangements created from fresh flowers.

Amira pointed out her room number. "Would you like to come in?" As soon as the words were out of her mouth, she felt flustered, not knowing why she'd asked him. Somehow it had just seemed the polite thing to do!

Brent hesitated. "Just for a few moments." Then he took the key card from her hand and unlocked her door. Opening it, he let her precede him inside. She was close enough to him to smell his cologne, to see the scar on the right side of his brow, to know that being alone with him in her room had been a foolish decision to make.

The small foyer led into a large room with a king-size bed, dresser and chest on one side, and a sitting area with a love seat, chair and entertainment center on the other. A maid had obviously cleaned the room and made the bed, but Amira's pink-and-green-satin nightgown lay folded on the side of the bed so she wouldn't have to look far for it.

Brent's gaze seemed riveted to the satin garment and the king-size bed. "You do know, Amira, it's not a good idea to invite strange men into your room."

"I've never done it before." Her experience with men was indeed limited. At seventeen she'd thought she'd been in love with the gardener, but after an uncomfortable groping session, she'd realized he was only concerned with getting her into bed. That had been her only "intimate" experience with a man.

Now Brent was looking down at her with a flare of heat in his eyes that seemed to consume her. Everything disappeared except Brent Carpenter and the longing inside her. He lowered his head very slowly. Then his lips covered hers and his arms enfolded her in an exciting embrace.

Swept away. Now Amira knew what the phrase meant. Nothing but his kiss mattered. The taut heat of him, the trace of his cologne lingering at the end of the day and his musky male scent brought to her mind visions of both of them naked, sharing a bed.

Passion she'd dreamed about, but never known seemed within her reach.

Instinctively her arms moved up to circle his neck, and he pulled her tighter against him. The amazing maleness of his body almost shocked her, but the shock gave way to pure pleasure as his tongue slid along the seam of her lips, coaxing them apart.

She wasn't sure what she was supposed to do, and he seemed to sense that because he murmured, "Open your mouth to me."

She didn't even think of denying his husky command. She wanted to know more about desire, more about becoming a woman, more about Brent. Something inside whispered that this man could teach her everything.

The tantalizing invasion of his tongue sent her senses reeling. Licks of fire seemed to reach deep into the center of her, and she became frightened by it, frightened by her reaction to him. She'd never met a man this sensual or this compelling.

Suddenly her hands were on his chest and she was pushing away. "I can't," she said as she looked up and saw the deep desire intensifying the green of his eyes.

What would he do? Would he be angry? He was in her room. What would her mother think about her daughter having a meal with a stranger and sharing a kiss before she really even knew the man? What would the queen think? Had she put herself in harm's way? Would her life be irrevocably changed?

She stood frozen with the fear of everything that could happen.

Brent must have seen it. "It's okay, Amira. It's

okay,'' he soothed again. "We both just got carried away.''

For the first time in her life she'd followed her instincts without propriety guiding her, and her instincts had been right. Brent wasn't the type of man to force his attentions on a woman. "I...I shouldn't have asked you in. It's not...proper.''

A wry smile curved his lips. "Being proper is important to you, isn't it?''

She just nodded and managed to say, "It's the way I was raised.''

Although he released her, as if he couldn't help himself, he touched the back of his hand gently to her cheek. "I never met a true lady before." He dropped his hand to his side. "I'd better leave." Then he crossed to the door quickly and opened it.

She stayed where she was, knowing she couldn't chase after him, knowing she couldn't ask him to stay. "Thank you again for dinner.''

"My pleasure," he said without smiling, and then he was gone.

After the heavy door closed with a click, Amira ran to it and secured the safety lock, sure that Brent Carpenter considered her the most naive woman he'd ever met...sure that she'd never see him again.

Chapter Two

Three loud raps on Amira's hotel room door awakened her. Glancing at the clock on the nightstand, she noted it was 8:00 a.m. She'd slept through the night again in a strange place! Maybe she'd left her nightmares in Penwyck. Maybe the news her mother had given her before she'd left—that her father's assassin was dead—had freed her.

There was another rap at the door.

Thinking the maid wanted to clean her room, she slid from the bed, pushed her hair from her eyes and grabbed her robe on the bedside chair. Slipping on the pink-and-green, flowered-satin garment, she quickly belted it.

When she looked out the peephole of the door, she blinked twice. It was Brent! With a room service table.

Opening the door, she couldn't keep from smiling or hide the breathlessness in her voice. "This is a surprise."

His grin was crooked and boyish. "It's a strategic move on my part to make sure you eat more than two crackers and tea. I don't want you fainting into another man's arms."

She knew he was teasing, but there was a serious glint in his green eyes, too. She was about to invite him in when she realized she was wearing her nightgown and robe. "Oh, I can't. I mean—"

Ignoring her reticence, he pushed the table inside. "You don't even have to tip me," he went on as if she hadn't interrupted.

Thoroughly flustered, unable to take her gaze from his broad shoulders, collarless blue shirt and his long jeans-clad legs, she stammered, "I...I have to dress."

Rolling the table to the sitting area, he set the covered platters on the coffee table. "You look fetching as you are. You don't have time to dress. The eggs and bacon will get cold, and don't tell me you don't eat bacon and eggs, because your figure doesn't need watching."

His appraising gaze raked over her, and she blushed to her toes.

With a chuckle he caught her hand and tugged her to the love seat. "Come on. I know you're a proper lady. I won't do anything improper. I promise."

His smile was so beguiling, his manner so offhandedly friendly, she couldn't resist. Missing her family and friends, she felt alone in a foreign land and she enjoyed Brent's company. More than enjoyed it.

Uncovering both their platters, he set the lids aside and settled his gaze on her. For a few moments he simply studied her with such intensity that she couldn't look away.

Finally he admitted, "I couldn't stop thinking about you."

His honest admission mandated she be just as honest. "I couldn't stop thinking about you, either."

He reached up to touch her then, to brush her tousled waves away from her face...

The phone rang.

The sound was a startling intrusion to the beginning of an intimate moment, and Amira really didn't know if she was relieved or perturbed.

"Excuse me," she murmured, and went over to the desk under the window to pick up the receiver. "Hello?"

"Good morning, Amira."

"Good morning, Your Majesty." Amira knew the queen's voice as well as she knew her own mother's.

"I hope I'm not calling too early. I forget about the time difference."

Glancing over at Brent, Amira noticed his surprised expression. Maybe he hadn't really believed she had connections to a royal family. "No, it's not too early. In fact, other mornings I was sitting in Marcus Cordello's reception area by now."

"How's that coming, my dear? Did you manage to meet with him?"

There was no point in beating around the bush. "I would have called you immediately if I had. I'm having a bit of a problem getting to see him. He's very...elusive and protected. I've been camping on his doorstep, but have only seen his staff going in and out. His secretary has informed me he'll be out of the office in meetings the rest of the week and away next week. So I'm afraid this might take longer than we planned."

There was a slight pause. "I see. Well, I know you're doing your best. Cole Everson is working on getting a few more details for you, including a picture of the man. That might help you spot him."

Cole Everson was head of the Royal Intelligence, and Amira knew Queen Marissa counted on him.

"What will you be doing today, Amira? Meeting with Marcus Cordello is important, but you need some time for yourself, too. Have you seen any of the city?"

"No, I haven't."

"It must be very lonely for you in Chicago. Do you want me to find a guide for you?"

Again Amira looked over at Brent. The queen was being so nice, and Amira suddenly felt as if she was doing something very wrong. There was a man in her room whom she hardly knew. She was in her robe. They'd been about to...

Suddenly she wished she weren't on a mission for the queen, and that she hadn't been raised quite so properly.

Marcus had begun thinking of himself as Brent Carpenter as soon as he'd rapped on Amira's door. He hadn't slept much last night, between thinking about her and dreaming about her, though *fantasizing* was probably the better term. The thing was—he felt more than a physical attraction to her. There was something about her that simply fascinated him. Along with rearranging his schedule and canceling today's appointments, he'd called a friend who was an expert at gathering information and asked him to check Amira's background. Now, listening to her phone conversation, he decided she must really be a lady in contact with the queen. This performance couldn't have been put on for his benefit, because she hadn't known he was coming.

He didn't need a dossier to know she was who she said she was and she was looking for *him*. He should leave right now…forget about breakfast, forget about spending the day with her. It would be safer never to see her again…to never let her meet Marcus Cordello. He didn't want his life disrupted again.

It had been disrupted when he and Shane were children and his parents divorced. The divorce had been bitter, and his mother had taken Shane to California while Marcus had stayed in Illinois with his father. They had just settled into that routine, seeing his brother one month every summer, when Marcus's life was turned upside down again because his father remarried. In a way, that was even more disruptive than the divorce because his stepmother insisted Marcus be sent to boarding school. She didn't want to be bothered with him. He'd weathered all of that and weathered it well, turning his interest to the financial markets, researching corporations and how they ran, beginning to invest any money he earned.

Then two years ago, when he'd thought his life was on track, when he'd already become wealthier than he ever dreamed, he lost his fiancée to diabetes. Rhonda had kept her condition from him, and he'd had no idea she was dealing with it. Since she'd died, he'd done nothing but work nineteen or twenty hours a day. He'd cut off all social contact and let his staff deal with the outside world.

But last night Amira had crashed through all the protective layers he'd built around himself, and he wanted to spend more time with her.

He saw her glance at him and also saw the guilty

flush that colored her cheeks. He might have to do some fast talking to get her to spend the day with him.

When she hung up, she looked pensive.

"Is everything all right?" he asked.

"The queen's always so understanding. She's like a second mother to me. She asked me if I want a guide while I'm in Chicago."

"What did you say?" If Amira ended up with someone the queen hired, the guide would surely be a bodyguard, too.

"That I don't."

"You don't want the queen's guide, or you don't want *any* guide? Because I'd be glad to show you a few sights today."

Amira looked uncertain. "Don't you have to work?"

"I haven't taken a day off in far too long. I can't think of a better way to spend it than showing you what I like best about Chicago. What do you say?"

A slow smile crept across her pretty lips. "The queen *did* say I should see some of the sights."

"A royal command if I ever heard one."

At that, Amira laughed and her hesitation seemed to vanish. "I have to shower and get dressed. Should I meet you somewhere?"

He didn't want to crowd her or make her feel uncomfortable. If he did, she'd run in the opposite direction. "I do have a few arrangements to make. Would you like to go to the theater tonight, or dancing at a club?"

"Dancing." She looked like a child who'd been given a Christmas present.

"Okay, dancing it is. Let's eat, and I'll meet you in the lobby in a half hour. Is that enough time?"

Their gazes caught and held.

"Yes, that's enough time," she murmured.

As they finished breakfast, Marcus knew he had to get out of this hotel room, away from Amira and that bed quickly before he kissed her and led her to it. She wasn't that kind of woman, and today he wasn't going to be that kind of man.

Still, she was so alluring, with her blond waves mussed and her flowered satin robe clinging so wonderfully to all her curves. He couldn't keep away from her. Covering the few steps between them, he lifted her chin and pressed a kiss to her lips. It was supposed to be a chaste kiss, a light kiss, but when he lifted his head, he was aroused. It was a good thing they'd be sight-seeing today. If they were on the move, he could restrain the desire to pull her into his arms.

He stepped away. "In a half hour," he reminded her huskily.

Then he left Lady Amira Sierra Corbin feeling more alive than he had in two long years.

The October day couldn't have been more perfect. The sky was blue, the air held a tinge of autumn, the sun gleamed off skyscraper windows. It was a day of play and fun and teasing. Brent found he could very easily rattle Amira with a seductive look, a little bit more than a friendly touch. When she'd appeared in the lobby in a forest-green pantsuit, he'd arched a brow and asked if that was her idea of casual. Very seriously she'd said that it was.

He'd taken her hand, slipped it into the crook of

his arm and said teasingly, ''One of these days we'll have to get you into a pair of jeans.''

His driver drove them to Wrigley Field. The ivy-covered stadium, one of the oldest in America, seemed to fascinate Amira. From there, Marcus directed his driver to the Shedd Aquarium, the Chicago Historical Society and the Lincoln Park Zoo where Amira was enchanted by the chimpanzees drawing on poster board with crayons.

Somehow throughout the morning, Marcus managed to keep himself from kissing Amira again, though it seemed to be constantly on his mind. He'd never felt this way—not even with Rhonda. Although they'd become engaged, he'd always been eager to get back to work, to hear about an exciting new investment opportunity. Today all he wanted was to be close to Amira, see her eyes come alive with the sights and her mouth break into that beautiful smile. Maybe he was so engrossed with her because he knew their time was limited.

They decided to have ice cream for lunch because they'd had a big breakfast. He discovered Amira's favorite was mint chocolate chip, and as she licked it from the cone, she nearly drove him crazy.

Late in the afternoon he had his driver drop them off along the Magnificent Mile, the stretch of Michigan Avenue created for shoppers. They ended up at Tribune Tower, home of the *Chicago Tribune*. Hungry after that, for food as well as Amira, Marcus took her to a small French café where nobody would know him. Flickering candlelight made her eyes shine with her enjoyment of the day. The intimacy between them caused him to reach across the table and touch her hand more than once.

It was almost 10:00 p.m. when his driver dropped them off at a casual club he'd frequented a few times. It was so crowded they couldn't find a table, and when he led her directly to the dance floor, they seemed to get bumped from every side. Besides that, the music was so loud, they couldn't hear each other.

As the band finally took a break, he held her close and whispered in her ear, "This isn't exactly what I had in mind. I want to talk to you, not shout at you. Would you like to see my penthouse?" He added quickly, "The housekeeper's there so we'll have a chaperone."

Amira seemed to debate with herself, but then she smiled up at him. "I'd love to see it."

At Marcus's building, the doorman opened the door for them. The man started to say, "Good evening, Mr.—"

Marcus cut him off. "Good evening, Charlie. How's your new grandson?"

"Three weeks old today and not a boy handsomer on this earth."

Marcus laughed and guided Amira to the private elevator that led to the penthouse. As soon as they stepped inside, she noted, "I think you live like royalty."

Her words surprised him. "Do you want to run that by me again?"

She listed the reasons why she thought so on her fingers one by one. "You eat in a private dining room. You have a driver. And you have a private elevator. Definitely earmarks of royalty."

He saw that she was teasing him, and he laughed. "I guess some people would look at it that way. But I don't have a dastardly twin ready to step into my shoes.'' Amira had told him again the whole story about Broderick's hostility toward King Morgan, and he still couldn't get over the idea of someone switching babies with the royal twins. He supposed anything was possible, yet he knew in his gut he and Shane weren't the twins the queen was searching for. They couldn't be.

"Do you have any brothers and sisters?" Amira asked.

"I have a brother." He wasn't about to tell her Shane was a twin. "And he couldn't be more unlike me. He's in construction—a contractor."

The elevator stopped at the top floor. Marcus was glad they'd arrived so he could put an end to the conversation. Family history wasn't a safe subject. She might know more about Marcus Cordello than she'd revealed.

After Marcus unlocked the door to the penthouse, he let Amira precede him inside and tried to see his condo through her eyes. There was chrome and glass and black leather, two original contemporary paintings on the walls as well as a contemporary wall hanging.

Her gaze swept the large sunken living room, the open dining area with its glass-topped table and wrought-iron chandelier. "You're not here much?" she asked perceptively.

"No, I'm not. It's a stopover where I catch a few hours sleep. My office down the hall has a more lived-in quality." He motioned past the living room. "In fact, you'd probably even find candy-bar wrappers on the desk."

He crooked his finger at her. "Come here. This is what I wanted to show you."

On his way to the French doors, he pushed a button on the wall and soft music flowed from unseen speakers. After he opened the doors onto the balcony, he held his hand out to her.

When she joined him outside, the city lay before them—twinkling lights, tall buildings, neon signs. "Now I know why you live here."

There were cushy outdoor chairs on the balcony, and she laid her purse on the table between them and went to stand at the railing. The air was much cooler than it had been during the day, but it felt great after being in the stuffy club.

"I guess we should have gone to the theater instead of the club." He was trying to think about something other than her slightly fuller lower lip, her long eyelashes, her satinlike skin.

Facing him, she murmured, "Then I might not have come here."

The way she said it, he knew she wanted to be here with him.

A slow dreamy melody poured from the speakers, and all he could think about was holding her in his arms. "Would you like to dance?"

Instead of answering, she just stepped closer to him. He took her into his embrace. He'd been waiting all day to do this, waiting all day to lean his cheek against hers, breathe in her wonderful perfume, and feel her body close to his. They danced together as if they'd been doing it for years. Maybe that was because they fitted together so perfectly. Maybe that was because they didn't really care about the music, but rather each other. As minutes ticked by, as the lights of the city below twinkled, they were hardly aware of one song passing into the next. Marcus only knew his heart beat in rhythm with hers, and the heat between them could have warded off the chill if it had been ten below.

Slowly Amira lifted her head and gazed into his eyes. "You gave me a wonderful day today. I'll remember it always."

She was talking as if she'd never see him again. That was what he'd planned. In fact, in the back of his mind, he'd decided he would take her to bed tonight if she was willing and say goodbye in the morning. But now he knew she was too innocent for a one-night stand, and he couldn't do that to her. He also knew that one day of being with her wasn't enough. She'd brought light and sunshine into his life again, and he wasn't ready to give that up.

"You told me you like to jog in the mornings, but you've been afraid to do it here. We could jog in Lincoln Park tomorrow morning if you'd like."

"Don't you have to get back to work?"

"Another day won't hurt. I'm going on a vacation on Sunday, anyway. I'll just start it sooner than I planned. Is eight o'clock too early?"

She shook her head. "Eight will be fine."

And then he couldn't be with her and not kiss her any longer. His hand slid to her neck into her luxurious hair. She'd worn it down today, and it was silky and soft. The style made her look a lot less proper.

As he held her, she tipped her chin up, and he knew she wanted the kiss as much as he did. Where they'd fallen into the first kiss with a ferocity that had stunned them both, he took this one slowly, easing them into it. When his tongue laved her lower lip, she opened her mouth to him. With the lights of the city below and music enfolding them, he felt bowled over by her. He'd never felt that way before. He'd always been the one in control, the one who called the shots. Danger signals went off in his head, but he quieted them with the idea that this could never be serious, that they'd never have the time to get truly involved. Even if they did go to bed together tomorrow or the next day, they both knew that would be the end of it. Their lives were an ocean apart. This was just one of those flings that happened on a weekend or over a holiday.

As he took the kiss deeper, the warning bells kept sounding.

Before his control snapped altogether, he pulled away. "I think I'd better introduce you to my housekeeper." Flora was just what they needed—a chaperone. Besides, he wanted to prove to Amira that he hadn't been lying to her and he *did* have a housekeeper.

You're lying to her about who you are.

No, I'm not, he thought quickly. I just haven't told her my real name.

Amira looked as dazed by the kiss as he felt. "That would be a good idea. Then I'd better go."

He saw she felt it, too—the need to be more than friends, the need to do more than kiss. But he wouldn't take advantage of her—not her shyness or her innocence or her proper upbringing.

Taking her hand, he led her inside to a snack of tea and cookies rather than their first night of passion.

Amira was as fascinated by the city as she was everything else about the United States—even more fascinated by Brent running beside her. He was wearing shiny black running shorts. His legs were hair-roughened, his thighs powerfully muscular. His soft black T-shirt was loose. As he ran, it molded to his well-defined muscles, and she could see the power in his body. She was sure he was slowing his pace so she could keep up.

Brent glanced over at her often, and she didn't know if that was because of her hot-pink running suit in the latest fabric for sportswear or because he just wanted to look at her. She knew she'd be a sight at the end of their run. She always was. She'd banded her hair into a ponytail, but strands escaped and floated around her face.

A few joggers passed them as they ran along a wide path. Amira tried to keep her attention on her breathing rather than on Brent and everything she remembered so vividly whenever she looked at him. He'd given her a perfect day yesterday—absolutely perfect. And that kiss last night...

His first kiss had thrilled her *and* scared her. Last night's kiss had opened a doorway and given her a glimpse of the kind of passion they could share. That was almost worse than being scared. It was a temptation from which she knew she had to turn away. Everything she'd been taught, all of her mother's counsel, warned her she was headed for disaster. Yet on this October day, with the sun shining so brightly on her head and in her heart, she couldn't heed the warning.

"Do you hear that?" Brent asked, suddenly stopping.

Caught up in her thoughts, she hadn't heard anything unusual. Now she listened and heard a low whine coming from a copse of bushes. "It sounded like an animal."

"My bet is it's a dog. Come on, let's go look."

Slowly…cautiously…Amira followed.

Pushing away the bushes, Brent hunkered down and looked beneath them. "Hello there, fellow. Are you hurt?"

"What is it?" Amira asked, crouching down herself.

Brent held his hand out to the animal that Amira still couldn't see.

"We're not going to hurt you," Brent said as if he expected the animal to understand. "Can I bring you out here?"

Since the animal stood perfectly still and didn't snarl or bark, Brent gently pulled the dog out into the sunlight.

Amira got her first good look. "Isn't she adorable? What do you think she is?"

The dog was small, brown—the color of hot chocolate—and bedraggled looking, as if she'd been on her own through days of wet and dry weather. Her fur was muddy and there were leaves clinging to it, but she seemed to like the idea of Brent scratching her between the ears. She barked a few times.

Brent ran his hands carefully over the dog's body. "Probably a mutt—looks like part beagle. She's too thin, but other than that, she seems okay. Nothing a good bath wouldn't fix." He examined her neck. "No collar or tags."

"What are we going to do about her?"

"We can't leave her here. She could eventually run into traffic, or someone might hurt her. She needs food and care."

"But if she belongs to someone…"

"In case she has one of those identifying computer

chips under her skin, we'll take her to a vet and get her checked out. Is that okay with you? I know it's going to cut short our jog."

"The jog doesn't matter. We have to take care of her."

The smile Brent gave her almost made her melt. "It looks as though we're both animal lovers."

"Yes, it does." She was finding so many things about Brent that she liked...too many things. Their gazes locked, and the intensity in his eyes should have scared her, but it didn't today.

Suddenly the dog barked again, and Brent laughed. "It seems she wants our attention." He scooped her up into his arms. "Come on, let's see if she has a home."

An hour later a vet had checked the dog over thoroughly and agreed that except for needing a bath, she seemed healthy. There was no computer chip in evidence, and he asked Brent what he was going to do.

"I'll take her home."

"You're going to keep her?" Amira asked, a bit surprised by that, since Brent worked so many hours.

"Just for now. I know of a place she'll be happy. In the meantime, I'll get her cleaned up and fed well."

Back at Brent's penthouse—a half hour later— doggy shampoo in hand, Brent led Amira into his bathroom. It was huge with black and white tiles, a shiny black enamel sink and a huge black whirlpool tub. He filled it while she cooed to the pup and fed her a biscuit they'd gotten from the veterinarian along with other supplies.

"Did you ever have a dog when you were a boy?"

she asked Brent now, as he checked the water to make sure it was the right temperature.

He didn't answer right away, just concentrated on the water flowing into the tub. Finally he said, "No, I didn't," and didn't elaborate. Something in his tone alerted her to pain behind the simple statement.

"You don't talk about yourself easily do you?" Even though they'd spent all day yesterday together, she hadn't learned much about him.

"Usually no one wants to listen," he said jokingly.

Again she caught some truth behind his words. What makes a man bring home a lost dog? Maybe a loneliness in himself? Maybe knowing what it's like to feel abandoned? "I'll listen to whatever you want to tell me," she said softly.

Time ticked by in heartbeats. "I think right now we ought to name the dog," he finally said. "Any ideas?"

She'd learned already that Brent was good at turning attention away from himself, and she let him do it this time. "I think she's the color of hot chocolate."

"How about Cocoa, then?"

"That's perfect!"

Unmindful she'd been given a name, Cocoa put her paws on the edge of the bathtub and peered into the water. Amira glanced at Brent. He wasn't watching Cocoa; he was watching *her*.

His gaze held her hypnotized as his voice lowered and awareness grew between them. "Thanks for being such a good sport about this. It's probably not what you envisioned for today."

With the huskiness in Brent's voice, the sparks of desire in his eyes, she felt breathless, hot and altogether excited. "I'm having fun, and I can't think of anything better to do than rescue a dog."

The crackle of electricity between them was so strong Amira tingled all over from it. Then Cocoa barked and Brent picked up the small dog, depositing her in the water. The pup looked startled for a moment and barked a few more times. Brent casually sprinkled water over her as Amira poured the shampoo into her hand.

A few minutes later, after a sudsing and rinse, Cocoa shook to whip the water from her fur. Amira and Brent laughed and again became caught up in enjoying each other's company. Amira had never before felt a bond like this with a man.

After they dried Cocoa, Brent said, "Let's go see what Flora's cooked up for lunch."

Cocoa wiggled away from Amira's hand and took off down the hall.

"Do you want to let her loose?" she asked, concerned for his obviously expensive furniture.

"Sure. She's clean. There's nothing she can hurt."

"You said you had a home for her. Where?"

As Brent stood and gathered up the wet towels, he was silent for a few moments. "It's a place called Reunion House."

Longing to know more, Amira patiently waited.

"When my brother and I were kids," Brent explained, "our parents divorced. I stayed with my father. My brother went with my mother to another part of the country. Each of us not only lost one of our parents, we lost each other."

"Brent, I'm so sorry."

He shrugged. "We did manage to see each other a month every summer in the house where we were once all together. It's on a lake about an hour and a half from here. Anyway, two years ago I bought the property adjacent to it, renovated the old house and called it Reunion House. It's for foster kids who are separated from their siblings. All they have to do is apply and they can come anytime and spend from a few days up to two weeks together.''

''The project means a lot to you, doesn't it?'' she asked, seeing that it did, hoping he'd tell her more.

''Yes, it does. So does seeing the smiles on those kids' faces when they're together. That's where I'm going for vacation next week.''

His words reminded her they wouldn't be spending any more time together. Brent would be going his way and she'd be...waiting until Marcus Cordello returned from wherever his jet-setting life took him.

Heading out of the bathroom, Brent asked over his shoulder, ''Do you want to take Cocoa for a walk after lunch?''

She should end this adventure right now. Her feelings for Brent were growing, and the more time they spent together, the harder it would be to say goodbye. ''I should probably be getting back.''

He stopped in the doorway. ''Should you?'' His green eyes were intensely dark, intensely questing. Taking her hand, he tugged her toward him and brought it to his lips, kissing her index finger, touching it sensually with his tongue.

Amira almost gasped from the pleasure, and she knew she was going to spend every minute she could with Brent and the consequences be damned.

''Let's have lunch, then take Cocoa for a walk,'' she whispered.

Chapter Three

As Marcus and Amira walked Cocoa, Marcus couldn't imagine having a more enjoyable afternoon. Cocoa did well on a leash, though she often tried to pull ahead. They took turns leading her, their hands brushing as they passed each other the handle. Marcus's state of aroused awareness made the afternoon exciting, but frustrating as well. He wanted to take Amira to bed, yet so many things stopped him, especially the innocence he saw in her beautiful eyes.

Cocoa saw a piece of wind-tossed foil on the sidewalk, jumped, barked and took off after it. Amira ran with her, and Marcus took longer strides to keep up with her. They laughed as Cocoa put her nose in the foil and pushed it.

After they walked at a leisurely pace again, Marcus's elbow rubbed Amira's, and he didn't move away from the contact. "I'm afraid she belongs to someone."

"She does seem leash trained. And she obeys 'sit' commands."

"Someone could really miss her. I think I'll take a picture of her and make up flyers. Fritz could distribute them and put them up on bulletin boards in the area. The pound is already on the alert if someone calls there. I can also notify other veterinarians."

Amira looked up at him with admiration in her eyes. "You're a nice man, Brent Carpenter."

He'd talked with both Flora and Fritz about calling him Brent Carpenter. They were used to doing whatever he wanted and hadn't lifted an eyebrow. He assured himself he had a good reason for keeping up the charade. He wasn't being completely honest with Amira because she was never going to meet Marcus Cordello. He'd make sure of that, because he wanted nothing to do with her whole fantastic story.

As Cocoa led them toward a tree, Marcus asked Amira, "What do you do as a member of royalty? I mean, do you just wander around the palace? Do you plan state events?"

"You must think I have a very useless existence."

He could tell she was half teasing and half serious. "I didn't mean to insult you. I just don't quite understand what it means to be a lady."

"In my case, it doesn't mean much at all. Yes, I live at the palace, but I lead a fairly normal life. I do assist the queen whenever I can, but thanks to her, I'm enrolled in a private academy and earning a degree in landscape design. I need meaningful work to do, too, Brent, just like everyone else. As far as the royal life goes, soon I'm going to move out of the palace and get my own place."

"How will the queen feel about that?"

"I don't know. I haven't discussed it with her. But I need my own life. I'd like to be an ordinary person—no guards, no escorts, no palace. I want to come and go as I please and not have to answer to anyone."

Those might be some of the reasons she wanted her own place, but a sixth sense told him there was more to it. "You don't want to be queen someday?"

She laughed. "Goodness, no. I don't even want to be a princess. Being a royal is not as easy as you might think. There are secrets and state responsibilities and a loyalty to Penwyck that comes before all else. When I marry, I want my marriage to be the most important thing in my life, not second to what the country needs."

That was the real reason she wanted to distance herself from the royal life, he decided. But her mention of marriage and how important it was to her disconcerted him. He'd never seen a marriage that worked. He'd never witnessed two people actually becoming one. He understood everything she'd said, though, and he admired her for knowing what she did and didn't want. Ever since he'd been a teenager, his studies, his investments and work had come first. That's how he envisioned his life. Yet Rhonda's death had taught him that work could blind a man to things he should see. Yesterday and again today with Amira, he found himself completely blocking work from his mind...something he'd never done before.

Cocoa stopped walking, came over to Marcus, looked up at him, then hopped up on two legs putting her paws on his knees. "Does that mean you want me to carry you?" he asked with a wry note.

She barked at him twice.

"That's a definite yes," Amira translated with a smile twitching the corners of her lips.

Scooping the dog up into his arms, Marcus laughed as Cocoa licked his face. Yes, if she had an owner he was going to do his best to locate them. He knew what it felt like to be displaced. He remembered the move from the home on the lake to the city with his father. He remembered the room at boarding school where he'd first found the financial world to keep himself from thinking about the stepmother who didn't want him and the father who didn't want to rock his new marriage. Most of all he remembered the tearing separation from Shane. Yep, he certainly wanted to return Cocoa to a home if she had one.

Home meant different things to different people. His home was still Shady Glenn. Because of the memories there? He couldn't imagine having a palace for a home. Thinking about what Amira had said concerning the life of a princess, Marcus was even more sure he was doing the best thing by keeping his identity a secret.

With Cocoa asking to be carried, Marcus and Amira ended their walk. When they reached his building, Charlie tipped the bill of his hat to Amira and winked at Marcus. He'd also asked the doorman to use his "new" name. Charlie had simply replied, "Whatever you say, sir."

Sometimes Marcus wished his employees would question him, talk back to him, stand up to him. But he'd learned at a young age that having money gave him power.

They took the elevator to the penthouse, and Flora came to greet them as they stepped inside. His housekeeper was in her fifties, a sturdy woman with a congenial smile that touched everyone she met. Her light brown hair was styled in a no-nonsense short cut, and she always wore jade earrings in her ears claiming they brought her luck.

Now she held out four pink message notes to him. "Barbra said these take precedence, sir."

Marcus quickly glanced at Amira. Had she caught the first name of his secretary when she'd sat in his reception area? Apparently not. She was removing Cocoa's leash, totally unconcerned with what Flora had to say to him.

Flora went on, "She said she wouldn't have bothered you, but these are important."

Taking the message sheets, surprised by the reluctance he felt to deal with them—he usually handled his responsibilities with alacrity—he realized he couldn't forget he was Marcus Cordello for very long.

Amira must have heard some of the conversation because she rose to her feet and approached him. "If you have business to take care of, I really should go."

He didn't want her to go, that was the heck of it. He couldn't help thinking of the possibility of having an intimate dinner with her and taking her to bed tonight, teaching her all about passion, slowly kissing her and touching her until he had his fill of her. Maybe then he could put her out of his head. Maybe then he could think about her going back to Penwyck without a sense of loss.

"Why don't you let Flora make you a cup of tea? I'll try to get these calls finished as quickly as I can."

Flora glanced from one to the other. "I baked fresh blueberry scones."

Amira smiled at the older woman. "You know how to tempt a girl. Scones are one of my favorite treats.

The cook at the palace always keeps them in the breadbox for me.''

''It's settled then,'' Marcus decided. ''I'll start a fire in the fireplace. You can have your tea and scones there.''

In his mind's eye he could imagine coming home to Amira at night, sitting in front of the fire, telling her everything he'd never told anyone else. That thought unsettled him. He'd never really confided in a woman. Not even Rhonda. He'd always put work first and kept serious thoughts to himself. Is that why Rhonda hadn't confided in him about her diabetes? He blamed himself for her death, and he believed he always would.

Cocoa ran over to the sofa, jumped up and curled in the corner.

Flora cast a wary glance at Marcus. ''Do you want her there?''

''She's free to go wherever she wants.'' The dog's comfort was more important than hairs on the couch.

''I'll remember that,'' his housekeeper assured him with a smile and then headed for the kitchen. ''I'll get that tea started.''

Marcus crossed to the fireplace, took out one of the long matches, and touched it to the kindling. The fire leaped up the chimney, and he glanced over his shoulder at Amira who'd curled up beside Cocoa. He couldn't believe how badly he wanted to carry this royal lady to his bedroom.

After one last long look at her, he said, ''I'll be back as soon as I can,'' and strode down the hall to his office.

As he sat at his desk, he told himself Amira was

here today and would be gone tomorrow. That was the reality of it. Just how involved did he want to get?

Two hours later Marcus emerged from his office, his second conference call finally completed. So much for finishing with business quickly. Maybe Amira *had* already left. Rhonda used to get tired of waiting for him and she'd take off to do whatever she wanted to do. They'd been together yet apart, were committed to sharing a life yet hadn't started doing that.

Part of him knew that if Amira *had* left, that would be best. But as he walked into the living room and saw her napping with Cocoa in her lap, he felt the peace and light she brought him return again. He found himself quietly going to the sofa and standing over her, watching the firelight play in her hair, noticing the brush of her lashes against her cheek, the delicate tilt of her nose, her soft, soft skin. She looked so peaceful in sleep. She was such a beautiful woman. Her beauty came from more than her physical appearance. There was a quality about her that was uniquely charming. Maybe it was her kindness... maybe it was her sincerity. Whatever it was, it drew him until he forgot about restraint, forgot about protecting himself from involvement. He bent toward her and gave her a slow, sensual wake-up kiss.

Her eyes fluttered open and she smiled up at him. "Just like in the fairy tales," she said in a dreamy voice.

He knew she referred to Sleeping Beauty being awakened by her prince. Straightening, he said gruffly, "I'm no prince."

He had already proved that. If he hadn't been so self-involved, Rhonda would still be alive. He never wanted to feel responsible for another life again, and he certainly didn't want the responsibility for a whole country. His conference call had reminded him who he was, what he did, and what his life was all about. It certainly wasn't about princes and fairy tales and ladies who thought men on white chargers could transform their worlds.

He was feeling too much for Amira and that was entirely too dangerous. It was time to put an end to this now. "Something's come up and I have to take care of it right away. It's been foolish of me to let responsibilities slide for two days. I hope you understand." His tone was cool, matter-of-fact, not at all personal.

She looked confused by his manner and his tone, and he was sorry about that. He was sorry he'd kissed her again because every one of those kisses were indelibly engraved in his mind. He needed distance from her now. If he had distance, he'd see how unimportant the past two days had been.

"I see," she said softly, transferring the sleeping pup from her lap to the sofa. "I guess I'd better be going then."

When he didn't dissuade her or say anything else, she stood and he could almost see her wrapping her pride around her. "I saved you a scone." She nodded to the dish on the table. "But I suppose it's stale by now. Thank Flora for me, will you?"

"I'll do that." It was killing him to let her leave without a touch or a kiss, but he knew if he touched her or kissed her again, he'd want her to stay. That wouldn't be good for either of them.

She self-consciously brushed back her hair. "I suppose your doorman could hail me a cab."

"There's no need for that. I'll have my driver take you back to your hotel."

"You don't have to—"

"I insist. I'll buzz Fritz and he'll meet you in the lobby in five minutes."

"All right."

There were questions in her eyes he didn't want to answer. There was confusion he couldn't address.

The silence drew long between them until she gave him a tremulous smile. "I had a lovely time yesterday and today. Thank you."

"You're welcome." He wanted to tell her about all the things he'd felt and thought in the past two days, but he couldn't do that. He wasn't used to opening up to anyone, and telling her wouldn't change anything. He was being more curt than he wanted to be, but he didn't know how else to end this, how else to let her know he couldn't see her again.

"It was a pleasure to meet you, Amira. I hope you have a good trip back to Penwyck."

His message must have gotten through loud and clear because her cheeks reddened. "I *will* have a good trip." Then she went to the foyer, picked up her purse and sweater and opened the penthouse door.

As she left, he felt as if he'd lost someone very important to him.

After Amira left, Marcus tried to work but he couldn't concentrate. When Flora came to his door and asked him what he'd like for dinner, he told her a sandwich would be fine. She returned a few minutes later with a turkey sandwich, a cup of coffee and her own special corn-and-pepper chowder. But the food didn't appeal to him any more than the work. Cocoa ate more of the sandwich than he did. He decided walking the dog might help clear his head.

When he took Cocoa outside, the crisp night air was welcome, the sights and sounds of the city as noisy as ever. But as he walked, he kept seeing Amira as she played with Cocoa, as she rewarded her with a dog biscuit, as she'd hugged her close.

As walks go, it was a short one. Twenty minutes later he was back in his apartment again still feeling restless and unsettled and all together out of sorts. Even Cocoa deserted him as she ran to Flora's quarters beyond the kitchen.

Marcus returned to his computer, answering e-mails. There was one from Shane, and he decided a phone call would be a lot more satisfying. He tried his brother's number in California, but no one answered. Shane's life was entirely different from Marcus's. He liked to keep everything plain and simple. He told Marcus he never intended to be rich, he just wanted to be happy. His contracting business kept him busy, and he was more likely to spend an evening in a honky-tonk with friends than in an upscale restaurant with business colleagues. Their lives were so different, yet there was a bond between them that could never be broken.

When Shane didn't answer his phone, Marcus decided that was par for the course today.

The papers on Marcus's desk needed his attention, but after he'd shuffled them around for another half hour, he decided he couldn't sign them. He hadn't read them thoroughly enough.

What had Amira done to him? Cast some spell?

No, that was something out of those fairy tales she

spoke of. She'd simply gotten under his skin and he had to do something about that. A jog would do it.

Checking his watch, he saw it was already nine-thirty. If he ran hard enough and long enough, maybe he could actually get some work done when he returned.

Marcus left his building and took to the streets in turmoil about the past two days, in turmoil about the past two years. Since Rhonda had died, he'd done nothing but work, and it had paid off. At twenty-three he was considered one of the hottest tycoons in the country.

Yet what did that mean?

He could make any deal, turn the tables in negotiations to his benefit, invest in an Initial Public Offering and watch it soar. The last forty-eight hours with Amira, thinking about her, fantasizing about her, seemed to make all the rest pale in comparison. Damn it to blazes, she was a lady and lived on an island across the Atlantic! To complicate matters more, she was looking for *him*, to try to prove he was a prince. He'd been out of his mind to think he could have a fling with her without any repercussions.

Yet when he thought about not seeing her again...

He ran. His sneakers hit the pavement hard as he pounded up and down streets that he knew as well as the back of his hand. He didn't even feel the chill in the air. Concentrating on the impact of each downward thrust of his athletic shoes, he tried to wipe all thoughts from his mind, all guilt from his soul, all feeling from his heart. It hurt too much to have bonds. He'd never had a bond that hadn't been broken in some way. He certainly wasn't going to go seeking an involvement that was surely going to be disastrous.

Yet as he ran, Amira's face appeared before his eyes. He couldn't block it, and he slowed his pace knowing he couldn't run away from his memory of her. All he could do was work and let time pass, then he'd forget.

He'd been running for forty-five minutes. Now he decided to walk to cool down. Still seeing the expression in Amira's eyes as she'd looked up at the Sears Tower, as she tried her first soft pretzel and gotten mustard on her chin, as she'd leaned over the bathtub while Cocoa splashed her with water droplets, he was hardly aware of the man he'd passed lounging in a doorway. Lost in thought, Marcus didn't sense the stranger following him or realize the danger.

Suddenly the mugger was upon him. There was a flash of the blade of a knife. One moment Marcus was walking, the next he was fighting off a mugger, holding his arm up in a defensive move to protect himself from the blade. It missed his neck and went into his shoulder. In spite of the shock of the burning pain, he managed to knee the man in the groin. He felt the knife again, this time in his arm, and he went down on the pavement on one knee.

Then there was a shout. Someone yelled, "Grab him." Marcus didn't know if the voice was talking about him or the mugger.

Everything went fuzzy and gray. He was on the ground. Someone was putting pressure on his shoulder. He was hot and then cold. Finally there was a ringing in his ears that turned into the wail of a siren.

When the phone rang in Amira's hotel room, she glanced at the luminous dial in the darkness. She hadn't been able to sleep. All she could think about was Brent and how he'd dismissed her. What had she done wrong? He'd become so remote...

The phone rang a second time, and Amira wondered who would be calling her at 1:00 a.m. She sat up in bed, suspecting someone had the wrong room. It couldn't be the queen. It would only be 7:00 a.m. in Penwyck. Unless— What if the king's condition had worsened? He'd still been in a coma the last time she'd talked with the queen. What if something had happened to her mother or Harrison?

Fully awake now, she snatched up the receiver and switched on the bedside lamp. "Hello?"

"Lady Amira?"

The voice sounded familiar, but it wasn't the queen or her private secretary.

"It's Flora. Mr....Mr. Carpenter's housekeeper. I know it's terribly late, but I'm worried about Mr. Carpenter."

"What's happened, Flora?"

"He went for a jog tonight and was mugged. The mugger had a knife."

For a moment she remembered the night her father had been killed, the member of the royal guard telling her mother what had happened. She could hardly get her words out past the lump in her throat. "Is Brent all right?"

"That's why I phoned you. He called Fritz to pick him up at the hospital, and he got home about ten minutes ago. He looks terrible. The doctor wanted to keep him overnight, but he insisted they let him come home. I'm not sure what to do."

"What do you need, Flora? What does *he* need?"

"That's just it, Your Ladyship, I don't know. He's closed his office door and says he doesn't want to be bothered. But he should be in bed. He doesn't have anyone here. His father's in Minneapolis. Since he won't let me near him, I thought maybe he'd let *you* help. I thought if you came over, maybe you could talk some sense into him.''

After what had happened this afternoon, Amira didn't think he'd listen to her any better than Flora, but she could give it a try. "I'll get dressed and catch a cab.''

"No need for that, Your Ladyship.''

"It's Amira,'' she said gently. The housekeeper had been impressed with her title ever since Brent had introduced them. But the title was an encumbrance now. She had a feeling her title and her connections to royalty were one of the reasons Brent had backed off.

The housekeeper went on, "I spoke to Fritz about what I was going to do. He'll be on his way to fetch you as soon as I hang up. You shouldn't be out in a cab alone at night.''

"Thank you, Flora. If you think that's best.''

"I do, Your...I mean, Amira. Thank you so much for helping. Mr. C-Carpenter shouldn't be alone right now.''

The housekeeper's words ringing in her ears, her heart pounding, Amira quickly dressed in black flannel slacks and a white pullover sweater. Hurriedly she brushed her hair and pulled it back into a ponytail, clipping it with a gold barrette. She tried not to think about what had happened to Brent tonight. Certainly the doctors wouldn't have let him come home if he was seriously hurt. Yet, on the other hand, she suspected his determination would have convinced any doctor to let him go.

When Amira reached the lobby, the hotel doorman was holding the door for Fritz. The chauffeur had a grim expression on his face. "I'm glad Flora called you, miss."

"I'm glad she did, too. Let's go."

The doorman at Brent's building recognized Amira and tipped his hat to her. Apparently in Chicago everyone came and went at all hours of the night.

Amira stepped into the elevator, beginning to worry about her decision to come here. What if Brent didn't want to talk to her? What if he thought she was meddling?

She *was* meddling, but she cared about him more than she wanted to admit. After the way she'd left tonight, she thought she would never see him again.

Flora was waiting for her and opened the door before Amira could knock. Her brows were creased with worry as she let Amira inside. "He's still in his office. I offered to bring him tea or soup, but he says he doesn't want anything."

Amira dropped her purse and sweater on the foyer chair. "I'll see what I can do." Then she crossed the living room and went down the hall to his office. For a few moments she stood at the door listening. She could hear nothing inside.

She knocked softly.

Brent's gritty voice came from within. "I told you, Flora, I don't need anything." He sounded strained, as if talking was an effort.

Instead of waiting for permission to enter, which he'd probably deny, she opened the door and stepped inside. "It's not Flora, Brent, it's me."

He was seated at his desk and had a glass in his hand. It was half-full of amber liquid. Whiskey, she suspected. He was shirtless, and his left shoulder was swathed in gauze and tape. There was another patch of gauze farther down his arm. His hair was disheveled and his face was ashen.

Staring at her, he asked, "What are *you* doing here?"

Chapter Four

Amira realized that, in a sense, she was seeing Brent naked. He looked like death warmed over and probably felt like it, too. That's why he'd ordered Flora to go away. He didn't want anyone to see him like this. If he felt vulnerable and weak, he was the type of man who would fight against that and hide it until his last breath.

Afraid for him, caring so deeply that she hurt along with him, she tried to keep her voice light. "I'm making the rounds of businessmen who got mugged tonight. A sixth sense told me you might not be listening to doctor's orders."

He scowled at her. "Sixth sense my foot. If Flora called you, I'll fire her."

His threat lacked conviction, but she still protested, "No, you won't. She did the right thing. She's worried about you, Brent. You should be in a hospital. All she had to do was take one look at you and know that. *I* know that. Why didn't you stay?"

He took a sip of the amber liquid as if to fortify himself before he set down his glass. "They insisted I had to wear a hospital gown. I don't *wear* hospital gowns."

Any other time she was sure she would have seen sparkles of amusement in his eyes with the words. Now he was just trying to make her believe he wasn't as hurt as he was.

He looked at the glass sitting on the desk, then picked it up again and took another swallow. "You didn't tell me why you're here."

"Once Flora told me what happened, I was worried, too."

She approached him slowly, not sure she *did* belong here. Standing at the side of his desk, she saw he was wearing running shoes and red jogging shorts. Wasn't he cold sitting there like that? Then she realized the whiskey was probably making him hot as well as dulling the pain.

She nodded to the glass. "Did the doctor prescribe that?"

"No," he drawled. "He prescribed pills. They might dull the pain, but they make everything else fuzzy, too. I need to be able to think straight."

He needs to be in control, she thought to herself. "What were the doctor's orders?"

He gave her a narrowed glance. "Something about not moving around too much."

"You should at least be in bed."

"I have work to do," he grumbled.

"You can't work in your condition!"

"You have no idea what condition I'm in," he muttered.

"Yes, I do. I can see the lines around your mouth

and on your forehead. They're telling me you're in pain. Your color isn't good, either. And from the size of that gauze patch, I'd say you were hurt more than you want to admit.''

''What were you, a nurse in a previous lifetime?''

She kept telling herself his gruffness was a protective shield. ''I might live in a palace, but I'm not a stranger to the human condition. I know you don't want me here, but I think you need me here.''

This time he merely glared at her in stony silence.

''At least let me help you to the sofa.''

''I don't need a nurse.''

''Then consider me a friend.'' Worrying that the heat coming from his body emanated from more than the whisky he'd drunk, she put a hand to his forehead.

He leaned away. ''I might not be taking the pain pills, but I *am* on antibiotics. I'm not so foolish as to disregard the possibility of infection. The doctor made sure of that.''

''I'm glad to see you have some common sense,'' she returned. She knew if she didn't stand up to him, she might as well go back to her hotel.

''What happened to the proper, demure lady I had dinner with the other night?''

''She came up against a stubborn male who doesn't know what's good for him.''

His gaze locked on hers, and then he closed his eyes and shook his head in frustration. ''Go away, Amira.''

Instead of doing as he commanded, she knelt by his side and covered his hand with hers. ''What are you going to accomplish by trying to make yourself work tonight? If you rest, if you give your body what it needs, you'll get better faster.'' She motioned to the glass. ''Or have you already drunk too much of that to see reason?''

Silent for a very long time, he finally responded, ''This is my first glass, and I haven't even had half of it.''

''Will you let me help you to the sofa?'' she prodded gently.

''There's nothing wrong with my legs. It's my shoulder that feels as if it has a branding iron on it.''

Rising to her feet, she stood, watching him expectantly.

When he pushed himself up from the desk, he winced. She imagined any movement would hurt right now. Avoiding her gaze, he moved slowly over to the leather sofa.

Before he got there, she hurried ahead of him, propping a pillow against the arm.

He gave her a long look, then sank down heavily onto the camel leather.

''I'm going to get you something to drink. Would you like anything to eat?''

''I don't need anything—''

''Liquids will help you heal.''

''All right,'' he gave in with a sigh.

Before he could change his mind, she hurried to the kitchen.

Flora had already boiled water for tea and had a tray ready with apple juice and a scone.

After Flora poured the tea, Amira picked up the tray. ''I need a cover for him, too.''

''I'm just glad he's listening to you.''

''I'm being persistent about it. At least if he lets me watch over him and he needs further medical attention, we can call Emergency Services.''

"I hope that's not necessary. He'd hate that."

"I know he would."

The two women exchanged a look that said they knew the man better than he thought they did.

Flora hurried ahead of Amira. When Amira was at Brent's door, the housekeeper handed her a light blanket.

"Thanks, Flora. Why don't you go to bed. If I need anything, I promise I'll come get you."

"Are you sure? I'll be glad to stay up."

"I'm sure. Where's Cocoa?" She'd forgotten all about the dog in the commotion.

Flora smiled. "Curled up at the bottom of my bed. She's been asleep for a while now."

"I'm hoping Brent will sleep, too. That will be the best thing for him."

The housekeeper nodded and headed for her suite on the other side of the kitchen.

Pushing the door open, Amira entered Brent's office again and set the tray on the desk. Glancing at him, she saw that his eyes were closed. With a shake of her hand, she unfolded the blanket and covered him with it. Then she unlaced his sneakers and pulled them off, one by one.

When she was finished, he looked up at her. "Why did you come?"

She decided to tell him the blatant truth. "Because I care about you."

"Don't," he rasped.

"Caring is just something that happens," she said simply as she pulled a chair close to the sofa and offered him the glass of apple juice.

He didn't take it, but instead gestured to the chair. "What are you doing?"

"I'm going to watch over you for a while. I told Flora to go to bed. She needs her sleep."

"And you don't?"

"Would you rather have the tea?" she asked sweetly when he didn't take the glass of apple juice.

"Juice is fine," he said with a dark look.

While he drank, she sat down beside him.

After he finished it, she took the glass from him and set it on the floor next to her chair. "Did they catch the man who did this?"

"Yes."

She reached out and touched his arm. "Brent, I'm so sorry this happened to you." And she was so very grateful his injuries hadn't been worse. She'd never forgotten the look on her mother's face the night she'd been told her husband was dead. Amira knew it wasn't the same at all because she'd only known Brent a short time, but she would have known terrible anguish, too, if his wounds had been fatal.

Brent gazed at her, the expression in his green eyes undecipherable. But then, as if he could no longer put up resistance, he covered her hand on his arm with his. "You're a special woman, Amira."

"Not so special. Anyone could bring you juice and tea."

"I wouldn't let just anyone be in here right now."

She knew that was true.

When he closed his eyes, she didn't know if it was because of the pain or because he was tired. "Try to rest," she said softly.

"You can't sit there all night," he mumbled, eyes still closed.

"I'll sit here until you fall asleep."

His fingers remained covering her hand as if he

needed the contact with her, but she felt the pressure ease a bit as he seemed to relax. "Thank you, Amira," he said huskily.

She didn't want his thanks. She impossibly wanted a whole lot more.

The first rays of light streamed in the office windows when Amira awakened the next morning. Brent had stirred and she was concerned he needed something. As she'd sat beside him last night, making sure he was asleep, she'd been so tempted to brush his hair from his brow and put her lips to his cheek. But she didn't feel the freedom to take such intimacies. What would he think of her if he'd awakened? So she'd satisfied herself with watching him, making sure his chest rose and fell with deep, even breaths. Only when she couldn't keep her eyes open a moment longer had she tucked herself into the corner of the sofa by his feet.

The weight in her lap made her smile. Sometime during the night, she'd heard Cocoa's paws on the parquet floor right before she jumped up and settled down with her. It had been comforting to have her there, keeping watch, too.

Now Amira's gaze met Brent's in the early-morning shadows. "Good morning," she said, her voice still fuzzy from sleep.

She was grateful that Brent's color looked better. His dark beard stubbled his chin, and he looked roguish and altogether too sexy. She suspected any bruises he'd gotten in the scuffle last night would make themselves even more known today.

When he hiked himself up against the pillow at the

arm of the sofa, he grimaced. She could almost feel his discomfort.

"Have you been here all night?" he asked.

"Yes. You didn't think I'd leave and take the chance you'd get up in the middle of the night and work did you?"

At that he almost smiled as he nodded to Cocoa. "I see you even brought in reinforcements."

Relieved his sense of humor was back in place this morning, proving he felt a little better, she said honestly, "I wanted to be here in case you needed something."

Cocoa sat up in her lap, jumped down to the floor and went over to stand beside Brent. When Brent leaned down and rubbed his hand over the dog's head, Cocoa put her paws on the sofa and licked Brent's face. That greeting and measure of comfort finished, she trotted over to the rug by the bookshelves and settled in front of them.

Brent's green eyes were intense as they returned to Amira's. "I still can't believe you came last night."

"Why can't you believe it?"

"Because we've only known each other a few days."

"It feels as if it's been longer than a few days," she mused. "Besides, Flora said you needed me. Not many people in my life have needed me." She sat up and swung her legs to the floor.

Brent hiked himself up further and tossed the blanket aside. She could still feel his gaze on her as he asked, "Have you ever been seriously involved with a man?"

"No, not seriously...though when I was seventeen I thought I was in love with someone."

"Someone at the palace?"

She knew he was thinking about the royal family, about the Royal Guard, about other men her mother or the queen might have deemed worthy for her. "He was the gardener. I remember the day I stopped to talk to him. I hadn't even been out on a date at that point. He was clipping the hedges, and he gave me one of those looks men give women when they want to stop them from walking by."

"You were seventeen and hadn't been out on a date?" Brent asked, astonished.

"Whenever I needed an escort to a royal function, the queen chose one of the Royal Guards to accompany me. Sean was so different from any of them. He wasn't stilted or formal. He acted as if he wanted to be with me."

"How old was he?"

"Twenty-four."

Brent grunted. "Old enough to know he shouldn't be fooling around with someone as young as seventeen."

"I didn't realize that then. I didn't realize the flirting and the compliments didn't mean anything to him. After I met him a few times in one of the gardens, he kissed me and tried...more. I figured out what he really wanted was to get me into bed, maybe so he could brag about it. When I rejected his advances, he got nasty and said I'd better grow up, that I'd better learn how to give men what they wanted or I'd be a very *lonely* lady for the rest of my life."

Brent muttered a curse, and she looked up at him, surprised.

"I'm not much better than that gardener," he admitted, his brows furrowed. "That first evening I met you all I thought about was getting you into bed."

The glimpses of desire she'd caught in his eyes had thrilled her. Now, having him admit the strong attraction he'd felt, too, her mouth went dry. Finally she managed, "You're the most honest man I've ever met."

Shifting against the sofa arm, he looked uncomfortable. "There's something I need to tell you."

She waited.

His gaze studied her for a very long time. Then releasing a pent-up breath, he decided. "Never mind. It's not important. I have to get a shower." Rubbing his hand over his beard, he added, "And a shave."

"You can't get your shoulder wet." She didn't know if he could make it to his room on his own steam, let alone take a shower.

Swinging his legs to the floor, he sat there for a few moments. "I'm still in my running gear, and I smell like sweat and antiseptic. I have to change the dressing on my wounds, too."

"You might need help with that."

"Are you going to help me with my shower, too?" he asked wickedly.

As if she answered questions like that on a daily basis, she shrugged nonchalantly. "That depends. Do you really need help or are you just trying to make me feel uncomfortable?"

Dropping his head into his hands, he thrust his fingers through his hair.

Amira wished she could do the same thing with her fingers. When he'd kissed her, she'd slipped her hand into the hair at the nape of his neck. It had seemed such an intimate gesture that she hadn't realized what she was doing at the time. Now she consciously wanted to do it.

"I don't know what I'm trying to do," Brent muttered. "My shoulder hurts and my pride took a beating. I can't believe I wasn't listening last night, wasn't watching out. I can't believe I couldn't stop him before he did this."

Sliding closer to him, her knee grazed his. "I can only imagine how frustrated you must feel, but it could have happened to anyone."

He glanced at her sideways. "That doesn't make me feel better."

"What would make you feel better?"

When his gaze locked to hers, she could see the desire in his eyes as well as a deep need maybe even he didn't know was there. "You don't want to know."

"Yes, I do."

"Don't tempt me, Amira, or I'll be just as brash as that gardener."

"You couldn't be."

He shook his head again. "You give me too much credit."

"Maybe you don't give yourself enough."

The atmosphere in the room crackled with the attraction they both felt as well as the memory of their kisses. The silence stretched too long, and she broke it. "I want to help you any way I can."

"You're asking for trouble. Men don't like to accept help from a woman. It makes them grouchy."

Laughing, she stood. "I'm not going to retreat just because you're grouchy. What would that say about my character?"

"It would say you're not a glutton for punishment." At that he stood, too, and when he did, his color faded.

"Brent?"

"I'm okay. I need to do this on my own."

"All right. But I'll follow you to your room. I think you really ought to eat breakfast before you attempt this."

"Maybe you're right. I'll make a stop in the kitchen and let Flora feed me."

"I could bring your breakfast in here."

"I'm not going to act like an invalid. It's not in me. You're welcome to join me for breakfast if you want," he said with a wink. "Come on, Cocoa. Let's see if Flora's up."

Then Brent strode from his office as if he hadn't been injured at all. His denial of his condition made Amira watchful as she followed him and Cocoa to the kitchen.

Flora was indeed up and already making breakfast. She took a look at Brent, though, and shook her head. "You should be in bed, sir."

The walk from his office seemed to have tired Brent out, and he sank heavily into a chair at the table. "Once I eat your French toast and hash browns, I'll feel like new."

Amira couldn't help but roll her eyes. "You'll have to patent that recipe, Flora. Every restaurant in the country will want it."

Brent just scowled at her, and she imagined even that took energy. He didn't argue when she crossed to the counter and poured coffee for him.

Fifteen minutes later he'd only finished half of everything on his plate. He was looking gray again, and she suspected this little excursion had tired him out.

As she pushed her coffee cup away from her, she advised, "Maybe you should rest for a while now."

Ignoring her concern, he pushed himself up from the table. "I told you—I'm going to get a shower."

She was determined to take care of him, even though he was determined to take care of himself. "All right. While you get your shower, I'll stand outside the door in case you need me."

"That's not necessary," he argued.

"It might not be necessary, but I think it would be a good precaution. I've had first-aid classes. I can change the bandages for you when you're finished."

His gaze caught and held hers. Then he headed for his room, not checking to see if she followed.

Brent could access his bathroom from inside his bedroom or from the hallway outside. While the shower ran, Amira stood in the hall, waiting to see if he needed help. He'd held his shoulder and arm stiffly this morning, but he'd seemed steady on his feet. It was obvious he was a proud man who didn't want to turn to anyone for help. That didn't mean he didn't *need* help.

When the shower stopped running, Amira listened for sounds of movement inside the bathroom. Ten minutes later Brent opened the door and faced her squarely. He was as pale as he'd looked last night, and he was holding on to the doorjamb. The pair of black flannel jogging shorts he wore now rode low on his hips. Her gaze passed up the length of all that tanned skin. His hair was still damp, and his creased brow and the expression in his eyes told her he was in pain.

How long could he stand there without leaning on her?

She ran her fingers over the edges of the shoulder bandage. It was dry. Somehow he'd managed to keep his shoulder and arm clear of the water. Her fingers not only touched the gauze but briefly grazed his skin, and the steamy atmosphere around them seemed to become electrified.

"I hate to ask you to do this, but I don't think I can handle changing the shoulder bandage on my own."

"Let's do it in your bedroom," she said softly, knowing asking for help was difficult for him. She knew he'd be more comfortable in his bed and by the time they'd finished he might need to lie down.

Amira saw the bandaging supplies on the sink.

"Everything's there that I need," he said gruffly. "The nurse got all of it for me from the hospital pharmacy."

He was standing in the doorway, and there was just enough room to slip past him to the sink. When she did, her breasts grazed his arm. Neither could ignore the jolt of awareness.

"I'll wait in the bedroom," he told her.

Amira quickly gathered up the supplies and followed him into his room. It was decorated in tan and navy and was as masculine as he was. The oak bed was definitely king-size. It was covered with a navy, tan and white geometrically designed quilt. The same fabric draped the windows. A triple dresser was empty except for a wooden valet that held Brent's wallet and change. With the door to the armoire standing open, she guessed his jogging shorts had come from one of the drawers.

"Sit there." She motioned to the edge of the bed. As he did, she realized there was only one way to get to his shoulder easily. She had to stand between his legs. He must have realized that the same time she did because he moved his thighs wider apart. When she stepped into the space, her heart was thudding so hard she could barely hear herself think. Then she concentrated on what she was doing and Brent's well-being...not the exciting, ferocious, scary feelings he stirred up in her.

When she removed the bandage from Brent's shoulder, she saw that the wound was long and deep. He glanced at her to see if she could handle the task, but she kept her mind focused and didn't meet his eyes. She worked quickly for her benefit as well as his.

After she'd finished, he was whiter than before and she knew he'd have to give in to the pain and the need to rest soon. "Would taking a pain pill be so terrible?" she asked.

"I'd rather feel the pain and know what's happening to me. Besides, looking at you is all the pain medication I need."

Along with his discomfort, she saw the passionate sparks in his eyes. What if he gave in to them? What if *she* gave in to them?

Emboldened by everything that had passed between them, by her night on the couch watching him and listening for his breathing, she asked, "If that's true, then why did you send me away yesterday?"

She was standing so close to him, she could smell the soap he'd used, see the line of his beard stubble even though he'd shaved, feel the heat from his body. They weren't even touching and she was trembling all over. They didn't have to be touching for her to feel the sizzle between them.

Brent let out a sigh. "I think you know the answer to that, Amira. If we keep seeing each other, one or both of us is going to get hurt."

Although she didn't want to believe it, she knew he was right. She knew if she stayed, they'd get closer and closer. Obviously, Brent didn't want that. Then she thought about their kisses, saw longing in his eyes now. Even if he did want to be with her, even if he let her into his life, what would happen when she had to go back to Penwyck? His work was here, his life was here. If they *did* become involved, they wouldn't be able to have anything more than a fling because of who he was and who she was. She'd never had a fling, and she didn't think she ever would. Her dreams were about a husband and marriage and children. A girl didn't get those by giving in to an attraction that was too hot to handle.

She thought about everything she'd done since she'd met Brent. She hardly knew him and she was standing in his bedroom thinking about what they'd do in his bed! What had happened to the values her mother had taught her?

Whenever she was around Brent, there was no black or white. There was only gray and the feelings that were deepening for him. She had to be true to who she was. She couldn't disappoint her mother or the queen.

"You're right," she responded in answer to what he'd said. "We would get hurt."

Quickly she stepped away from him and picked up the gauze, tape and scissors. "After I put these in the bathroom, I'm going to leave. I'll tell Flora you're resting. If you need anything else, I'm sure she can get it for you."

He didn't look surprised or disappointed, and he didn't ask her to stay. "Thank you, Amira...for everything you've done. I'll never forget it."

"I'll never forget you," she whispered, tears coming to her eyes.

Then she turned away from him and left his bedroom, before she crawled into that bed beside him and gave him any comfort he wanted.

Chapter Five

Empty.

Since Amira had left the penthouse a few minutes ago, he'd felt empty.

It was a feeling Marcus had never had before and one he didn't like. Being the man of action that he was, even in his present condition, there was only one thing to do.

Fill the void.

Picking up the phone on his bedside table, he decided Shane should be up. In fact, he might already be at a construction site. Marcus kept telling his twin he should get a cell phone, but his brother just wasn't that type.

Shane answered on the first ring. "About time I hear from you," he chided. "Did you buy the State of California yet?"

Marcus laughed. There was no jealousy between them. Shane did his thing and Marcus did his. They supported each other, happy in each other's successes, sympathetic at each other's losses.

"Not yet. Do you have a few minutes?"

"I should have been out the door a half hour ago. But I always have time for you. What's up?"

Marcus knew how the business clock ticked. If Shane said he should be on the job, then he should be. Marcus didn't want to have a rushed conversation about Amira's story. But he did have a question.

"Tell me something. Do you remember Mother or Dad telling any stories about labor and delivery?"

"Ours, you mean?"

"Yes, ours," Marcus responded patiently. "You've been around Mother more than I have. Did she ever talk about it?"

"Not that I can recall. Why?"

Why, indeed. Even a long phone conversation wouldn't handle this. He needed to talk to Shane in person. They hadn't seen each other for a while... "What does your schedule look like for the next few weeks?"

"I'll be starting a new project. Long days, short nights. You know the drill. Why?"

"I thought I might fly out. There's something I want to discuss with you."

"So discuss. You're asking odd questions."

"I know. I met a woman who started me thinking about some things. That's all."

"A woman? A pretty woman?" There was amusement and hope in Shane's voice.

"Yes, a very pretty woman. But she's not from the U.S. and she's leaving soon. I've decided it's better if I don't see her again. I was going to have Fritz drive me up to Shady Glenn today, but..."

Something in Marcus's voice must have alerted Shane that something was wrong. "You're not leaving today?"

"I was mugged last night."

"You mean your wallet was stolen?"

"Not as simple as that. The mugger had a knife."

"Blue blazes, Marcus! Are you all right?"

"If I don't move too fast. He got my shoulder. I should feel a lot better by tomorrow. Today I'm just a bit wiped out."

"You went to a doctor, I hope."

"I didn't have any choice. Somebody called an ambulance. But I came home last night. I couldn't stay in that place. You know how I feel about hospitals." After Rhonda had slipped into a coma, he'd sat by her bedside for two days. Then he'd lost her. Shane knew that.

"Yeah, I know how you feel about them. At least Flora was there to look after you. Wasn't she?"

"I wouldn't let Flora look after me so she called in reinforcements."

"Fritz?"

Marcus laughed. "He was in on it. She called Amira—the woman I told you about—and he drove her over."

"And just what does this Amira look like?"

"Blond hair, violet eyes."

"And..." Shane probed.

"And she's as innocent as an angel. Not like any twenty-year-old I've ever met. She's been protected and chaperoned all her life."

"Uh-oh. It sounds like more than a little interest there."

"It's impossible," Marcus said in frustration. "She lives on an island an ocean away."

"Are you sure you're not going to see her again?" Shane asked.

"It's not a good idea."

"Good idea or not, it sounds as if maybe you should." There was a lengthy pause before Shane asked, "Is she in your dreams?"

Marcus knew what his brother meant. "Yes."

"Is she in your thoughts when you're awake, too?"

He didn't answer that one.

"You might have to see her again to get her out of your system."

Marcus knew his brother might be right. "She's something else, Shane. She really is. Like no woman I've ever met. I can forget about deals and investments and whether she's with me because of who I am and what I have."

"Then see her again."

Marcus heard a loud male voice calling for Shane.

His brother said, "Uh-oh. One of my subcontractors is at the door. Must be an emergency. Do you want to talk later?"

"I'll phone you next week. We'll see if we can coordinate our schedules."

"Sure thing. You can always help me dig a footer."

Marcus could hear the grin in his twin's voice.

After Marcus hung up, he thought about what Shane had said about seeing Amira again. Should he take the risk?

For the rest of Saturday, long into the night and all day Sunday, Marcus thought about Amira—how special she was, how much he liked being with her, how much he wanted her. She was alone in Chicago, and he was the only person she really knew. If he went away, he'd feel as if he was deserting her.

He wasn't just going to Shady Glenn for a vacation, but to spend some time at Reunion House. He liked being with the kids and making repairs on the old house. It gave him a different kind of satisfaction from the usual work he did, the kind of satisfaction Shane had all the time, he imagined—working with his hands, building. Marcus suspected that Amira would like Reunion House and enjoy meeting the kids there. Yet, after the way they'd left things yesterday, he didn't know if she'd accept his invitation. His father would be at Shady Glenn, so having a chaperone wouldn't be a problem.

But he needed an enticing way to ask her to join him.

Cocoa ran into his office then, barked at him and stood on her hind legs.

Marcus smiled. He did have an idea, and one he suspected would work very well.

On Monday morning Amira was debating how she would spend the day. She'd dressed in a blue, tailored pantsuit ready to go sight-seeing. Yet the thought of doing it without Brent didn't seem very satisfying. She knew she had to stop pining for him. She knew she had to forget about him. It was very hard, especially when she had a week on her hands that she didn't know what to do with.

The knock on her door was unexpected. Crossing to it, she looked out the peephole and saw a yellow wagon with Cocoa sitting in it!

Opening the door, she didn't know what to expect. There was Brent standing two feet from the wagon, grinning at her.

"What are you doing here?"

He nodded to the wagon and the envelope propped beside Cocoa. "Read it," he suggested.

Stooping down, she patted the dog on the head and ruffled her ears. Then she picked up the envelope and opened it, her heart racing. The invitation inside read, "Come along with me to see Shady Glenn and Reunion House. Cocoa."

She looked up at Brent, confused.

Taking the handle of the wagon, he pulled it inside. When he straightened, his hand went to his shoulder and she could tell he was still in pain.

"What are you doing up and out?" she asked, concerned.

With a shrug he smiled. "I have things to do, places to go, people to see."

"You need a keeper," she muttered.

"How would you like to be my keeper for a few days?" His green eyes said the invitation was a serious one.

She didn't know how or what to respond to that.

"I'm going to Shady Glenn to recuperate until next weekend. I know how you worry about chaperones. My father's going to fly in this evening. So he'll be there. While you're there, you can check out Reunion House. The kids love visitors and you can help me present Cocoa to them."

The whole idea seemed like another wonderful adventure. Did she dare go with him?

His smile fading, he leaned toward her, slowly combed his fingers through her hair and smoothed his thumb over the side of her cheek. "Amira, I know we live in different worlds and all we'll ever have is this week. But having it could be better than not having it. Don't you think?"

She knew she was falling in love with Brent, and she also knew love came along maybe once in a lifetime if you were lucky. Her mother had been twice blessed, but not everyone was. Amira knew what she felt for Brent was special, and if she stayed here and didn't go with him, she'd regret it for the rest of her life.

"I don't know what I'll tell the queen."

He continued to stroke her cheek as if he garnered as much pleasure from it as she did. "I'm sure you'll think of something. You could tell her you're seeing some of the state while you're here. That's true."

Yes, it was. And the queen *had* told her she should see the sights. "I'll have to give her the number at…Shady Glenn, is it?"

"That's no problem. Do you really think she'll be calling?"

"Only if there's something new to report. I can check in with her secretary and then she won't worry about me."

"So you'll go?"

She realized the decision had been made as soon as he'd asked. "Yes, I'll go."

They were gazing at each other, and neither of them seemed to be able to look away until Cocoa barked a few times.

Brent chuckled. "I'll translate for her. She says to pack light and to bring jeans and sweaters."

"I don't have any jeans along. When do you want to leave?"

"Whenever you're ready."

"Can I have a couple of hours to go shopping first?"

"Sure. I can even recommend a few stores."

Amira's phone rang then. Cocoa trotted over to the instrument and barked at it as if she didn't welcome the intrusion, either.

"I have to get that," Amira apologized. "It might be the queen...or my mother."

Brent nodded, but she could tell from the look in his eyes that he really didn't understand her being on-call and what this mission to find Marcus Cordello meant to Penwyck.

After she picked up the receiver, a strong masculine voice asked, "Miss Corbin? This is Cole Everson."

Cole Everson, the head of the Royal Intelligence Institute, had coordinated the efforts to find Marcus Cordello and his brother. "Hello, Mr. Everson. The queen told me you might be phoning. Have you found a picture yet?"

Out of the corner of her eye, Amira noticed Brent take Cocoa into her sitting area and stand by the window.

"Unfortunately, I haven't. This man protects his privacy with a vengeance and so does everyone else around him. I can't even get hold of a home address. Mail that doesn't go to his business is sent to a P.O. box. I've decided to initiate surveillance on the P.O. box so we can follow whoever picks up the mail to wherever Marcus Cordello lives. I understand he's going to be out of the city this week."

"That's what his secretary told me, and I don't think it was a ploy. She seemed sincere."

There were a few moments of silence. "I discussed

this with the queen, Miss Corbin, and if you'd like to return to Penwyck, I can find someone else to try to meet with the man.''

"Is that what the queen wants?"

"I think the queen wants what's best for you. If you'd rather not be in Chicago alone for a week, or feel this is getting too frustrating for you—"

"I want to do this for Queen Marissa and King Morgan," she told Cole. Glancing at Brent, she saw he was watching her intently. "I'm going to take the next few days as a...holiday and see some of the countryside. I'll inform the queen's private secretary where I can be reached."

"When will she have that information?" he asked.

"Later today."

"All right. If I need to contact you, I'll get it from her. I'm hoping to have a photograph by the end of the week. Cordello attended a private school and graduated when he was sixteen. I'm trying to obtain a yearbook from the school. If we can just get that, I'll have an artist age his features properly so you can at least know what he looks like now."

"Mr. Everson, is Marcus Cordello a recluse?"

"No. He just guards his privacy and the details of his life carefully. That's not unusual in men of his wealth and stature. Tabloids can get hold of photos and use them to their own benefit. But we'll track something down. That's my job. By the time you return to the city, I should have a home address for him, too. In the meantime, you have a good holiday. Will you be needing an escort or a guide? I'm sure the queen will provide one."

"No. I don't need an escort. I'll be staying at

a...guest house someone recommended. I'll be quite safe."

"You're sure about this, Miss Corbin? A young woman alone in a strange country—"

"I'm sure, Mr. Everson."

"All right, then. As soon as I have more information, I'll be in touch."

After she hung up the phone, Amira crossed to the sitting area where Cocoa was sniffing the rug and the furniture and anything else that looked interesting.

"What was that all about?" Brent asked, looking concerned.

"Just an update from the head of the Royal Intelligence. He's trying to find a home address for Mr. Cordello. They're going to stake out his post office box."

Brent glanced out the window as if he was looking for the man himself. "I see. Did I hear you mention something about a photograph?"

"Mr. Everson is having trouble locating one. He's hoping to have something by the end of the week. When I told him I was going to take a holiday, he wondered if I wanted an escort or a guide."

At that Brent turned from the window and gazed at her. "What did you tell him?"

"That I don't need one."

"And that you're staying at a guest house."

"Yes. I'll be a guest at your house, right? I don't want to mislead the queen, but...she just wouldn't understand. Neither would my mother."

Approaching her slowly, Brent held her gaze with his. "Are you sure you want to come with me? I don't want you to do anything you'll regret."

"This is my decision to make, Brent, no one else's. I'm sure."

Marcus felt guilty as hell. He'd known what that conversation with Everson was all about, and as soon as Amira had hung up, he'd considered telling her the truth. But if he did, that would be the end of whatever was starting between them. He wanted this week with her. He wanted it more than he'd ever wanted anything in his life. If he told her who he was now, she'd call the queen...she'd call Everson. Lord knew who else she'd call. His life, as well as his brother's and his parents', might never be the same. Any sparks between him and Amira would smother in the ashes of the search for twins and royal obligations. He didn't understand royal obligations, and he didn't want to be any part of them.

So instead of telling her his true identity, he offered, "Fritz will drive you to wherever you want to shop and then bring you back here to pack. I'll try to clear my desk so I can leave the city with a free mind."

As free as it could be, knowing that when they returned, they'd both have to deal with Marcus Cordello.

"This is beautiful country," Amira said as Fritz drove her and Brent to Shady Glenn. "The leaves are gorgeous!"

"Oaks and maples, sycamores and elms. Fall is always a spectacle here. I never tire of this drive."

He might never tire of the drive but the drive was tiring him out, she noticed. He was pale again, and lines of fatigue etched his brow. No matter how hardy he said he was, he needed time to recover from the knife wound and the mugging.

Amira thought about Princess Anastasia, her best friend at the palace, and how well she'd recovered from the unexpected trauma in *her* life. Anastasia, who was five years older, had taken Amira under her wing when Amira and her mother moved there. Everyone had been worried about Anastasia the last few weeks. She'd been in a plane crash and had gone missing. Thank goodness Jake Sanderstone had found her. Although amnesia had complicated their relationship, she and her knight in shining armor had found the kind of love that would last a lifetime...the kind of love Amira dreamed of.

The kind of love she was beginning to feel for Brent?

Concerned for him, she hoped his father might convince him to take it easy for a few days.

About an hour away from Shady Glenn, they stopped at a pleasant restaurant for dinner. Amira noticed how Brent always turned the conversation away from himself, and she wished he'd let down his guard a little. She wished he'd let her get to really know him.

They arrived at Shady Glenn as darkness fell over the rolling hills. Fritz parked beside the old three-story stone house, which was surrounded by blue spruce. Floodlights illuminated the outside of the house, and Amira could see its high double-wide windows and the broad front porch with dark brown railing and balustrades. A detached garage sat at the end of the gravel drive.

"It's elegant," she said simply.

Brent attached Cocoa's leash so the dog wouldn't

run off into strange territory. "I've never thought about it that way. It was always just home. Even after we moved to the city, I thought of it as home."

"Maybe that's because you were your happiest here."

That brought his gaze to hers. "I guess. We were a family here, and my brother and Dad and I still are."

"And your mother?"

He stared at the front door of the house as if he was seeing his mother there. "My mother is never satisfied with what she has. She's on her fifth marriage."

Glancing back at Amira, he asked, "You said your mother remarried?"

"Yes. But I like Harrison. I didn't know how much I missed having a father until he married my mother. When they return from their honeymoon, I'm hoping the three of us can spend more time together."

Fritz had taken their luggage from the trunk while they were talking and now went ahead of them to the porch steps. Brent climbed out of the car with Cocoa and came around to the passenger side, opening Amira's door. They walked up the brick path to the house.

A few moments later they were standing inside. Amira didn't think she'd ever seen a house that looked more inviting. The furniture was large and overstuffed in colors as bright as the rainbow. Braided rugs were surrounded by beautiful, polished hardwood floors. There was a full-size quilt hanging on one wall, and Amira went over to it, studying the workmanship.

"This is beautiful," she murmured.

"My grandmother, my father's mother, made it

along with some of the stitcheries you'll see on the walls upstairs.'' There were a few paintings of pastoral scenes and a copper sculpted flight of birds hanging beside one of them.

"I thought Dad would be here by now. I'm going to check the machine. My cell phone signal is weak in this area."

Amira wandered around as Brent went into what she presumed was the kitchen.

He was back a few moments later, a scowl on his face. "I have some news that might change your plans. My father's been delayed for a few days, some type of management crisis. That means you won't have a chaperone here."

Amira's pulse beat faster. "What about Fritz?"

"I keep a car in the garage. Fritz is going to take a few days off and visit family in the area. We'll be here alone."

Was there really a message from Brent's father? Had he planned this? Did she know him well enough to trust him?

"I know what you're thinking, but I *didn't* plan this. Do you want to hear the message?"

Instantly she felt guilty for her thoughts. Why couldn't she trust her instincts with Brent? Maybe because he was still so guarded. "No. I don't need to hear the message."

"I can have Fritz drive you back to Chicago if that's what you want."

She saw how tired Brent looked, remembered how kind he'd been to her the past few days, recalled every detail of every one of his touches and kisses. She almost felt as if it were her duty to take care of him.

Because she cared about him so much?

She felt a lot more than duty. Over the years in the palace, she'd learned about loyalty and faithfulness and always being ready to serve. But all these feelings for Brent took everything she'd learned to a new realm. Still, she shouldn't make a rash decision. She'd been taught that, too.

"I'll stay the night and decide what happens after that in the morning. I can always hire a driver to take me back." They weren't too far from De Kalb and she suspected there was a car service there.

"That sounds good to me." Brent looked relieved.

Fritz interrupted them as he came down the stairway. "Sir, I took the luggage upstairs. The master bedroom is made up, but the other two aren't."

"That's all right, Fritz, I'll take care of it. You get going."

"Thank you, sir. I'll check on the Jaguar before I leave. It was serviced two weeks ago and it should be in great condition. But I'll make sure."

"I'm sure it's fine. Tell Estelle I said hello."

"I will, sir." He gave Brent a smile and then headed for the door.

Brent glanced at the stone fireplace. "Would you like a fire?"

She could imagine sitting in front of the crackling fire with Brent and no one else around except Cocoa. She wasn't sure she should take the chance and put them in temptation's way. Not tonight.

"I think I'm going to turn in early." Maybe if she did, he would, too. He certainly needed the rest.

"All right. I'll go make up your bed then."

"You know how to make beds?" she teased.

"When my brother and I were kids, we had chores

just like everyone else. Do *you* know how to make up a bed?''

She grinned at him. ''I didn't move into the palace with my mother until I was ten. Like you, I knew the realities of running a home. Even at the palace I make up my own bed so Delia doesn't have to.''

''Who's Delia?''

She felt a bit embarrassed by admitting, ''She's sort of a valet for both me and my mother. She keeps our rooms clean, makes sure my clothes are pressed. That sort of thing.''

''It seems you and I have a lot in common,'' he said pensively as he started up the stairs.

Brent showed Amira to a pretty room decorated in shades of aqua and yellow. The curtains were lacy as was the bedskirt. The Aubusson rug on the floor showed wear, but was still very beautiful.

''I'll be right back,'' he said.

In a few minutes he brought sheets and a blanket to the room. Removing the patchwork quilt, he laid it over the cane-back rocker. Together they made the bed. When he stretched the blanket across the top sheet, his gaze caught hers. They went to smooth out a wrinkle at the same time and their fingers brushed. Backing away, Brent lifted the quilt from the rocker.

As he tossed it across the bed, he grimaced.

Amira warned, ''You shouldn't be doing this.''

''I'm not an invalid,'' he brusquely reminded her once more and tossed the pillows on top of the quilt.

''No, you're not. But you were hurt only three days ago, and you're trying to act as if it didn't happen. You can't do that, Brent.''

He faced her with his jaw set. ''Why not?''

''Because you need time to heal. You're not a superhero, even though I forget that sometimes,'' she added with a smile.

His annoyance dissipated, and he slowly came around the bed and took her hands in his. ''You're very good for me, Amira. When I'm with you, I feel peaceful. I haven't felt that way in a very long time.''

''Do you only feel peaceful?'' she asked tentatively, not knowing if she should.

''If only you knew,'' he murmured as he folded his arms around her, bringing her close to him. ''In one sense I feel peaceful. In another…''

He let his words trail off as he lowered his head and covered her lips with his. She knew in every kiss he was acknowledging how innocent she was, how inexperienced. He seemed to use that to awaken the fire in her, to awaken passions she never knew she'd feel. His tongue taunted her upper lip, and she tightened her arms around him. Then he angled his head so he could take the kiss deeper, and she moaned softly, feeling prickles of fire in every part of her, longing for satisfaction she'd never known. The pure sensuality of his hands passing up and down her back, his scent, his slow, enticing ravishment of her mouth weakened her knees and made her feel as if she were drowning in Brent.

Suddenly he stopped all of it and lifted his head. ''I don't know what this week's going to bring, but I do know I won't take advantage of you. I want you to realize what you're doing every step of the way. Since we don't even know if you're going to stay, I think I'd better go to my room.''

She admired so much about Brent Carpenter—his honesty, his sincerity, his kindness. He was real yet noble, as noble as the soldiers who protected the king, as noble as the military who fought to keep Penwyck free.

Should she stay here alone with him or shouldn't she? If she did, she knew what might happen. She welcomed the thought of truly loving Brent, yet she didn't know much about him. What if he often picked up women and brought them home? What if she wasn't special to him? What if she gave her heart and he kept protecting his?

"Have you ever been seriously involved in a relationship?" she asked him.

Stepping away from her, his face changed, and she could no longer see the desire in his eyes. She could see nothing there now and that scared her.

"Yes, I've been seriously involved. But I don't want to discuss it, Amira. It has nothing to do with you and me being here now."

"I don't think that's true," she protested. "Whatever happened in your past shaped who you are, just as mine shaped me. While we're here, I'd like to get to know you better. Isn't that why you asked me along?"

His response was quickly emphatic. "No. I asked you along so we could enjoy each other's company, go out on the lake, appreciate the children."

"And?" she prompted, knowing what else was on his mind because it was on hers.

"And…maybe do whatever comes naturally to a man and a woman."

Suddenly she had to know the truth. "Did you bring me here to seduce me?" she asked bluntly.

At first she saw anger flash in his eyes, but it disappeared and all that was left was exasperation. "Where is this coming from?" he asked. "I told you

I won't take advantage of you. If and when we have sex, we'll both want it. Seduction isn't part of that.''

''I see,'' she said softly, more confused than ever. He wouldn't seduce her, but he wanted to have sex with her. He wanted her company, but he didn't want to go any deeper than surface chatter.

Cocoa ran up the steps then and into Amira's room.

''I'd better take her out for a walk,'' Brent said gruffly. ''Feel free to turn in. I'll keep her with me.''

There had been a wall around Brent before, but it had cracked here and there and she'd seen glimpses into his soul. Now it seemed he'd patched up all the cracks and she couldn't see into him at all. Maybe she should leave in the morning...or maybe she should work at tearing that wall down.

''I'll see you in the morning, then,'' she murmured.

''In the morning.''

When he left her room, he shut the door. She felt he'd also shut it on the feelings that were growing between them because maybe they were just too uncomfortable for him to handle.

Chapter Six

When Amira came downstairs the following morning, Brent was already sitting at the kitchen table, a mug of coffee in front of him, Cocoa at his feet. "Instant," he said, grimacing. "If we want breakfast, we'll have to buy groceries. I waited in case you'd like to come along."

Cocoa ran to Amira, and she bent down to pet her. "Where do we have to go?"

"About two miles up the road there's a general store. They sell a little bit of everything. You might enjoy the uniqueness of it. Even if you decide to go back to the city, you need to eat before you go."

She latched on to the practicality of that. "I'd like to see your general store."

Standing, he took his cup over to the sink and dumped the coffee down the drain. "Nice outfit," he said with a nod and a hint of a smile.

Because she wasn't used to wearing the type of clothes she'd put on, she felt a bit self-conscious. The

royal-blue leggings hugged her body from her waist
to her ankles. Her cashmere sweater was the same
color blue, short, only coming to her waist. It swung
a little when she walked. According to the salesclerk,
the black, tie-shoes on her feet were all the rage. They
felt a bit clompy to her, but fashion was fashion.

"It feels a little bit odd," she admitted.

"What do you wear when you attend classes?"

"Slacks and sweaters. Nothing like this. It would
raise more than a few eyebrows."

"Do you have men in those classes?"

"Sure we do."

"Then it would raise a few temperatures, too."

She knew she was blushing and couldn't help it.
"Are we taking Cocoa?" she asked, changing the
subject because it reminded her too much of what
they'd said to each other last night.

"We'd better leave her here. They might not let
her inside. She'll be fine. I'll go get the car. Just turn
the button on the knob and the door will lock when
you shut it."

After Amira found her sweater in the living room,
she said goodbye to Cocoa, then locked the door and
waited for Brent. They rode to the general store in
silence. She felt a tension between them this morning—a different kind of tension than the one that had
hung between them since they'd met. It had to do
with her decision to stay or go, with her question last
night about Brent's serious relationship. He obviously
didn't want to reveal anything about his personal life.
If she stayed, maybe she'd figure out why.

The general store was a clapboard building situated
next to a gas station. Four concrete steps led to the

wooden screen door. The inside door was open even though the temperature outside was cool.

Brent went in first and took a quick look around. When he saw the salesclerk, he seemed to relax. He picked up the top plastic basket from a stack inside the door. "What would you like for breakfast?" he asked her.

"Can we make pancakes with blueberries?"

"We can if there are blueberries in that case over there." He pointed to the refrigerated section.

She went to the case and peeked inside like a kid in a candy store, not knowing whether to pick up the blueberries in the box or the ones in the bag.

"I don't do much grocery shopping," she admitted as he came over to join her.

"I don't, either. We make a good pair. We're both out of touch with the real world."

Slanting him a glance, she saw he was serious. "Coming to the United States has given me a whole new perspective on a lot of things."

"Like?" he asked.

"How sheltered palace life is, how much of the world I haven't seen, how much freedom I've never really had...how very protected I've been. This trip, succeeding in meeting Marcus Cordello...it's like a rite of passage for me."

A shadow seemed to cross Brent's face.

"What's wrong?" she asked.

"Nothing. I'm hungry, that's all. I'll pick up a few provisions, then we can go stir up those pancakes."

When they returned to Shady Glenn, Marcus grabbed both bags of groceries and wouldn't let Amira help carry them. Their conversation about the real world had troubled him, reminding him of

Rhonda and the life he'd led with her. She had been hip and sassy, lighthearted and fun. It had been convenient for them to be together, convenient for them to care about each other, convenient to think about a future. She'd loved everything his money could buy her, and he'd loved giving her presents and a taste of his world.

What he regretted was not giving her enough of himself. If he had, she would have told him she had diabetes. She wouldn't have hidden the fact that she had to give herself insulin twice a day. If he'd known about her condition, he would have watched her more carefully.

Everything he was feeling about Amira was bringing back all of the old baggage he'd fought to leave behind.

Amira's questions last night had made him defensive, and he'd handled all of it badly. He'd had to ask himself honestly—had he brought her here to seduce her? The answer to that was yes, so he knew he had to back off, treat her like a friend and answer some of her questions. That's the conclusion he'd come to in the middle of the night.

Cocoa greeted them both as if she hadn't seen them for years.

Afterward Brent found a griddle in one of the cupboards and then started coffee brewing. Silently Amira took a large bowl from a cabinet and began to mix the pancake batter.

Once he'd poured the water into the coffeemaker, he leaned against the counter, deciding to take the bull by the horns. "You asked me last night if I'd ever had a serious relationship."

She stopped stirring.

"When I was twenty-one I was engaged. Her name was Rhonda."

Amira lifted her eyes to his. "What happened?"

Crossing his arms over his chest, he began, "I wish I could tell you we had an argument and went our separate ways. That would have been easier than what happened." He thought about his life a few years ago. "I met Rhonda at a party. I went to a lot of them back then. I was a bachelor looking for a good time, earning a master's degree in finance. Rhonda was in an undergraduate program in the same field so we had a lot to talk about. She was one of those women who never ran out of things to say or suggestions for fun things to do. We had a fast life. I worked at my business during the day, earned my master's at night. She was in her senior year, determined to become an investment banker."

"It sounds as if the two of you fitted together well," Amira said quietly.

"I thought we did. But she didn't tell me something very important about herself, and I still can't decide if that was my fault or hers. She had diabetes and she wasn't taking good care of herself. I didn't know that. I thought she was losing weight because she wanted to be model thin. I didn't realize she sometimes skipped her insulin or didn't eat when she should have. And when I found out, it was too late."

"She became ill?"

He pushed away from the counter and jammed his hands into his pockets. "She passed out in class one day and slipped into a coma. I sat by her bed with her parents for two days, praying and hoping. But her kidneys failed and she died."

"Oh, Brent."

"I felt responsible, Amira. Why wasn't I the type of man she could confide in? Why hadn't I seen what was happening to her? Why hadn't I questioned her more thoroughly about the weight loss? Why didn't I see something was wrong with her?"

Amira took a few steps closer to him. "Did you ever consider that maybe she didn't want you to see?"

"Why not?"

Her violet eyes were wide and steady and compassionate. "For the same reason that you wouldn't admit your shoulder hurt. Why did you have to carry both grocery bags in here today? Why couldn't you let me bring one of them in?"

"I didn't want you to think—"

"That you weren't strong? That you were taking too long to heal? That I'd think less of you if I had to help?"

He'd never talked about this with anyone. His dad and Shane knew what had happened, of course, but he'd never discussed it with them. He'd never told them how devastated he'd felt or how guilty. Now Amira was making him take another look at all of it. "Women don't have an image or ego to protect," he protested.

"Don't they? Oh, Brent. She probably wanted to keep up with you in every way. She wanted to look good for you. She wanted to be what you wanted her to be."

"Then it *was* my fault."

Shaking her head emphatically, Amira protested, "No, it wasn't your fault. Even in Penwyck, girls see magazines, read articles about what men supposedly want. They make themselves into a package. It's only when a woman really trusts a man, deep in her soul, that she can leave off the makeup, dress in sweats and not brush her hair.''

If only he could believe that. If only... "We dated for a year. We were going to get married. She should have trusted me.''

"Did you trust her?''

He thought about that. He'd been building his empire, wheeling and dealing. He and Rhonda had talked about finance, but he'd never told her details of his work. He'd never given her specific names of companies he was working with or thinking about buying. Was that because he thought she might use the information to further her own future? To get herself a better job?

On a deeper level, he had never told her what it had been like to be separated from Shane when they were kids. Yet he'd already told Amira how difficult that had been. He could see himself sitting down with Amira, explaining a merger he wanted to accomplish and letting her bat ideas back to him. And now this conversation they were having...

"I guess I didn't trust her any more than she trusted me. I don't know why. I never told her about Mother and Dad's fights. Or the affair Dad had that broke up my parents' marriage.''

"Maybe you both were trying to be what you thought the other person wanted.''

"This is heavy stuff before breakfast,'' he said gruffly, and went over to the window to look out at the backyard where a wooden swing hung from the tall oak. That swing had been there since he was a child.

Following him to the window, Amira stood very

close, her elbow brushing his. "What do you see out there?" she asked, seemingly out of the blue.

"I see—" He stopped before he said Shane's name. "I see my brother and me climbing the tree, shimmying to the top branches. I can hear our mother telling us we were going to break our necks, and see Dad putting up a ladder against the tree just to be on the safe side." He pointed to a patch of land in the rear corner. "See that area that looks like it's overgrown with vines?"

Amira nodded.

"Every June my mom and my brother and I would pick strawberries. When Dad came from the city on weekends, we'd make ice cream on the front porch and put the strawberries over it. I guess it's silly now to think about that, but I do often."

"That's because you were happy then."

Turning away from the window, he left the past and found the present. "I haven't been happy for a long time. I've been busy—not happy."

"And you haven't been involved with anyone since Rhonda?"

"No. After she died, I decided personal relationships carried too high a price. Being responsible for another person's life and happiness is just too great a burden." He still believed that even now. That's why he'd wanted Amira to come and spend this week with him. He wanted to be happy without the responsibility of thinking about the future...because there could be no future between the two of them.

After she studied his face, she quietly said, "I know loving can sometimes be a burden. But when I hear my mother talk about my father, I know she would have given up anything for that love. Seeing her with Harrison now, I can tell she's found love all over again and the two of them complete each other's lives."

Brent shook his head. "I only see heartache when two people connect. My family broke up because my father turned to another woman and my mother found out. Because they couldn't repair their marriage, they separated me from my brother. Rhonda and I cared for each other, but apparently not deeply enough."

He paused for a moment, then asked very soberly, "What does it take to make a successful relationship? What kind of love do you have to have? I don't know, Amira. Most of the time I believe men and women are supposed to be ships passing in the night. It's much easier that way. Last night you asked me if I brought you here to seduce you, and I got angry because you put it into words. I did bring you here for that. But I promise you now, if you stay, we'll become friends before anything else happens. I don't want you to have regrets when you go back to Penwyck."

Gazing into her eyes, he could see what her answer would be before she said it. "I'll stay."

He knew it took courage for her to make that decision. She was going against an upbringing that would make staying alone in a house with a man a scandal. But she wanted more time with him as much as he wanted it with her.

More than anything, he wanted to take her into his arms and kiss her, yet he knew kissing could easily get out of hand and he intended to keep his word to her. "Let's go for a walk after breakfast. I want to show you everything I like best about being here."

Before he realized what she was going to do, she

rose up on her tiptoes and kissed his cheek. That simple gesture touched him in a way nothing else could. "What was that for?"

"Your honesty. Our friendship."

His honesty. What would happen when she found out he was Marcus Cordello?

Right now it didn't matter. For the next week he was Brent Carpenter.

And he'd deal with the rest later.

At first Brent captured all of Amira's attention as they went out the back door and through the yard. The blue sky had become overcast and there was dampness in the air. But she hardly noticed all that. Her world was filled by the man beside her who had finally given her a piece of his soul. She could understand better now why he closed himself off and had been slow to share personal information. Several times in his life, he'd had to fit the puzzle pieces back together again.

Now she could understand why he immersed himself in his work and hadn't looked for another serious involvement. He wasn't looking for one now. He felt responsible for his fiancée's death, even though he wasn't. Love brought with it responsibility so he didn't want either. Amira knew she had to take this week for what it was, an interlude—time to spend with a man she was beginning to care about deeply. She had to accept the fact that that was all it was. Could she do that?

As Brent's large hand clasped her elbow, she didn't have time to formulate an answer. "Over this way," he directed her.

Cocoa ran beside them as they came to the end of

the pathway in the yard and entered a copse of weeping birches.

"Through here." Brent's hand went to the small of her back.

She could feel its imprint through her sweater. She felt small beside Brent, protected by him, excited by being so close.

"Where are we going?"

"In a few minutes you'll see," he said with an easy grin.

Emerging from the birches, they came into a small clearing bordered by pines. In that clearing sat a lopsided little building that Amira supposed could be a utility shed. Except, she could make out a shade at the window, and the door was somewhat unusual. It was a Dutch door such as she'd seen at a stable. Then she saw the slab of wood nailed above the door. It looked as if it had seen many winters. She could just make out the letters that spelled Private and she suddenly knew what it was.

"You had a clubhouse."

"A clubhouse for two. My brother and I built it. We found the plans in a magazine and it gave us something to do the summer we were eleven."

"May I?" she asked motioning toward the door.

"You'd better let me open it first and see if it's safe to go inside."

When Brent opened the door, there were only a few cobwebs and the smell of damp leaves. "You're too tall to fit," she teased.

He stooped, then folded his legs and sat on the floor. When he patted the boards next to him, she laughed and ducked through the doorway.

Then she sat on the floor beside him with their

shoulders brushing. Cocoa wiggled inside beside Brent and settled on the wooden floor, too.

"You and your brother did a good job if this is still standing," Amira remarked.

"It's been through a few repairs, but it's held up well."

In the small quarters Brent was more than ever aware of her. He took her hand in his and held it, interlacing their fingers. The silence was only broken now and then by birds chirping and by the breeze blowing stray leaves across the threshold.

"I spent a lot of time here," he said. "Although my brother was far away, I felt closer to him in here."

"Did you live at Shady Glenn all year round?"

"Before the divorce, yes. After the divorce, my father got an apartment in the city and we stayed there during the week and came out here on weekends. After he remarried, I didn't get home for months at a time."

"Why? Where were you?"

"At boarding school...prep school...whatever you want to call it. Someplace where my stepmother didn't have to deal with me."

Her indignation caused her cheeks to flush. "That's a *terrible* thing to do to a child. Didn't your father realize that?"

Brent shrugged. "My dad wanted to keep peace with his new wife. By the time I was ready for college, they'd separated and divorced, too. The truth is, I don't think my dad ever stopped loving my mom. If she'd been able to forgive his affair, they might still be together."

Amira was quiet for a while. "When trust is broken, it's difficult to get it back again."

Brent thought about his first night with Amira and why he hadn't told her he was Marcus Cordello. "There are reasons why people do the things they do. There are always two sides...two points of view."

"I guess if two people love each other enough, they can overcome anything," Amira mused.

Cocoa had put her nose on Brent's leg. Her eyes were closed, and to lessen the intensity of the moment, Amira nodded to her. "I think we tuckered her out."

"Just as well. That means we'll have a few moments of privacy," Brent said, his voice low and intimate. Taking Amira's chin into his hand, he tilted her face up to his.

When he kissed her, she felt there was a new depth to it, a richness that hadn't been there before. Maybe it was because of everything he'd shared with her. Maybe it was because their friendship was growing into so much more...at least on her part.

Suddenly there was the rat-tat-tat of rain on the roof.

Cocoa scrambled to her feet, and Brent lifted his head. "Uh-oh. We'd better make a run for it."

Holding on to the leash with one hand, Brent hurried out of the clubhouse and held his hand out to Amira. "Come on. If we hurry, we might not get soaked."

Brent held Amira's hand as they ran. Moments after the drizzle started it changed to a downpour. When they reached the back door to the house, Brent held it open for Amira and she rushed inside.

Cocoa purposely shook, and water splattered everywhere.

"I'm not much better than Cocoa," Amira said. "I'm dripping all over your floor."

With a smile Brent nodded to the bathroom. "Go ahead and get out of those clothes. I'll light a fire, then change in the laundry room. I have a pair of jeans in there."

Cocoa trotted behind Brent to the living room.

Amira had stripped off her clothes in the downstairs bathroom when she suddenly realized she had nothing to put on. Not only that, but her hair was wet and she needed to brush it out while she dried it or it would frizz all over.

Wrapping herself in one of the bath towels, she opened the door and peeked out. She thought she heard the dryer door close in the laundry room. She could scurry upstairs, put on fresh clothes, then do something with her hair.

But she'd barely made it to the stairway when she heard Brent's footsteps. Before she could start up the steps, he was there, his gaze raking over her as he took in her bare shoulders, the towel tucked at her breasts, her bare legs and feet.

"Come sit by the fire," he said, his voice husky. "I'll go get you some clothes."

She hadn't even noticed the kindling taking off in the fireplace. Her hand went to her hair. "I need to fix up a little."

"You don't need to fix a thing. Go on. Sit on the sofa and cover up with the afghan. Do you want jeans?"

"I laid a sweat suit over the chair upstairs. That'll be fine."

He couldn't seem to take his eyes off her, and she couldn't stop staring at his chest. He was shirtless and so very masculine. His shoulders were so broad. The dark brown hair running down the middle of his chest whirled around his navel. He hadn't even snapped his jeans, she realized, and quickly brought her gaze back up to his. The fire couldn't be warming the room already, but she felt very hot, very excited, very…much a woman.

Breaking the silence, he murmured, "I'll be right back," and then he was up the stairs, and her knees were shaking as she made her way to the sofa where she curled up in the corner and covered herself with the afghan. Only this morning they'd spoken of being friends first…before anything else happened between them. Yet their attraction to each other, the pull toward each other, was stronger than logic or good intentions.

Her heart beat faster as she heard Brent's footsteps in the upstairs hall, heard him descend the steps. Suddenly he was standing before her with her clothes. She noticed his eyes dipped to her breasts covered modestly by the afghan. Then his gaze returned to her face. There was such a deep need and longing there in his eyes.

He held out the clothes to her, and his voice was husky. "I'll go into the kitchen. Let me know when you're dressed."

She could let him walk away. She could build on their friendship. She could get dressed and pretend she didn't feel the longing and the need, too. But was that honest when all she wanted was to be held in his arms? When all she wanted was to let him awaken every womanly desire she'd never felt?

Taking the clothes from him, she set them aside. "Will you kiss me?"

"Amira." His voice was a pleading groan, telling her she was pushing him too far. "You don't know what you're asking. I can't turn my desire for you on and off like a light switch."

"Then don't turn it off," she suggested softly.

Sinking down on the sofa beside her, he took her into his arms, afghan and all, kissing her eyes, her nose, trailing kisses down her cheek to her neck.

"You are so sweet," he murmured. "Like a Christmas gift someone surprised me with when I didn't believe in Christmas any longer. I can't wait to unwrap you." Keeping his eyes on hers, he reached for the corner of the afghan that had been thrown over her shoulder. He'd almost uncovered her breasts when the phone rang.

He swore. "I'll let it ring."

But when it rang a second time, Amira looked worried. "It could be for me. If it is, I should answer it."

The expression on Brent's face changed from desire-filled to remote, and he shifted away from her. "I have Caller ID. I'll check it. If it's not someone I recognize, you can pick it up."

While Brent went to check the phone on a small bench by the dining room, Amira quickly wrapped the afghan around her again.

"It's for you. It's an international area code that I don't recognize."

Making sure the afghan was securely fastened around her like a huge bath sheet that dropped to her ankles, she knew only her shoulders were showing. Yet as she moved toward the phone, she had the afghan wound so tightly that she knew Brent could see every curve and every wiggle. When she picked up the receiver, he moved away, over to the window and stared out at the rain.

"Hello?" she said, not knowing who to expect.

"Hi, darling."

"Mother! It's so good to hear your voice. Are you still in Greece?"

"We've been out on a sailboat Harrison hired for the past three days. Now we're on Santorini. There are cafés, vineyards, black sand beaches. Our suite has a view of the Aegean Sea. It's so beautiful, Amira. I wish you could see it."

"Maybe I will someday," she murmured, thinking how perfect the Greek island sounded for a honeymoon.

"How are you getting along? When I called the palace, Mrs. Ferth gave me this number."

"I'm not in Chicago right now. I haven't seen Marcus Cordello yet. He's on vacation somewhere this week and nobody knows where. So I thought I'd take a holiday until he comes back."

"That's a wonderful idea. Except you're all alone. Are you sure it's safe?"

"Oh, it's safe. I'm in the country at this wonderful house. It's raining now and there's a fire going."

"Won't you be lonely?"

"Oh, no. Really, Mother, it's a treat. Doing what I want, when I want to."

"Sometimes I worry about you, honey. I didn't realize how lonely *I* was until I met Harrison. Now I know the rest of my life, I'll never be alone again. I love him so much. More each day. I can hardly imagine my life before I met him anymore."

Amira could hear the happiness in her mother's voice and it made her heart ache. She glanced over at Brent. What had she been about to do? She knew he didn't want a serious relationship. She knew after she accomplished her mission, she'd never see him again unless she flew to the United States or he flew to Penwyck. They could have a few days together every few months. Once a year? What kind of relationship was that?

"I'm glad you found Harrison, Mother. I'm glad you're not lonely anymore."

"I didn't mean to suggest that being with you, having you, wasn't enough. You understand that, don't you?"

"Of course. The bond between a man and woman isn't like any other."

"You sound as if you know that from experience. Have I been too involved with palace affairs to notice something going on in your life?"

"No. You haven't been too involved. I...I guess I just dream about that kind of bond. You talked about having it with father, and I see you have it with Harrison. It's just something I want, too...along with children." She glanced over at Brent again and saw he was watching her intently.

"You must be careful, Amira. I never told you, but I knew about your meetings with Sean in the garden."

"You never said anything."

"It seemed to end as fast as it started. And you were only seventeen then. Now, at twenty, you might be ready for something more serious. When you're on Penwyck, you have lots of people to look out for you. But on your own in Chicago... Be careful. There are men who would take advantage of a beautiful young woman like you."

Amira was aware she was standing in Brent's living room with only an afghan wrapped around her. A few minutes before she'd welcomed his attentions and encouraged him. Now she felt ashamed that she'd been so bold. Was she mature enough to act on her feelings? Was she mature enough to listen to her heart?

"When will you be flying back to Penwyck?" Amira asked, changing the subject.

"Probably tomorrow. Harrison must get back. We've decided to look for a house in the country but keep Harrison's apartment since it's so convenient to the palace."

"I think when I return, I'd like to find a place of my own."

Silence met her words, then her mother said, "If you think you're ready for that, then that's what you should do. I'd love to go apartment hunting with you."

Amira knew she and her mother would always be close, no matter what happened, no matter how their lives changed. She was so grateful for that. "I'd love for you to help me decorate. Your taste is as good as mine."

Gwen Montague laughed. "You take care of yourself, honey. I hope I see you as well as Marcus Cordello sometime next week."

"I'll do what I can to make that happen. Has King Morgan's condition changed?"

"No. It's the same. All we can do is pray and try to figure out who is the true heir to the throne. Take care, and I'll see you soon."

When Amira hung up the phone, tears pricked her eyes. She missed her mother. She missed everyone at the palace. But most of all she felt as if by being here with Brent, she was becoming a different person. She didn't know what was right and what was wrong, what was best or what would lead her into trouble.

Brent broke into her train of thought. "That was your mother, I take it."

"Yes, she's having a lovely honeymoon, but... she's worried about me." Awkwardly Amira walked to the sofa and picked up her sweat suit. "I'm going to get dressed."

"Amira, we weren't doing anything wrong. You're not a child. You have a right to make your own decisions. Don't let your mother make you feel guilty—"

Amira held up her hand to stop him. "She'd never intentionally make me feel guilty. This isn't about what I should or shouldn't do according to anyone else's standards. It's about me and you and what I want for my life. When I was talking to my mother, I realized I always imagined my first time with a man would be with my fiancé or my husband."

"I can't offer you more than this week," Brent said honestly.

"I know that. That's why I'm going upstairs and getting dressed."

Then she crossed to the stairway with as much dignity as she could muster and let the afghan trail behind her like a train. She could feel Brent's gaze on her as she ascended the steps, and she just hoped she could make it to her room before she started crying.

She wanted more than a week with Brent, but that's all he could give.

At the top of the stairs she paused and glanced over her shoulder. He'd turned away and was staring into the fire. What did he think about her now?

Chapter Seven

After Marcus made sandwiches and opened deli containers from the general store, he went to Amira's room and knocked. She came to the door without her usual smile, then she rushed in. "I'm sorry, Brent. About what happened earlier. I shouldn't have been so forward. I…"

She was altogether flustered. He could tell she'd showered and dried her hair because it was fluffy and soft around her face. The raspberry-colored sweat suit complemented her creamy complexion.

Unfulfilled desire rushed through him again and he got a grip on it. "I expected your suitcase to be packed."

"It should be," she murmured.

Even though he'd expected it, the thought of her leaving was disagreeable. Frustrated, trying to understand her, he asked shortly, "Can't you put aside what you *should* do for once in your life?"

Her violet eyes were very wide, but she squared

her shoulders. "I have to be true to who I am and what I believe. You said you wouldn't push."

So he had, but he hadn't realized how being close to her, talking with her, staying under the same roof with her would affect him. He felt peaceful one minute and turned inside out the next.

"I made lunch," he said gruffly. "Are you staying for it?"

He saw her lip quiver, and he wished he didn't feel so deeply about everything concerning her. Softening his tone, he added, "The rain stopped. I thought we could take Cocoa to Reunion House after lunch."

"You still want me to go with you?" she asked, as if she expected him to throw her out.

"Of course I want you to go with me. I think you'll enjoy the kids."

She worried her lower lip for a moment. "I'll change and be right down."

"You don't have to change. You look fine the way you are. These are children. They don't care what you're wearing."

Her gaze passed over him as if assessing what he'd said. He was wearing jeans and a black polo shirt. He found that having her look at him with those sparks in her eyes was damn arousing. "Change if you want...or don't. Come down when you're ready." Before she stirred up his insides anymore, he went downstairs.

To Amira the tension between her and Brent as they ate lunch was palpable. He was treating her like a polite stranger, and Amira wished there was something she could do about that. But as she'd told him, she couldn't go against everything she'd been taught or put her dreams aside. She wanted to be more than an object of desire.

When they drove to Reunion House, Cocoa sat on Amira's lap. "I'm going to miss her," Amira said.

"So am I. But the kids will keep her better occupied than we can, and she'll have a backyard where she can run and play. Marilyn loves animals as much as she likes kids. She's always said she wished Reunion House had a mascot. I still wonder about Cocoa's owner, though. Flora's supposed to let me know if anyone calls."

When Brent had spoken of Marilyn, the housemother at Reunion House, Amira hadn't known what to expect. But she instantly liked the lady who came out to meet them on the porch. She was in her forties with short black hair and sparkling hazel eyes.

She gave Brent a hug. "It's been a while." After he agreed that it had been, she leaned back and studied him. "How are you feeling?"

"Almost back to normal," he assured her. "Now I want you to meet somebody. Lady Amira Sierra Corbin, this is Marilyn Johnson, chief mom and bottle washer of Reunion House."

Marilyn gave Amira a comprehensive look that sized her up as she smiled and extended her hand. "It's good to meet you, Lady Amira. Brent told me he'd be bringing you along to show you around."

"Please call me Amira."

Marilyn nodded. "And I'm Marilyn." To Brent, she said, "We have seven children here right now. They'll all love Cocoa." She grinned at the dog that Brent held in his arms and scratched the animal under the chin. "We're so glad to have you here."

Cocoa barked as if she understood exactly what Marilyn had said.

They were all laughing when a pretty young redhead came to the door. "Marilyn, excuse me. I'm sorry to interrupt, but I wanted to know if you want me to put the baked potatoes in the oven for supper tonight."

"It's all right, Joanie. There's somebody here I want you to meet. Our benefactor, Mr...." She stopped. "Brent Carpenter. He's the one who makes Reunion House possible."

Joanie seemed to hesitate only a second before she came outside and stood close to Brent. "How do you do? It's so good to meet you. I just started working here two weeks ago. I know I'm going to love it."

Marilyn explained to Brent, "Joanie has a degree in elementary education, but hasn't been able to find a teaching position yet. She thought Reunion House would be a nice substitute."

Brent put Cocoa down on the porch and shook the young woman's hand. "It's good to have you with us." Then he introduced Amira.

When Joanie took a closer step to Brent, Amira thought it was a proprietary step. She might not be experienced in the ways of men, but she knew the ways of women from growing up with three princesses. Joanie already had a look in her eye that said she was going to get to know Brent better if she had anything to say about it. Amira found herself not liking that idea at all.

Cocoa looked up at Joanie beseechingly as if she wanted the young woman's attention. Joanie scratched the dog's head. "Come on inside." Her smile was mainly for Brent. "I'll introduce you to the kids. There's a great batch of them here right now, except for one little boy who's kind of belligerent.''

''I think we should let Mr. Carpenter make up his own mind about the children,'' Marilyn said wisely.

Joanie blushed. ''Well, sure. They're all in the kitchen having a snack. It's a good time to meet them.''

The rambling old house was spacious and welcoming, and Amira thought anyone could feel at home here. As they crossed the living room, they heard laughter and guffaws coming from the kitchen. There was a shout and what sounded like a dish falling to the floor.

''It sounds like more is going on than snack time,'' Marilyn said with a frown.

They all hurried to the kitchen, Cocoa trailing behind.

Amira knew she shouldn't, but she smiled at the sight of the three girls and four boys participating in a food fight. One of the youngsters dressed in a red oversize T-shirt and baggy jeans—a baseball cap turned backward on his head—stood on one of the chairs, breaking pieces off a cookie. He'd flung a tidbit at one of the girls who squealed and retaliated by tossing a raisin at him. It was the kind of scene Amira would never find in the palace. These kids had energy to burn, and they were doing that instead of repressing it.

Of course the chaos couldn't be allowed to continue.

Marilyn stepped right into it, giving them all a silent reproving look. Shrieks of laughter and food tossing stopped immediately.

Brent nudged Amira's arm and whispered, "Wish I knew how she did that."

Amira could see the amusement dancing in his eyes and she saw the little boy he must have once been before all the changes in his life.

Apparently thinking she should do something with her new position as assistant, Joanie looked up at the boy and said, "Jared, get down from that chair now."

He gave the redhead a defiant look. "We was just having a little fun."

Marilyn shook her head. "What you were doing was making a mess."

He didn't move from the chair, but cast a glance at Brent and then Amira.

Marilyn went over to him. "Jared, if you'd like to get down from there, I'll introduce you to our guests...before all of you clean up the kitchen."

There were groans and grumbles. Jared just gave Marilyn a sheepish look and hopped down to the floor. Then he looked up at her. "Do we really have to clean the kitchen?"

There were crumbs and raisins and bits of cookies from one end to the other. Cocoa was happily licking at them. Unable to see the dog from where he'd been perched, Jared now spotted Cocoa.

Without waiting to hear if he'd have to do unexpected chores or not, he ran over to the dog but didn't get too close. Looking up, he asked Brent, "Is she yours?"

"Not exactly. My friend and I," he nodded to Amira, "found her. Her owner still might claim her. In the meantime I thought she could make some friends here. Would all of you like to take care of her?"

There was a variety of agreeable confirmation that they would.

Picking up Cocoa, Brent directed, "Why don't each of you tell her your name."

Amira decided Brent had chosen a clever way to meet the children, and she listened carefully, too, as Paul, Shara, Jimmy, Glenda, Amy, Mark, and Jared told Cocoa who they were. Brent let each of them pet the dog, and they all did so freely except for Jared. When it was his turn, he hesitated.

Amira stepped closer to the young boy. "She's quite gentle. She won't hurt you if you're nice to her."

Jared's big brown eyes were wary, and he studied Amira for a long time to see if she was telling the truth.

"You saw the others pet her," she reminded him.

"They're them. I'm me. Maybe she won't like my smell."

"There's only one way to find out," Brent said casually.

Beside the plate of cookies on the table was a dish of cheese cubes. Amira picked one up and broke off small pieces. She said to Jared, "Open up your hand."

When he did, she laid the cheese in it. "Just hold it out to her and let her lick it off. She likes table food, but you can't give her too much of it because it might make her sick."

"Dogs get sick?"

"Yes, they do."

Instantly Jared held his hand out to the dog. Cocoa gladly licked up the cheese scraps and Jared's hand, too.

The boy broke into a wide smile. "She likes me."

Paul shrugged. "She likes the cheese."

Everybody laughed, but Jared was petting Cocoa by then, and she was obviously enjoying it.

Joanie went to the closet and took out a broom, dustpan and brush. She handed them to Paul, Glenda and Jimmy. To Jared she said, "You can wet paper towels and wipe off the table. Mark and Shara, you can wash up the dishes."

"Real sport," Jared mumbled under his breath. Amira realized he'd taken a dislike to the younger counselor.

As soon as Joanie had dispensed the chores, she came to stand by Brent's side again. "We'll make sure Cocoa's well taken care of. Would you like to see the bedrooms Marilyn and I wallpapered? We think they're quite an improvement."

"I'd like to give Amira a tour and then I want her to look at the yard outside. She's earning her degree in landscape design and I thought she could give us a few pointers."

"That's an excellent idea," Marilyn agreed. "We could use some color out there and decide where to put a birdbath."

"I ordered a jungle gym. It should be arriving in the next day or so. We'll have to decide the best place for that, too."

"Will it have monkey bars?" Jared asked as he swiped across the tabletop with a paper towel.

"It will have monkey bars and ladders and a rope to climb, too."

As Joanie took Brent and Amira on a tour of Reunion House, she stayed very close to Brent. Amira began to get annoyed. Brent listened to the cute redhead as she explained how she and Marilyn had chosen the wallpaper. She told him they were going to paint the beds and bookshelves, too, in bright colors. But Brent was less interested in the furniture and more interested in the kids.

"I understand Paul and Shara are brother and sister, Glenda and Amy are sisters, Jimmy and Mark are brothers. Who's Jared meeting here?"

"His sister is supposed to arrive tonight." Joanie shook her head. "It'll be a good thing, too. He's a troublemaker."

"Exactly what has he done?" Brent asked.

"He just stirs up the other kids. You saw what he was doing when we went into the kitchen."

"They were all participating in that," Amira interjected.

Joanie gave her a sharp look. "You can bet Jared started it."

"He's probably excited about seeing his sister and has a lot of extra energy," Amira said helpfully, thinking a positive attitude toward Jared would be better than Joanie's negative one.

"Are you around kids much?" Joanie asked.

Amira had to admit she wasn't. "No."

"I have been—between observation field trips and student teaching. Jared's the type of boy who enjoys making trouble."

Thoroughly annoyed with Joanie now, Amira took a deep breath. "Maybe so. But I'd imagine each child has to be treated as an individual. If Jared is acting up, there's probably a reason."

"Well he's not telling any of us what it is. He's quite sullen at times."

The boy hadn't seemed at all sullen to Amira, and she wondered if he was just that way with Joanie.

Joanie placed her hand on Brent's arm. "Let me show you the play stations I've set up. I think you'll approve." Her brown eyes flashed the message that she was quite impressed with him.

Brent looked down at Joanie with a smile. "I'm sure I will."

Amira couldn't tell if he was just being polite or if he was attracted to the teacher. Then she thought about what had happened on the sofa this morning and Brent's needs as a man. With an attractive, willing woman not very far away, how long could he resist?

Amira hated the thought of it, hated the thought of him making love to anyone but her. She realized she was capable of deep, deep jealousy for one very complicated reason. She was in love with Brent Carpenter. She wanted to make love with him more than she'd ever wanted anything, but knowing he didn't want a serious relationship, knowing he didn't want responsibility for anyone other than himself, she knew she'd have to keep her feelings to herself.

During the rest of the tour, Joanie talked animatedly to Brent. Even though he cast Amira a glance every once in a while, she definitely felt like the third wheel.

When they returned downstairs, Joanie took Brent into the living room where there were games and books and CDs. She was showing him the most recent when Amira wandered into the kitchen. The children had finished cleaning up and were outside with Marilyn...except for Jared.

He was standing at the door looking out at all of

them. Not knowing what else to say, she said something obvious. "I'm glad the sun came out again."

He glanced at her and turned to look outside once more. "I can't think of nothin' except seeing my sister."

"How long has it been since you've seen her?"

He shrugged. "A year. My pop ran off and left us. Someone called the cops and they took us away. It's the last I saw her." Facing Amira then, Jared's face broke into a smile. "She's coming tonight."

Amira could see and feel exactly how much this meant to Jared. She could imagine how much it had meant to Brent to be reunited with his brother every summer. He was doing a wonderful thing here with these kids.

"I'm sure your sister can't wait to see you, either. What's her name?"

"Lena. You got any brothers or sisters?" he asked suddenly.

"No, I don't. I often wish I did. I have good friends, though, and that helps."

"It's not the same," he offered with a shake of his head, as if he were much older than ten.

"No, I guess it's not. I'll have to make do, won't I?" She found this little boy engaging, much more mature than his language and his age would predict.

"I wish you were staying here with us instead of Joanie," he mumbled.

"I think I'd like that," Amira responded sincerely. "But unfortunately I'm only visiting for a little while. I don't live around here."

"Where do you live?"

"On an island named Penwyck. It's near Wales. Have you ever heard of it?"

He screwed up his face. "In school. It's over there near England, isn't it?"

"That's exactly where it is."

"That's far away. Maybe someday I'll get to go someplace like that. I want to go to Australia where they have crocodiles."

"It's good to have dreams. If you hold on to them long enough, they'll come true."

"You have to do more than hold on to them," a strong masculine voice maintained.

Amira had been so concentrated on Jared that she hadn't heard Brent come into the room. Now she saw that both he and Joanie were standing at the table.

"You have to do everything you can to *make* them come true," Brent added.

"Like saving up money?" Jared asked.

"That's one way. Learning everything about the place where you want to go is another. Maybe you can learn something in school that could help you get there."

"Like what?"

"Australia has sheep and horses and mines. If you would learn skills that would help with any of those things, someone might hire you over there."

"Really?"

"I'll see if I can find some books on Australia," Brent said. "I'll send them to you. In fact, if I can order them on the Internet when I get back, they might be here by the end of the week."

"Then Lena can read them, too."

Joanie checked the clock above the sink. "It's time for the kids' group session," she said almost apologetically to Brent. "You're welcome to stay if you like."

"I just came over today to give Amira a tour, but I'll be back. The back porch railings need a coat of paint. I have to clean out the spouts, too. I'll be around all week."

And Amira suspected Joanie would be right by his side as often as she could be.

"You going to be here, too?" Jared asked Amira. "I mean longer than today. You can meet Lena."

She made a decision without analyzing it any more. "Yes, I'll be here for a few days, too. I'd love to meet your sister." She glanced at Joanie. "I'll take a more analytical look at the yard the next time we're here."

Brent's gaze settled on her and it was filled with curiosity. But he didn't ask any questions about why she'd decided to stay.

A half hour later when they returned to Shady Glenn, he said, "I can run up to the general store and get steaks for supper. I'll make them on the grill."

She remembered their first night together and sharing a steak. "That sounds good. Maybe I can make something for dessert if you buy a basket of fresh apples."

"You can really cook?"

"Of course I can cook. All I have to do is follow the recipe. I'm not a hothouse flower, Brent. I might have advantages others don't, but no one waits on me hand and foot." It ruffled her feathers to have him think she wasn't just like everyone else, like all the other women he dated or had attracted him before. When he looked at her as an oddity she didn't like it at all.

"Did I strike a nerve?" he asked, brows arched.

"Sometimes I feel as if you're looking at me as if

I'm some kind of specimen. I don't live on another planet.''

He fought back a smile. "No, you just live in a palace.''

She was beginning to wish she didn't. She was beginning to wish she lived in Chicago.

"It's a building," she said feebly.

Brent rolled his eyes. "A building with a throne room," he teased.

For some reason she was sensitive to all of it right now, and she felt silly tears prick at the back of her eyes. Not wanting him to see, she started for the living room. "Yes, it has a throne room...and a throne...and a king and a queen. Are you satisfied?''

She didn't know where she was going, but her bedroom seemed like a good idea.

Brent caught her before she made it to the stairs. Holding her by the shoulder, he nudged her around. "What's wrong?''

She bit her lower lip, then decided to tell him how she felt about his attitude. "I never minded being part of a royal family until I came here. You're acting as if it's something to ridicule, something that doesn't mean anything at all. It means a lot to me and to our country.''

Gently he brushed her hair away from her cheek and looked deep into her eyes. "I'm not ridiculing you. Your life is very different from ours. You've got to admit that. I'm sorry if I poked fun at it. I never meant to upset you.''

Amira realized she was more upset about the way Joanie had looked at Brent. "I'm sorry I overreacted.''

His gaze was penetrating and questioning as if he

could see something deeper was bothering her. "What made you decide to stay here with me? Spending time with the kids...meeting Jared's sister?"

She could tell him those were the reasons, but those wouldn't be honest. "I'd like to do both. The reason I'm staying though, is because I care about being with you." She remembered what Brent had told Jared about his dreams—that holding on to them wasn't enough. He had to do something about them. She was doing something about her dreams by staying with him.

Brent must have seen her dreams evident in her eyes because he suddenly became very serious. "Amira, I like having you here with me. You know that. And I want you. You know that, too. But don't get starry-eyed about me. It's not practical. We *do* live in different worlds with an ocean between us, and that's not going to change."

She wanted to tell him it could change. She wanted to tell him that she might consider moving her whole world for him. But she knew he didn't want to hear it. She knew if she even broached the subject of love, he'd back off and send her packing.

"I think we can change whatever we want to change if it's important enough."

The phone rang, interrupting their conversation. After a dark glance at it, he went over and checked the Caller ID. "Not anyone I know, so it must be for you. I'll go to the general store and give you some privacy. I won't forget the apples," he added, as he picked up the receiver and handed it to her.

By the time she greeted the caller, Brent had closed the kitchen door.

"It's Cole Everson," the man on the phone stated.

She took a trembling breath. "Hello, Mr. Everson. You have more information for me?"

"Some. I wanted to make contact with you to make sure I had the proper number. We discovered that Cordello's brother's name is Shane, and he's living in California. I decided to go about this one brother at a time. It has to be handled delicately or the whole world will know how upside down everything is in Penwyck. We want to prevent that from happening. Once you make contact with Cordello, I'd like you to convince him to ease our path to his brother."

"I'm sorry I didn't manage to see Marcus Cordello before he jetted away somewhere."

"That's not your fault. From what I understand, this man is as elusive as they come. As I mentioned before, unlike most wealthy men, he stays out of the limelight, no pictures in the newspapers or anything like that."

"Have you found out his home address?"

"Not yet. Apparently no one's fetched his mail from his post office box. If they have, they've been damn good staying out of sight. I should have that picture soon and a few more details. I can overnight everything to you."

When Brent had given her a tour of the house, she'd noticed a fax machine in his office. "There's a fax here. Would that help?"

"That would help a great deal. The photo won't be as good, but you'll get the idea. You have the number?"

"Hold on a minute."

Going into Brent's study, she found the number on the handset of the fax and told Cole what it was.

"We're all set then," he said. "I'll fax it as soon as I have it."

When Amira hung up the phone, she thought about what the next prince of Penwyck might look like. Would he be tall and handsome, befitting the prince's stature?

In a day or two she'd know.

Then again, in a day or two her feelings for Brent Carpenter might overtake her heart completely and she might not even care about the prince of Penwyck.

She'd only care about loving Brent.

Chapter Eight

Bang! Rustle, rustle.

The loud noise awakened Amira with a jolt. She began to tremble.

Rustle, rustle. Bang.

Someone was climbing the wall. He was coming to kill her and her mother.

Automatically, from fear, panic and practice drills in the palace, Amira dropped to the floor as she'd been taught, seeking cover...seeking refuge. Disoriented, she tried to peer through the blackness all around her. She couldn't see a thing. How close was the assassin? This time her father was gone. He couldn't protect the king or her, her mother...

Still lost in fear, Amira cowered when she heard the rapping on the door.

"Amira? Are you awake?"

She knew that voice. It wasn't the voice of a stranger or anyone in the Royal Guard. It was—

It was Brent. Her heart was pounding so fast she couldn't speak.

The doorknob turned and the banging started again.

Light from the hall streamed into the room through the open door. Brent saw Amira crouched on the floor between the nightstand and the bed. Immediately he hurried to her, hunkering down. "Amira, what's wrong?"

Relief flooded through her, and tears burned in her eyes as she realized she was safe. She wasn't in the palace. She wasn't even on the island. "I...I...nothing's wrong," she finally managed in a whisper.

Reaching out, he clasped her shoulder. "Like hell, it's not. You're trembling."

"It'll pass. It always does."

Apparently, he wasn't going to wait for it to pass, because he helped her to her feet and led her to the bed. After she was seated, he sat beside her, his arm tight around her.

She took a few steadying breaths. "Really. I'm all right."

"You're still trembling," he murmured as he pressed his lips to her temple.

During the years when she was a child and she'd had a nightmare, her mother had held her. They'd come often after her father's death. Since her teen years, she'd handled the panic and the fear herself. She didn't let anyone see her fear of having an assassin kill her the way he had killed her father.

"Why were you on the floor?" Brent asked gently.

"That's what I was taught to do."

"Taught?" he looked totally perplexed.

"There have been assassination attempts on the king."

"At the palace?"

"Yes. At night, if I hear anything strange or running in the halls, shouting or alarms going off, I'm supposed to take cover…find someplace to hide until someone can take me to safety."

"Are you telling me security at the palace has actually been breached?"

"Yes." She cleared her throat, fighting off the remnants of her fears.

"What happened, Amira? Why are you so scared?"

That night was what she didn't want to remember, but apparently blocking it during her waking hours pushed it into her dreams.

"My father was major of the Royal Guard and part of the king's personal contingent. He died intercepting an intruder climbing the wall beneath the king's bedroom window."

"How old were you?"

"Ten. But I wasn't living in the palace then. I remember a soldier coming in the middle of the night. I heard him tell my mother what happened. She went white…she…"

Tears welled up in Amira's eyes and she tried to blink them away. But there were too many of them.

"What happened to the man who killed your father?"

"For years we thought he'd gotten away. After my father was shot, the queen offered my mother the position of lady-in-waiting, and we moved to the palace. The nightmares began then. When the queen learned about my fear, she moved us as far away from the king's chamber as possible. My mother used to hold me at night, and I think she was as afraid as I was that the assassin would climb the wall again and somehow get into our rooms, murdering us like he'd murdered my father.''

"You said for years you thought he'd gotten away. Were you wrong?''

She studied Brent for a long moment and then knew she could confide in him. "I still don't know the whole story, though I think my mother and her new husband do. While I was away on holiday in the Scottish Highlands in August, Owen, one of the royal twins was kidnapped. My mother and Harrison Montague, Admiral of the Navy, got very close and fell in love. He told her the man who killed my father had been wounded the night of the assassination attempt and later died.''

"Why didn't anyone tell you that before?''

"I don't know. It has to do with state secrets and conspiracies. When I learned the man who murdered my father had died, I thought my nightmares would be gone for good. But even after Owen was returned unharmed, I still had them.''

"That's because you're living at the palace. You're still involved in all of it.''

"With Mother married now, I'm going to find a place of my own. I just hadn't found anything suitable before I left.''

"The sooner you move out, the better.''

She shook her head. "The palace has been my home. The royal family has been my family. When the king bestowed the title of lady-in-waiting on my mother for her position with the queen, he bestowed the title of lady on me, too. I was companion to the princesses. Of course, the titles were also given to us because my father gave his life for King Morgan. It's not easy to leave them all.''

Brent's gaze was filled with compassion for her. He brought her into his body, holding her, rocking her. ''Here I thought you were a privileged lady with not a care in the world.'' The wind blew outside, and the banging began again. Amira started and Brent stroked her hair. ''It's just the shutter,'' he said. ''It came loose in the storm. The only way I can get to it is through the window in this room.''

''It's storming?''

Earlier tonight, after dinner, Brent had gone to his study to work, and Amira had come up to her room to read and to write in her diary about all the feelings she was having for him. She'd gone to bed early around ten o'clock.

''It started raining about eleven. But the wind just picked up not so long ago.''

Amira's cheek lay against Brent's bare chest. She loved the feel and the scent of his skin, the taut strength of his muscles, the deepness of his voice. She loved everything about him.

His breath was warm against her temple as he murmured, ''I don't want to ever see you afraid.''

''I'm not afraid while you're holding me,'' she confessed.

''Then maybe I should hold you all night.''

Amira realized she would like nothing better. Brent's hold on her became less comforting and much more sensual. His lips nudged her hair aside as he kissed from her temple down to her ear. She moaned softly at the scalding-hot flickers of his tongue.

''Brent.'' It was a plea. All the fear was gone and

all she could think about was Brent's smell and his taste and his heat.

With erotic care, he tickled her earlobe with his tongue and then sucked it into his mouth. The sensation started a keening ache inside of her. She ran her hand over his chest, sifting through his chest hair, feeling the muscles underneath. When he groaned, she felt power she'd never felt before.

He laid her back on the bed, kissing her face, her eyes, her nose, her lower lip. She laced her fingers in his hair to bring his mouth to hers—

The phone rang.

She went still, and Brent lifted his head. "That better not be the wrong number," he grumbled. Then he pushed himself away from her. After he stroked her hair away from her brow, he said, "I'll be right back."

Amira could hear Brent on the phone, but not what he was saying. She rebelted her robe and went to sit in the cane rocker.

He returned in a few minutes. "It was Marilyn. She's having trouble with Jared."

"What kind of trouble?"

"Jared's sister didn't arrive as planned. Her foster mother had car trouble and they won't get here until tomorrow evening. Jared's afraid she won't come at all, and he won't settle down for the night. Marilyn thinks I might be able to talk him into a calmer mood. I'm going to head over there now."

She thought about the nightmare, about what had just happened with Brent, Jared's eyes as he'd asked her— "Can I come with you?"

"Are you afraid to stay here by yourself?"

Standing, she squared her shoulders. "No. I've

been dealing with these nightmares since I was ten. It's over now and I'm fine. Thank you for comforting me.'' She knew she sounded formal, but she didn't know what else to say.

''Comfort was the least of it,'' he admitted wryly.

''You don't give yourself enough credit. I needed to be held. No one has held me for a very long time. But now it's over, and if I can help with Jared in any way, I'd like to.''

Taking Amira's hand, Brent tugged her into his arms and hugged her. His kiss was light, but the look in his eyes wasn't, and she knew if the phone hadn't rung, they'd be making love right now. Instead, they were going to reassure a little boy that he wasn't alone.

''Is he upstairs?'' Brent asked Joanie without preamble when he and Amira stepped inside Reunion House.

She frowned. ''Yes, and he has everyone else awake, too. I don't know what Marilyn thinks *you* can do when neither of us can get him to settle down.''

''Let's go see.''

Ever since she'd met Jared, Amira didn't like Joanie's attitude toward the boy. It was as if she'd written him off as a troublemaker and didn't even intend to try to help make things better. Amira had noticed she was quite competent and related to the other children well. Maybe it was just a personality clash.

''They're in the playroom upstairs,'' Joanie explained and then glanced at Amira as if she didn't belong there.

Brent was already intent on his mission and started up the stairs.

When Amira reached the second floor, she saw the children gathered in the playroom with Marilyn. The housemother was reading them a story. When Amira listened, she realized it was a passage from *Treasure Island*.

Jared was sitting in a chair, his knees pulled up on the seat, his arms circling them. He was hunched up as if he'd withdrawn into himself, not caring about what was going on around him.

Crossing to Jared, Brent capped the boy's shoulder with his hand.

Marilyn closed the book. "Why don't we all get ready for bed, again."

Jared still didn't look up as Marilyn ushered the boys into their bedroom and Joanie ushered the girls into theirs.

"I think we should talk," Brent told Jared.

"There's nothin' to talk about," the boy mumbled.

"I think there is. You're upset about Lena not arriving and you're taking that out on everybody else. Do you think that's a good way to handle it?"

"What am I supposed to do?" Jared asked defiantly.

"You can start by telling me what's going through your head," Brent suggested.

Jared's gaze met Amira's, and she got the feeling he didn't want her to leave. Sinking down on the floor beside Jared's chair, she crossed her legs. "Sometimes talking helps," Amira offered softly.

"Talking's not going to help. It won't bring Lena here."

"She'll be here tomorrow, Jared," Brent assured him.

"No, she won't! They're just telling me that. I know she's not coming."

"Her foster mother had car trouble. That's all. They'll be here tomorrow around dinnertime."

Jared's eyes met Amira's. "When our pop left, they told us they'd keep us together. They didn't. Why should I believe you?"

"Mr. Carpenter wouldn't lie to you," Amira responded with a certainty she felt.

Jared thought about that for a little while. Then he asked, "I'm supposed to believe she's coming and hold on to it like one of those dreams you told me about?"

She nodded. "Just like that."

After a few moments of silence, he asked, "You really think she'll come?"

"I think she will," Amira assured him.

"Tomorrow night's far away," he mumbled, sounding younger than ten.

Brent crouched down beside him. "I suppose it would help if you had something to make the time go faster. How about a ride on the pontoon boat. Have you ever been fishing?"

Jared shook his head.

"Would you like to go?"

The boy thought about it, then glanced at Amira. "Are you coming, too?"

"Would you like me to come?"

"Yeah." Jared's face reddened a little.

"Then I'll come. I'll pack us a picnic lunch and we can eat on the boat."

"Cool!" Jared said with a grin.

"If you want to go out on the boat with us tomorrow morning, then you're going to have to get some sleep," Brent said firmly.

"Maybe if you have trouble falling asleep, you can count all the fish you're going to catch," Amira suggested.

Jared smiled at them both. "I'll try it. Before, I just couldn't stop thinking about Lena...where she was... not seeing her again..."

Brent straightened. "I know how hard it is to be patient, but you can do it."

When Amira rose to her feet, she saw Joanie standing in the doorway and wondered if she'd heard the whole conversation.

After Jared had bid them good-night and went into the boys' bedroom, Joanie looked up at Brent, her eyes wide, her long lashes giving a little flutter. "You were so good with him. I know if you hadn't come over, we wouldn't have gotten *any* sleep."

There was an element of truth in Joanie's words, but Amira could see through the blatant flattery, too.

Brent just smiled at the young teacher. It was the kind of smile that always made Amira's heart flip, and she was envious of him bestowing it on Joanie now. "Sometimes a little understanding goes a long way. Amira helped. I'm not sure he would have gone out on the boat with me if she hadn't agreed to come along."

"Oh, I'm sure you could have convinced him," Joanie said. "I'll bet you can be very persuasive."

There was an undercurrent in her words that had more to do with the vibrations between a man and woman than convincing a little boy to go fishing.

Brent looked over at Amira. "We'd better be get-

ting back if we're going to get up early. I still have
to fix that shutter outside your bedroom.''

Amira thought she saw Joanie's face light up because she'd just learned Amira and Brent weren't
sharing a bedroom—they each had their own. Did the
young woman think that made Brent fair game?

After Brent talked briefly with Marilyn, he drove
Amira back to Shady Glenn. They were silent, lost in
their separate thoughts. Brent let Amira out at the
door and drove the car to the garage. She went
straight up to her bedroom, knowing he'd meet her
there to fix the shutter.

Ten minutes later she worried about him as he
leaned outside the window, a flashlight and screw-
driver in hand.

''Be careful,'' she murmured, wanting to hold on
to him, to make sure he didn't lean too far.

A short while later he pulled his head inside and
shut the window. ''You worry too much, Amira. I
wasn't in any danger of falling out.''

''You never know,'' she murmured.

He came closer to her then, and they both thought
about everything that had happened earlier. ''Are you
sure you'll be able to get to sleep?''

''I'm sure. I'll probably have less trouble than
Jared.''

Brent gave her one of those smiles like he'd given
Joanie. ''I think he has a crush on you.''

''Don't be ridiculous.''

''I'm not being ridiculous. You're a beautiful, kind
lady. He couldn't help but fall for that.''

Before she could stop herself, she said, ''Joanie has
a thing for you.'' She didn't exactly want to call it a

crush, because if Brent felt attracted to the woman in any way, it was more than that.

"A thing?" His grin made Amira angry.

"You know what I mean."

"No, I don't."

"Men," Amira said with some disgust, turning away.

But he wouldn't let her escape, and he caught her arm. "Yes, I'm one of them. What makes you think Joanie has a 'thing' for me?"

"I can read women. It's in the way she looks at you, the way she flutters her lashes, the way she stands within six inches of you."

His smile grew wider. "And that bothers you?"

"No." She'd said too much already. Pulling away from him, she went over to her dresser.

Following her, he clasped her shoulder this time, and turned her toward him. "I don't want Joanie, Amira. I want you. More than anything I want to kiss you right now. But if I do that, we'll wind up in that bed and I'm still not sure that's what *you* want."

Earlier she'd been vulnerable. Earlier his comfort had slid into something else. It would have swept her away if the phone hadn't rung. He seemed to know that and she appreciated that about him. Her admiration for him grew every day.

"You're an honorable man, Brent Carpenter."

A shadow passed over his face, and his eyes became sad. "Not as honorable as you think. I wish—" He stopped abruptly.

"What do you wish?"

"I wish lots of things were different." Stepping away from her, he crossed the room to the door. "But they aren't. If you have another bad dream, feel free to call me."

"I'll be fine." She knew she wouldn't call for him...couldn't call for him. If she invited him into her room again, it wouldn't be for comfort after a bad dream. She'd only invite him into her room again if she decided to make love with him.

"Good night, Amira," he said gently.

"Good night."

When she heard the door to his room close, she sank down onto the bed, knowing any further dreams she had tonight would be of him.

There was a cloud cover when Amira and Brent went to fetch Jared from Reunion House the next morning. It seemed to Amira that a cloud also hung over her and Brent, and she didn't know how to dispel it. Every time he looked at her there was something in his eyes. Sadness maybe? But as soon as she glimpsed it, it was gone and his guard was firmly back in place.

Jared was full of excitement and energy as they walked through the backyard. A Jet Ski bobbed there from the gentle lapping water on the lake. Farther along a blue pontoon boat was moored. It had a circular front deck and high-backed, padded admiral's chairs.

Brent stepped onto the boat first carrying the picnic basket. Jared hopped on before Brent could give him a hand. When it was Amira's turn to board, Brent turned to her and offered her his hand. She took it, feeling such a sense of rightness that it almost overwhelmed her. Whenever she was with Brent, she felt safe. That was so odd since she hadn't felt safe since the night her father had died. Her life in the palace had been pleasant, full of advantages most people didn't have. Yet remembering what had happened to her father, she had never felt safe there. When she'd traveled to Chicago alone, some of that fear had come with her. But when Brent had scooped her into his arms that first night and she lay against his chest, the sense of security had been overwhelming. She realized now that was one of the reasons she was so drawn to him. One of the reasons she'd fallen in love with him.

As Brent helped her into the boat, his arm went around her waist, and he looked as if he was going to kiss her.

"This is so cool," Jared called from under the canopy where he was examining everything. His enthusiasm broke the moment, and Amira stepped away from Brent breathless, knowing this day wasn't about the two of them. It was about keeping Jared occupied.

The breeze ruffled Amira's hair as she sat on one of the chairs, watching Brent teach Jared how to prepare a fishing rod. When Brent's cell phone rang, he grinned at Amira and asked, "Hold this?"

She took the fishing rod, glad that Brent was using corn as bait and not worms. Absently she listened while she watched Jared attach two kernels of corn to his hook.

"The papers have to be signed today?" Brent asked. "All right. I'll be back at the house by five at the latest." He glanced over at Amira. "You've brought Quentin up to speed as far as I'm concerned?" He listened to his secretary for a few moments, then added, "Just tell him not to forget."

A few moments later he attached the phone to his

belt again. Meeting her gaze he explained, "One of my employees is driving up to give me papers to sign."

"Even when you're on vacation you're not really on vacation, are you?"

He shook his head ruefully. "No."

"Do you have a very large staff?"

"Large enough. They're all very capable and do their jobs well." Taking the rod back from Amira, he asked Jared, "Ready to see if those fish are biting?"

The boy grinned at him, and Amira could see Jared was having a terrifically good time.

The morning passed pleasantly and swiftly as Amira sat with Jared and Brent, watching them fish. Jared was fascinated by everything—the boat and how it ran, the fishing rod, the type of fish in the lake. The breeze tossed Amira's hair. It was nippy with the sun still dancing behind the clouds, and she shivered.

Brent must have noticed. He unzipped his jacket, shrugged out of it and put it around her shoulders.

"I can't take this. You'll get cold."

He was wearing a sweatshirt with his jeans, and he shook his head. "I'm fine. My sweatshirt is heavier than your sweater."

Brent's jacket carried his warmth as well as his scent. She liked being wrapped up in both.

"If you get too cold, we'll go back."

Seeing the disappointment in Jared's eyes, she quickly shook her head. "I can always sit inside. I'm not going to spoil this fishing trip."

Brent's gaze was approving as he reached over and took her hand and warmed it under his. Sitting here with him and Jared, Amira could imagine a similar day with her own children. As she thought about being pregnant with Brent's child, a sense of pride and well-being blossomed inside of her.

Could she give up her life in Penwyck if he asked her to? It was all she'd ever known. Still, a future with Brent was becoming her heart's desire.

You can't base your future on knowing a man for only a week, her better sense told her.

Yet she felt she knew Brent in every way that mattered.

Nevertheless, if all Brent felt was desire, what did they have to build on?

Throughout the morning Amira looked for signs that Brent felt more than physical attraction. She thought she saw a few. He was kind to her, cared about her comfort and seemed to enjoy being with her. But love consisted of a lot more than caring.

It was almost four when Brent piloted the pontoon boat back to the dock and tied it down. He swung the almost-empty picnic basket as he took Amira's hand and Jared ran ahead of them. They were about twenty yards from the house when the back door opened. A girl of about eight stepped outside. She had long brown hair tied in pigtails and a wide smile on her face.

Jared took off with a loud whoop, and moments later he was on the porch hugging his sister.

Tears sprang to Amira's eyes as she and Brent stopped and watched. "I can see why you put your time and heart into Reunion House," she murmured.

"I remember the reunion my brother and I had after being separated for nine months. Even though I knew we'd be separated again eventually, that first moment was pure hope and happiness and everything we'd ever meant to each other."

Brent's barriers were down and Amira felt honored that she could share this moment with him. He was a man who could love deeply. The question was— would he let himself love her?

Brent must have felt the closeness between them, too, because he draped his arm around her shoulders and they walked up the path to Reunion House together.

They only stayed at the house long enough to meet Lena and see that she and Jared, as well as the other kids, were well occupied. Cocoa seemed to be at home there already and thoroughly satisfied with her new environment.

When Brent pulled into the drive at Shady Glenn, there was already a car there.

"Quentin's early," Brent said brusquely as he unfastened his seat belt.

After Brent came around and opened Amira's door for her, they approached the porch. A man had been sitting in one of the cane rockers and rose to greet them. He was about five-eight, stocky, with brown hair. His suit and tie seemed out of place here.

As Amira smiled at him, she thought he looked familiar. Had she seen him somewhere before, or did he simply look like somebody she might know?

On the porch Brent introduced Amira to the man. "Quentin Franklin, Amira Corbin."

She shook his hand still trying to place him. Where had she seen Quentin Franklin before?

Chapter Nine

As Marcus sipped from his first cup of coffee for the day, he heard the shower running upstairs. Last evening had been one of the most frustrating of his life, but one of the most satisfying. It had been frustrating because he'd been close enough to Amira to kiss her as they'd sat on the sofa in front of the fire and played Scrabble. It had been satisfying because she was quick and bright and funny and had not only played the game, but talked and teased and laughed, too. He couldn't remember ever being that relaxed with a woman—comfortable enough to take off his shoes and not worry about what he should say or do or be. He could just be himself.

Only…she didn't know who he really was.

The phone rang and he automatically picked it up. "Hello?"

"I'd like to speak to Amira Corbin."

Now Marcus checked the Caller ID and saw the international code. "I'm sorry. She's not available right now. Can I give her a message?'' he asked smoothly as if he was a clerk at a desk.

There was silence and then he heard, ''This is Queen Marissa of Penwyck.''

This was the woman who might want to place the responsibility for a country on his head. ''Hello, Queen Marissa. What would you like me to tell Miss Corbin?''

''Do you know when she will be available?''

All he wanted to do was get the woman off the phone. Thinking about how long it usually took Amira to dress, he answered, ''She'll be here for breakfast in about half an hour.''

''I imagine she's taking her early-morning jog?''

''I don't think she ran today, but I'm certain she'll be here for breakfast in a half hour.''

''All right. Please tell her to call me immediately.''

''I'll do that. It was an honor to speak with you, Your Majesty.''

When Marcus hung up the receiver, he felt relieved but unsettled, too. That had been the woman who thought she might be his birth mother.

Twenty minutes later Amira came into the kitchen looking beautifully fresh and casual in jeans and a sweater. She was wearing her new shoes and had her hair tied back in a ponytail.

He poured a cup of coffee for her and set it on the table. ''You had a phone call.''

Amira lost her relaxed look and asked, ''Who was it?''

''It was the queen.''

Her eyes widened. ''Why didn't you come and get me?''

''Because you were in the shower.''

"That doesn't matter. If the queen wanted me—"

He felt impatient with her and the whole impossible situation. "Don't be ridiculous, Amira. What would you have done? Answered the phone dripping wet?"

"Yes!"

Immersed in the vision of her answering the phone that way, he shook his head. "I didn't think a few minutes would make a difference. In fact, you could probably eat breakfast first and the world won't fall apart." He was frustrated by her royal connection, knowing what it could mean to his life. He could also feel the sand in their hourglass running out, and not seeing her again disturbed him more than he wanted to admit.

"What did she say?" Amira asked, her voice strained.

"She said to call her immediately."

Amira went to the phone and asked coolly, "May I have a bit of privacy?"

"Fine," he said, exasperated with her. "I'll be in my office."

As Amira blinked away tears, she was angry with Brent for dismissing the call as if Queen Marissa had been a phone solicitor. She'd seen the exasperation and frustration in his eyes and knew full well what it was from. When he'd given her a good-night kiss last night, it had been a question. She'd ended the kiss before she'd been swept away again, and he'd left her at her bedroom door, wanting him.

Trying to push her relationship with Brent to the back of her mind, she dialed the queen's number. Her secretary, Mrs. Ferth, answered and then she transferred the call to the queen.

"Amira?"

"Yes, Queen Marissa. Has something happened?"

"Indeed it has. Prince Dylan has finally returned home. He's been traveling through remote areas of Europe. That's why we couldn't reach him."

"But he's home now?"

"Yes. He made a stop in Paris and heard about the king's health, Megan's pregnancy and marriage, Owen's kidnapping and return. He was very surprised his brother has a child and that Owen actually got down on his knees to ask Jordan to marry him."

Everyone had been surprised at that! "Had Dylan heard about Princess Anastasia's plane crash?"

"No, he hadn't. But he's pleased to see her with Jake Sanderstone. He thinks Jake can keep her in line. His words—not mine."

"Does he know about…?" Amira didn't know how to put the mix-up with the royal twins delicately.

"Does he know he might not be the true prince?" Queen Marissa formed the question for her. "Yes. I told him what Broderick says he did and how I tried to foil his machinations. But Dylan doesn't seem too concerned. He has always felt Owen outshone him in everything and assumed his brother would eventually be named king. That's why he took off on this trip of his in the first place. So the idea that Marcus and Shane Cordello might be the true heirs doesn't faze him. He was more disconcerted by the possibility that King Morgan and I might not be his parents. As with Owen, I assured both of my sons that I will always be their mother no matter what DNA reveals."

Amira felt compassion for the queen and the whole situation. She had worried in silence about Dylan while he was gone. "I'm so glad Dylan's home and that you can stop worrying about him."

"I'll always worry about my children. Dylan did say he'll help us any way he can to get to the bottom of Broderick's plot. I think he's quite eager to meet Marcus Cordello himself."

"I'll do everything in my power to speak to Marcus Cordello when he returns to the city. I'll be on his office doorstep Monday morning ready to confront him. Somehow I'll get through those doors into his office. I will not let my country down."

"We know you'll do your very best, my dear. Are you finding your accommodations suitable where you're staying?"

Amira looked around the kitchen and into the living room. She was very comfortable here. "It's very casual, Your Majesty, but very peaceful, too."

"None of us have had much of that lately. You get your fill of peace and quiet while you can and enjoy yourself."

After Amira hung up the phone, she knew she had to get something straight with Brent and get it straight now.

She found him at his large mahogany desk, his laptop computer switched on. When he heard her, he swiveled toward her. "Well? Is the country still in one piece?"

"You can make fun of me if you like," she said coolly. "But if I receive another call from the queen, please let me know immediately. A subject should never keep Her Majesty waiting."

Brent stood, his eyes stormy. "No one is that important that you can't take a breath before you return their call. You act as if she owns you."

Amira's feelings for Brent, somewhere between a hope and a dream, brought tears to her eyes. "You'll

never understand my duties, my world…my life.''
Spinning around, she headed for the kitchen and went
outside, not knowing where she was going. She just
knew she didn't want this idyll with Brent to end. She
didn't want to go back to her duties, her world and
her life, but yet she had to. She had no choice. Penwyck was where she belonged. Brent would never
understand that…never understand what her life was.

She took off at a run when she left the house, and
before she realized it, she'd followed a path through
birches and elms and found herself at the edge of the
lake.

Brent caught up to her as she stood on the bank
edged with laurel, staring at the pontoon boat a quar-
ter of the way around the lake.

She could hear his feet rustling the leaves as he
came up behind her. ''Help me understand the world
you come from.''

When she turned to face him, he was hardly a
breath away. She could see his annoyance with her
was gone now.

''I *don't* understand, Amira,'' he said gently. ''But
I'd like to.''

The intensity in his eyes was more than she could
handle at the moment, and she looked away. ''It's
difficult to explain.''

Tenderly, so very tenderly, he cupped her face in
his hand. ''You don't run away from 'difficult.' I
know that about you.''

No, she didn't. So she tried to do as he asked. ''On
Penwyck, everything revolves around the royal family. They can hardly take a walk without newspapers
wanting to cover them. Although my father was part
of the Royal Guard, he never talked about the family.

In his silence I sensed his loyalty, the attitude of discretion everyone around him followed. My father was a wonderful man—kind and gentle, yet strong and sure. I was always so proud of him when I saw him protecting the king. That's what I remember most— how he stood, handsome in his uniform, flanking the king wherever he went.''

"Like our Secret Service," Brent responded.

"Yes, exactly like that. I always knew that if he had to my father would give his life for King Morgan. But I never believed that would happen. When I was a child I saw the palace as a fairy-tale castle and believed nothing bad could happen in King Morgan and Queen Marissa's kingdom. Then in one terrible night I learned I was all wrong."

"You learned about real life."

Amira realized that just as her father's death was a life-changing event for her, Brent had had a similar one when his parents divorced and he was separated from his brother. "I learned about reality," she agreed, "but I also learned about loyalty and kindness. The royal family took in my mother and me and gave us new lives. The queen invited my mother to become her lady-in-waiting. My mother became her confidante. Queen Marissa arranged for private tutors for me, and Princess Anastasia, especially, became like a big sister to me. Princess Meredith and Princess Megan were older, but they never acted as if they resented me. Neither did Prince Dylan or Prince Owen. It was as if the queen and king had decreed us part of the family, and all of them appreciated the sacrifice my father had made. Because of him, the king lived. Because of him, Penwyck still had its monarch."

"I'm beginning to understand," Brent said, and she could see from his expression that he was.

"They gave me my life. After my schooling was finished, Queen Marissa found a place for me in the academy. Everything at Penwyck is about loyalty and honor."

"So it's natural for you to be on call, to fly to the United States to meet a man who's a stranger, to return a phone call immediately. Tell me something, Amira. Do you like your life?"

Again she felt she had to be honest. "Before I came here I thought about getting my own apartment but not changing my life. Now...I don't know. Sometimes all of it is a burden, and sometimes it gives my life meaning."

"I could never live like you do. Never."

"Most people can't," she admitted, thinking about a life here with Brent. But he didn't want to share his life on an ongoing basis. No matter what she did or what she changed, that wouldn't change.

Brent's cell phone beeped and he glanced at it askance. "I'm supposed to be on vacation," he muttered, taking it from his belt and slipping it open. "Yes?" he asked tersely.

Amira watched his face go grim. Taking her hand he started tugging her toward the house, and she hurried along beside him, worried.

She heard him say, "We're headed for the car now. We'll be there in two minutes." Snapping the phone shut, he clipped it back on his belt, not slowing his stride.

"What is it?"

"That was Marilyn. She can't find Jared and Lena anywhere. Apparently Lena's foster mother and father are getting a divorce. No one knows where Lena will be placed. Both kids are terrifically upset. I think Jared's afraid they'll ship her even farther away.''

''Where do you think they'd go?''

''He might take her to the woods with him, or he might hide out somewhere for a while. I just don't know. I *do* know ten-year-olds don't usually plan ahead.''

When Brent and Amira arrived at Reunion House, they searched it again with Joanie and Marilyn.

''We're wasting our time,'' Brent said as they stood in the foyer once more. ''He wouldn't take the chance of us finding them here. I'm going to the woods. Marilyn, call Emergency Services, and tell them we need to find these kids.''

''I'm going with you.'' Amira ran beside Brent as they hurried to the kitchen and out the back door into the yard.

Brent had his eyes peeled to the woods as they ran toward them. Suddenly he pointed. ''There. Did you see a flash of yellow?''

Amira had missed whatever Brent had seen. ''No, I didn't, but that doesn't mean it wasn't there.''

As they met the tree line, Brent tugged her along it. ''There. I saw it again. I think he's headed for the dock.''

Lena and Jared were a good hundred yards ahead. All Amira could make out were colors. One was definitely moving slower than the other. ''She's not running as fast as he is. Maybe she's hurt.''

''That's what I meant about kids not planning. I don't know what he thinks he's going to do on the dock. Unless—'' Brent swore and Amira guessed what Brent was imagining.

''I showed him how to do it,'' Brent muttered. ''I showed him where I keep the key. Damn.''

They heard the pontoon boat's engine start when they were still fifty yards from the dock. Brent surged ahead of her. ''Wait on the dock for me.''

''What are you going to do?''

''Go after them,'' he called over his shoulder, and she suddenly realized exactly what he intended. Her heart almost stopped.

The pontoon boat was chugging fast and picking up speed.

Afraid for Brent, Amira watched as he hopped on the Jet Ski and started it. She thought about his shoulder, about the wound that wasn't yet healed. What did he think he was going to do? He certainly couldn't stop the pontoon boat with a Jet Ski, could he?

Watching in fear and dismay, she saw him race on the surface of the lake, speeding so he could catch up with the boat. He looked as if he were flying. As he pulled up beside the pontoon boat, she saw with dread what he was going to do. He was going to jump onto the deck! What if he didn't make it? What if he fell between the two vehicles? Good Lord, she loved this man and she wanted nothing more than to spend the rest of her life with him. There was no doubt in her mind.

With bated breath, she saw Brent jump to the pontoon boat's deck, teeter for a moment, then leap over the rail. She had never been so relieved, never been so grateful. But what had it cost him? What if he had torn his shoulder open again?

Waiting on the dock was the hardest thing she'd

ever done as the Jet Ski skipped over the water until
it hit the shore then fell on its side. In the meantime,
Brent piloted the boat back to the dock. As soon as
she could, she caught the line and helped him tie it
up, noting Jared's and Lena's expressions. Lena
looked scared, but Jared looked defiant.

Brent pointed toward the dock. "Out," he said
gravely.

Jared hopped onto the dock first, and then Brent
put his hands around Lena's waist and carried her to
Amira. "She turned her ankle. Thank goodness or
they would have been across the lake before we could
catch them."

Jared turned on Brent then. "You shouldn't have
brought us back. We're just going to run away again.
You wait and see."

"If I hadn't caught you, where would you have
gone? The lake is about three miles round. You
wouldn't have gotten very far. What would you have
done for shelter tonight. And food?"

The ten-year-old produced four cookies from his
pocket. "We had food."

Brent shook his head and took Jared by the shoulders. "Running away is not going to solve anything."

"It'll keep us together," he almost shouted, his
voice trembling between anger and tears. "I don't
want them putting Lena somewhere where I can't call
her, where I can't see her. We want to be together,
Mr. Carpenter. Please."

Amira's heart went out to the two children, and she
knew Brent's did, too.

Crouching down in front of Jared, Brent studied the
boy for a long time, then he looked at Lena. "I can't

make you any promises, but I do know people in the system. Let me see what I can do.''

"You mean we'll be together?'' Jared asked, wariness in his tone.

"I'll try to make that happen. Can you trust that I'll do my best for you?''

Jared and Lena exchanged a look. "I guess we can't stay at a motel without a credit card.''

The corner of Brent's mouth turned up. "Not unless you have a bunch of cash.''

"Don't have much, just five dollars from chores.'' It seemed to take a very long time for Jared to decide what he was going to do. "All right. We'll give you a chance.''

Brent extended his hand to the boy. "Shake on it?''

Jared put his hand into Brent's, and Amira felt her throat constrict. The brother and sister had such hope in their eyes, such trust in Brent's power to reunite them. What if she trusted Brent, too? What if she trusted what she felt and gave in to it?

After Brent called the dispatcher to let them know Jared and Lena had been found, he sat down with the brother and sister and Marilyn again, getting specific information from them so he could make a few calls.

Amira tended to Lena's ankle, putting an ice pack on it and propping it on a stool. Although she kept close to Jared, Lena's eyes were filled with a thank-you, and when it was time for Brent and Amira to go back to Shady Glenn, Lena waved to her. Amira felt as if she'd made a friend.

Thinking about everything that had happened, Amira was quiet on the drive back to Shady Glenn. When Brent pulled up in front of the house, he didn't cut the engine. "I'm going to go around the lake and see about that Jet Ski."

"You're not serious."

"Of course I am." He studied her carefully. "What's the matter?"

"I was worried about you. I still am. You should let me check your shoulder."

"I'll tell you what. Why don't you go in and make us some hot chocolate. I'll make sure the ski didn't damage anyone's property and I'll be right back. Promise."

"You'll be right back?"

"Fifteen minutes tops."

She didn't want to act like a meddling fussbudget. "Okay. I'll put something together for us for lunch."

As Brent drove off, Amira went inside and fixed a tray of sandwiches, covered them and set them in the refrigerator. True to his word, he returned fifteen minutes later. When he took off his jacket, she noticed the nerve in his jaw working. That meant he was in pain.

"The gauze patches and tape are upstairs. Let's go tend to your shoulder."

"You have a one-track mind," he said with patient amusement.

If he only knew what track her mind was on.

As they mounted the steps, she could feel his gaze on her. At the top of the stairs he asked, "Bathroom or my bedroom?"

"This will be easier if you're sitting on the bed." She remembered the last time she had done this and how she had left him afterward. She could see he was remembering, too.

As she'd done before, she stood between his legs to change the bandage. But this time something was different. This time she wasn't denying everything she was feeling. This time she secured the last piece of tape and then looked into his eyes.

"You scared me to death on the dock. I was afraid...I was afraid something terrible would happen to you."

He didn't make light of what she'd felt. Rather he took her hands in his. "I didn't know what was going to happen out there. I just knew I had to get on that boat and stop them before they hurt themselves."

"You're a hero," she said, her admiration obvious.

"Oh, Amira..." He shook his head. "I'm not a hero. I just did what I had to do." He lifted her fingers to his lips and kissed them one by one.

She never knew her fingertips were connected to her heart. She never knew her heart could feel so full or so sad at the same time. "We only have a few days left," she murmured.

His green gaze was questioning as he raised his head. "I know. What would you like to do with those days?"

"It doesn't matter...as long as I'm with you."

Releasing her hands, he slid his arms around her and brought her closer. "I want you," he said, his voice deep with need.

"I want you, too," she whispered.

"Are you sure?" he asked, and she knew if she hesitated at all, he would restrain himself and pull away.

Remembering how she'd felt on that dock, thinking about everything she'd learned about him over the past week, how she was going to feel leaving him when she returned to Penwyck, she said boldly, "I'm sure."

Brent tugged her down onto his lap then and kissed her as if he'd never kissed her before and would never kiss her again. Parting her lips, he ravished her mouth with the inflamed desire of a man who had waited too long. When she moaned softly, overwhelmed by the sensuality of the kiss, she wanted to give him everything she was.

Breaking away, he took a deep breath. "I want to do this slowly, Amira. I want you to know the full pleasure of everything a man and a woman can do for each other."

"We don't have to go slow." She had read books about what was going to happen, but her first time with Brent couldn't be found in any book. "I trust you," she said simply.

He kissed her again and eased her back onto the bed. "This is going to be good, Amira. I promise you that."

She wasn't exactly sure how he defined *good,* but as soon as he trailed kisses across her mouth, down her chin and throat into the vee of her sweater, she was trembling. While his mouth worked its magic, his hands slid under her sweater and pushed it up. His skin on hers was hot, taunting, so deliciously erotic that she couldn't help but move restlessly so he would touch more.

"Easy," he said to her, "let's take this off." With slow care he lifted her sweater over her head, admired her breasts in the lacy bra, and then he was unfastening it, touching her, putting his lips to her nipple.

She'd never felt anything so exquisite, and she cried his name.

His hand went to her jeans. "It's going to get even better, sweetheart. I promise."

He was about to unfasten her zipper when his hand stilled.

At first she was so caught up in what was happening between them she barely noticed. But then he shifted and sat up, and she felt bereft without him covering her. "What is it?"

"I heard something downstairs—"

"Is anybody home?" came a deep male voice at the foot of the stairs.

Amira plucked up her sweater and held it in front of her breasts. "Oh, my gosh. Is it Fritz?"

"No, it's not Fritz. It's my father. I'd better get down there before he comes up here."

Sliding off the bed and pushing himself to his feet, Brent took a deep breath. Then he bent down to her, kissed her hard on the lips and assured her, "You'll like Dad and he'll like you. Tonight after he goes to bed, we'll finish where we left off."

As Brent went into the hall and called down to his dad, Amira couldn't wait for tonight to come. She loved Brent Carpenter and she was going to show him exactly how much.

Chapter Ten

Glancing outside the kitchen window, Amira saw Brent and his dad deep in conversation while Brent cooked the hamburgers on the outdoor grill. She liked his father very much. He'd immediately told her to call him Joe, and his hazel eyes had been friendly. She'd been embarrassed a little while ago when she'd descended the steps and her gaze had met Brent's. But his smile had been as intimate as before. It told her he wanted to be with her as much as she wanted to be with him.

As she mixed an olive oil and lemon juice dressing for a pasta salad that Owen's wife Jordan had taught her how to make, she thought about the night to come. She wanted to know Brent in every way, and she wanted him to know her. Maybe tonight she could tell him how she felt. Maybe tonight she could tell him she wanted to see him again after she returned to Penwyck. Maybe tonight they could talk about her moving to the United States permanently. It would be a risk for her, but it would be worth it if Brent could come to love her. Maybe the idea was altogether fool-hardy, but she was tired of living a protected existence.

When the phone rang, she thought about letting the machine pick it up, but then the Caller ID showed the number that Cole Everson had used.

The head of the Royal Intelligence Institute got straight to the point. "I have a picture, Amira. I'm going to fax it to you as soon as we finish here. I also have Cordello's home address. Watching the post office box didn't work. No one picked up the mail after I began surveillance. It was as if he knew we were watching. But we found a deed for a purchase of a house near De Kalb and that gave us his home address in the paperwork. I'll also fax that information to you."

"A house near De Kalb?" At first a frisson of fore-boding skipped down her spine. But then she told herself she was being silly. Lots of inhabitants of Chicago must have houses in the state and maybe De Kalb was a popular area.

"With this information," Cole went on, "you'll know who you're looking for and have a second place to look. But the queen doesn't expect you to take on the role of a private investigator. If you still can't corner the man after a few days, I'll bring in a pro-fessional. As soon as we hang up, I'll fax you what I have. Good luck, Amira."

When Amira hung up the phone, she no longer gave a second thought to the dressing for the pasta salad or to the frozen vegetables on the counter. Rather she went to Brent's study to wait for the faxes.

* * *

The aroma of hamburgers wafted into the fall air as Marcus stared at his father in astonishment. "Shane and I are adopted?"

Joseph Cordello had gone along with his son's wishes to call him Brent when he'd arrived at Shady Glenn. But as soon as they stepped outside and had a bit of privacy, he wanted to know why. Marcus had filled him in, giving him the tale Amira had related, adding the rest of what she had told him about life on Penwyck. Then his father had revealed the secret he'd been keeping for twenty-three years.

Joseph's eyes were anguished. "I never wanted you to find out like this. So suddenly."

"Suddenly? Dad, I'm twenty-three years old!" Marcus was feeling more than shock now. Anger mixed with it. His world had just been rocked again by his father's revelation.

Joseph Cordello took a deep breath but kept his gaze steady on his son's. "When your mother and I divorced, we felt you were too young. We decided to wait until you and Shane were eighteen. But the time never seemed right. We wanted to tell you and Shane together, but the four of us were rarely in the same state..."

Although Marcus was keeping a tight rein on all of his emotions, his turmoil must have shown because his father stopped then and said, "You have every right to be angry. But we didn't tell you because we love you both. In every way that matters, we *are* your parents."

Unable to watch the pained look in his dad's eyes, Marcus took a few steps away from the grill and looked toward the lake. "Who *are* our birth parents?"

His dad answered quickly. "According to our lawyer, they were a young couple who were in a terrible accident. They both perished. An aunt was baby-sitting you and Shane at the time.''

''Why didn't the aunt take us?''

''She was elderly and knew she couldn't handle bringing up twins. She also didn't want to separate you. She wanted a good family to raise you.''

Marcus swung around and faced his father again. ''Did you ever meet the aunt?''

''No. No, we didn't. We were told traveling was difficult for her. Our lawyer and his wife transferred you to us.''

The full realization of everything his father had told him hit him. ''Then Amira's story *could* be true.''

Since his father had arrived and Marcus had had to leave Amira in his bed, he'd thought only of her and what they'd been about to do. As he'd introduced her to his father, he'd decided he couldn't make love to her without telling her who he was. He'd decided to ask her to help him keep the world outside at bay with him until Monday.

Now he had to tell her the truth not only to restore real honesty to their relationship but because he might very well be one of the Penwyck heirs!

As he heard the back door open, he turned and saw Amira coming down the steps with her head bowed. It was crazy, but he always missed her when they were apart, even if it wasn't for very long. In the midst of all that he'd learned, honesty between them became the priority. Deciding supper would have to wait until he revealed the truth to her, he became aware of the papers in her hand.

She raised her face to him, and he didn't have to ask her what they were. He knew.

He'd decided to tell her the truth hoping nothing would change between them. That had been optimism at its worst. Her wounded expression tore at his heart and the look of betrayal in her eyes lanced his soul.

"Why did you do it?" she asked, her voice rising as she shook the papers at him. "Why did you tell me you were somebody else?"

He stepped closer to her, but she backed away and he stilled. "I didn't intend for it to go this far. Let me explain."

"Explain? There *are* no explanations. You're Marcus Cordello! I poured my heart out to you. I told you how much I needed to see him and why. You sat there and listened, being sympathetic, learning how much it mattered to me and everyone at Penwyck. And still you didn't say a word. You deceived me all this time, playing with my emotions, leading me on. I can't believe I wasn't intelligent enough to put it all together. I met you in the hotel where your offices are. Your secretary's name is Barbra. How could I have let that pass?"

For the time being, he buried his feelings about his father's revelation and concentrated on Amira. "You let it pass for the same reason I couldn't tell you the truth. We were getting to know each other and nothing else mattered."

"My mission mattered."

He could see the tears glistening in her eyes as the strength of her emotions shook her voice. "Amira…"

"The first time we saw your doorman," she went on, "you cut him off. He was going to call you by your real name. And that man who came here yesterday…I knew I'd seen him somewhere before. One of those days I was sitting outside your office, he came out. You've played me for an utter fool. This afternoon I thought—'' Her cheeks grew red, her lower lip trembled, and Marcus had never felt so low in his life.

"It's not the way you think."

"It's *exactly* the way I think. You saw me as some shy little twit who didn't know the first thing about men. You thought you could take advantage of me—"

Marcus knew he had no defense. But he *had* struggled with becoming involved with her because of who he was and where she was from, and the fact that she was shy and innocent. "I never took advantage of you."

"What about this afternoon? If your father hadn't arrived, you wouldn't have stopped."

Suddenly uncomfortable with having this discussion in front of his father, Marcus knew it was where they had to have it because Amira would never let him talk with her about this calmly inside. Still he had to give it a try. "Let's go inside and discuss this."

"I'm not going anywhere with you."

That's the response he'd expected. "This afternoon, Amira, we were both in that bed. Neither one of us would have put a stop to it if my father hadn't arrived. You might be shy sometimes and you *are* innocent, but you're your own woman, too. You made the decision to be with me."

Her gaze darted to his father and, as she realized they were discussing their most private matters in front of him, she looked thoroughly mortified.

Marcus wished he could put his arms around her, persuade her to believe that his father wouldn't judge anything. But he knew she wouldn't let him get close to her. He knew she'd never let him touch her again.

Although her eyes glistened with unshed tears, she squared her shoulders. "I'm leaving here tonight. When I get back to the city, I'm taking the first flight out. Someone from Penwyck will be in touch with you. I hope you don't play the same games with them that you played with me." Then she turned and practically ran into the house.

Marcus didn't think he had ever heard a more earth-shattering silence. As the door slammed, he started to go after her, but his father put a restraining hand on his shoulder. "I don't think another confrontation is a good idea."

"I can't let her leave like this."

"I think you're going to have to. In the state she's in, you set a foot near her, and she's going to *walk* back to Chicago. I'll offer her my driver. He's at a motel in De Kalb. He can be here in half an hour."

"I can't let her leave," Marcus said again.

"If you don't let her leave, you might never get her back. *If* that's what you want. I think you'd better be sure exactly what you want before you talk to her again."

Marcus took a long look at Joseph Cordello, remembering the man wasn't his biological father. Yet, hearing his advice, Marcus felt his anger at being kept in the dark for twenty-three years vanish. This man was his "real" father in every definition of the word. "All right. Offer her your driver."

As Joseph Cordello went inside, Marcus felt as if the foundation of his life had cracked in two and nothing would ever be the same again.

*   *   *

The Jet Ski skimmed the surface of the lake, but Marcus got no pleasure from the speed. He'd felt turned inside out since Amira had left. Making repairs at Reunion House hadn't helped. Taking long drives hadn't helped. Assembling the jungle gym hadn't helped. Running until he'd dropped hadn't helped. Talking to his dad hadn't helped. No matter what he did, he thought about her, about who she was, about who they could be together.

The day after Amira had left he'd tried to put her out of his mind by having a talk with Jared's foster mother and dad and then the authorities. The family who had taken Jared in would also take Lena. They'd been unable to do that a year ago, but since then they'd moved to a larger house and Mr. Brinkman had gotten a promotion. The satisfaction in what he'd been able to do had come when Jared hugged him. Even then all he could think about was having children of his own with Amira as their mother.

He gave the Jet Ski more power, seeking to outrun the pain and the feeling of emptiness. But he couldn't outrun it, and he knew he should stop trying.

When he returned to the dock, his father was standing there waiting for him. His dad had come along to Reunion House this morning to help him with the jungle gym. "You had a call," Joseph said.

"Amira?" he asked, knowing that was improbable but hoping nonetheless.

His father shook his head. "Sorry, no. It was a Mrs. Dunlap, Cocoa's owner. Apparently she called Barbra and Barbra gave her the number here. She phoned a veterinarian, who told her that you found Cocoa. Only her name isn't Cocoa, it's Brownie. I told her where you'd taken Brownie and how much the kids loved her. She said her arthritis is getting worse and she can't walk Brownie as much as she'd like. Brownie slipped her collar one day when they went for a walk. I think Mrs. Dunlap would like to visit Reunion House and see if the dog really has a good home. If she does, she'd like to visit now and then.''

"That would be a good solution for everyone,'' Marcus said. "I'll have Fritz drive her up here as soon as I get back to the city.''

"Are you going back tomorrow?''

Tomorrow was Sunday. He'd promised to have dinner with Marilyn and the kids before he left. "Fritz will arrive in the late afternoon, and we'll start back then. What about you?''

"I'll leave first thing in the morning.'' He paused, then asked, "Are we all right, Marcus? Can you still think of me as your father?''

Having a few days to let it all sink in had helped. He realized his dad was the same man he'd always known, and he still felt admiration, respect and love for him. "We're all right, Dad. I could never think of anyone else as my father.''

His dad capped Marcus's shoulder, and there was moisture in his eyes. He cleared his throat. "Are you going to tell Shane?''

"I have to decide the best way to do that.''

"I'm surprised you haven't received a call from Penwyck.''

"I don't even know if Amira flew back yet. Maybe she stayed. Maybe she'll be at my office bright and early Monday morning to meet me in an official capacity.'' His heart lifted at the thought.

"Do you really think that's likely?'' His dad made him face the impracticality of that possibility.

In his mind's eye he could see Amira waiting for him at Shady Glenn, holding their child in her arms. "No, it's not likely."

"You know, son, I was a fool where your mother was concerned. We had problems, and I thought I wanted more than she could give me. I made a terrible mistake that she could never forgive. But I also didn't try very hard to win her forgiveness. My pride kept me from telling her that I still loved her. If Amira is the woman you want or need, don't let her simply fly away."

"She'll never forgive me."

"You don't know that, do you?"

No, he didn't know that. His mother hadn't been able to forgive, but maybe Amira could.

Suddenly Marcus realized he didn't just want to ask Amira for forgiveness because that was the right thing to do. He wanted her to forgive him because he loved her. He hadn't wanted to fall in love. He'd fought against it from the moment he'd met her. Her heart called to his and now he wanted to answer that call. He just hoped it wasn't too late. He just hoped he could convince her not only to forgive him but to trust him for the rest of their lives.

Filled with resolve, he said, "I'm going to ask Marilyn if I can change our dinner plans to tonight. Then I'm going to make reservations and see when I can get a flight out."

"This is serious, then," Joseph remarked as he and Marcus started walking toward Reunion House.

"This is it, Dad. The real thing. I found a woman I can't do without. Now I just have to convince her she can't do without me."

After discovering Amira had checked out of the

hotel, Marcus also found out that she'd made flight arrangements through the concierge and returned to Penwyck. Throughout Saturday night, he went over persuasive arguments in his mind. None seemed right, none seemed good enough. In spite of that, he got an early flight out the next morning.

Fortunately, he had time to stop in a jewelry store in the airport before he left.

His flight landed on schedule. Due to the time change, it was early evening when he arrived at the palace. As his taxi pulled up, he saw a gray limestone edifice three stories tall. Actually it looked like two buildings joined by a covered glassed-in walkway that was illuminated from the curved ceiling inside.

At the main entrance he gave his name to the guard, who called someone in the palace. Another guard dressed in the same red jacket and black slacks with a red beret escorted him through a garden to the covered hallway. The floor was marble as were the columns. There were floor-to-ceiling arched windows.

When they exited the walkway, they came to another long hall. Finally they stood before a large door. The guard opened it and Marcus stepped inside.

Marcus barely noticed the hand-carved plaster and gilded wainscoting, the marble fireplace with columns, the cream velvet sofa, the chairs covered in silk damask. The walls were decorated with paintings, water lilies by Monet, a Renoir, and a large photograph of what Marcus supposed was the royal family with their horses. Amira wasn't in the picture so he didn't stare at it very long. He glanced at the desk and saw no one was seated there.

Suddenly a door opened and two women walked in. The first woman looked to be in her forties. Her blond hair was pulled into a chignon at her nape similar to the way Amira had worn her hair the first night he'd met her. She had blue eyes that were very serious. The second woman was older, in her fifties. Her hair was dark and she wore it in a corona on the top of her head. She, too, had blue eyes and was strikingly beautiful. Her maroon silk blouse and tailored wool slacks suited her understated elegance.

The guard bowed and said formally, "Her Majesty, the Queen, and her lady-in-waiting, Gwendolyn Montague."

Marcus had asked to see the queen or Amira's mother, not knowing if an audience was that easily obtained. Apparently his name had carried some weight. Maybe a very lead weight.

Still, he bowed to the queen. "I'm honored." Then to Mrs. Montague, he said, "It's a pleasure to meet you, too."

Neither woman spoke so he addressed the situation immediately. "I've come for two reasons. First and foremost, to find Amira and convince her I'm not the blackguard she thinks I am. Secondly, I came to find out if my brother and I might be royal heirs. I had no idea we were adopted until a few days ago, so I had put the idea out of my mind since Amira first told me about it because I didn't want any part of it. I didn't want my life disrupted." He looked squarely at Amira's mother. "But your daughter did disrupt my life quite completely, and when she left I realized it was empty without her."

The queen and Gwen Montague exchanged a look.

"Well, Mr. Cordello," the queen finally responded. "You've deflated our indignation on Amira's behalf.

I think we were both ready to roast you over hot coals.''

Marcus thought he saw a twinkle of amusement in the queen's eyes. ''I think Amira would like to do something much worse,'' he said with complete seriousness.

The queen motioned to the grouping of furniture.

Marcus waited until the women were seated, and then he sat on the edge of one of the silk damask chairs that was as uncomfortable as any chair could be. But there was no way to make this conversation comfortable, antique chair or not.

Gwen Montague looked him straight in the eye. ''You haven't known my daughter very long, Mr. Cordello. Am I supposed to believe you care deeply for her after less than two weeks?''

''Amira told me the story of how you and your first husband met at an embassy ball. She said you knew from the moment you looked into his eyes that he was the man you belonged with. It was that way with me and Amira, although I didn't want to admit it. There are a lot of reasons for that—reasons why I pushed her away at first.''

''I know this might seem a bit indelicate,'' Gwen told him, ''but Amira seems to think you were only interested in getting her into bed.''

The queen's brows arched, and a bit of a smile lurked at the corner of her mouth as she saw how uncomfortable Marcus was with discussing this with Amira's mother.

He deserved this grilling and met it with honesty. ''That was my intention. When I asked her to go to Shady Glenn with me, I knew we'd have a week to be together. But I also never tried to take advantage of your daughter, Mrs. Montague. If she's honest with you, I think she'll tell you that.''

The queen's lady-in-waiting paused for a moment. ''She did tell me that, but I needed your explanation before I decided if she'd had the wool pulled over her eyes or not.''

''I imagine you'll have to get to know me before you can make any decisions about my character and my feelings for your daughter. But I am going to ask her to marry me.''

Again the queen and Amira's mother exchanged a look.

''Amira's still quite upset,'' the queen interjected. ''She's changed since her trip to the United States. She's talking about moving out of the palace, living on her own. If you're not the prince, as you hope you're not, your life in Chicago will remain as it has always been. Would you expect Amira to give up everything she knows here?''

''I'm not sure what we'll do. We'll have to work it out…together.''

''Mr. Cordello, I don't know what Gwen thinks, but I believe you're an honorable man. Since she's Amira's mother, though, it's up to her to decide whether or not she'll tell Amira that you've come.''

''Is she here now?'' he asked, determined to search every room in the palace for her if he had to.

Gwen Montague must have seen that determination in his eyes and maybe some of what he felt for Amira, too. ''I have the feeling you'd tear the palace down to find her,'' she said, her voice a bit friendly now.

''I would. I know how special she is.''

Silence reigned for a moment.

''All right, Mr. Cordello,'' Gwen Montague decided. "I'll tell you where you can find her. The rest is up to you. She's having dinner in town at the Artist's Place. It's a small café."

"Yes, she told me about it. They have new artists' work on display."

"Yes, it's one of her favorite spots to go when she wants to think. She just left about half an hour ago, so you should be able to catch her there. Do you need a driver?"

"I asked the cab to wait." He stood, not knowing if it was proper or not, but wanting to be on his way. "I'm glad I had the opportunity to meet both of you."

"We'll need to discuss DNA testing," the queen reminded him.

"Yes, I know we will. If you want to set something up, that's fine."

"Then you will stay at the palace tonight?" the queen asked.

"If that's what you'd like."

"That's what I'd like. No matter how things go with Amira. You might be the next heir, Mr. Cordello. You deserve to be here."

After he bowed to the queen, he shook Gwen Montague's hand. "Thank you for being open-minded."

"Amira's young but she knows her own mind. I wish you luck, Mr. Cordello."

"Marcus," he said automatically.

Gwen nodded. "Marcus."

The guard escorted Marcus out of the palace the same way he'd come in. As he descended the steps, he realized that these guards probably had stories to tell, but they never would. Their loyalty was obvious in their demeanor.

Marcus gave the cab driver the name of the restaurant and then he tried to organize his thoughts, tried to come up with the best arguments, tried to hope Amira wouldn't turn him away.

As the cab neared the center of Marleston, he couldn't help but remember his mother's inability to forgive his father. He remembered Amira saying when trust is broken it's hard to repair the damage. He'd broken her trust, and the damage had been great.

In front of the Artist's Place, he paid the driver and got out of the cab. He decided not to have the man wait. One way or another he'd get back to the palace.

He pulled open a heavy wooden door and stepped inside a dimly lit foyer. The place looked like a quiet pub. Artwork hung on all the walls and sculptures stood on pedestals. The heavy wooden tables were surrounded by black leather barrel chairs. There was a sign on the lectern before the archway that led into the restaurant: Please Seat Yourself. Apparently, Sunday nights were quiet ones here. Only four tables were occupied.

He spotted Amira immediately to the rear of the restaurant at a corner table where the light was the dimmest. Her blond hair reflected it. There was a sandwich before her, but she wasn't eating. She was just staring at the pictures on the walls. His heart hammered so hard he couldn't think. He could only feel.

He strode through the room quickly, coming to stand at Amira's table. "Lady Amira Sierra Corbin?" he asked formally.

At the sound of his voice, her chin came up and her astonishment was evident in her eyes.

"I'd like to introduce myself," he went on. "My name is Marcus Cordello, and I'm searching for the most incredible woman I've ever met. I did something foolish by not revealing to her who I really was as soon as I realized she was looking for me. Once the die was cast, I didn't know how to turn it around.''

Dropping the formality, he spoke from his heart. ''I wanted that week at Shady Glenn with you in case I never saw you again. But when you left, the idea of never seeing you again was intolerable.'' He went down on one knee beside her, ''I never meant to hurt you. I never meant to take advantage of you. I never meant to fall deeply in love with you, but I did.'' Dipping his hand into his pocket, he brought out the small black box. ''If you agree to marry me, I'll spend the rest of my life making up to you for my deception. I promise you I will never tell you anything that isn't true again. I love you, Amira. I can't imagine my life without your laughter, your sincerity, your compassion. Will you honor me by becoming my wife?''

Amira looked absolutely stunned. She stared down at the ring in the box. It was a large heart-shaped diamond with smaller diamonds swirled on either side. It was a ring fit for a princess...a ring fit for the woman he loved as much as life.

Finally she looked up at him with tears slipping down her cheeks. ''Marcus?''

''What, sweetheart?'' he asked gently.

''I was just trying out your name. It fits.''

His pulse was racing fast and hope seemed to overtake his whole heart. ''Can we see if the ring fits, too?''

Taking it out of the box, he slipped it onto her finger. Looking up at her again, he asked, ''Can you forgive me?''

''I forgive you, Marcus. I love you.'' And then she was in his arms. They were both standing, and he was kissing her with all the love and fervor and commitment that he couldn't give her before.

The kiss went on and on and on until there was applause from other patrons in the restaurant.

Marcus lifted his head, hoping Amira wasn't too embarrassed. "I should have done this privately," he murmured. But I couldn't wait."

"I'm glad you didn't wait," she managed shakily.

Pulling his chair close to hers, he sat down beside her, holding her hand. "Are you sure?"

"I'm sure. I know what kind of man you are."

He winced at that.

"Although, when I found out who you were," she continued, "I felt betrayed and disappointed and didn't know if anything we'd experienced was real. I didn't know how I was going to ever see you, look at you again, if you came here to get the prince dilemma straightened out. I had decided to fly to Paris and enroll in school there. But tonight, sitting here, I realized that would be running away, and I didn't want to run away from you. I was going to stay here until you came to Penwyck, and then I would find out if you felt anything for me or if my imagination had just gone wild."

She was beautiful and courageous...and his. "Your imagination didn't go wild. I began falling in love with you from that first night. Sure I felt desire and I wanted you in my bed. But I wanted so much more and didn't even realize it. As each day passed and I thought about you leaving, I grabbed on to whatever we could have."

"Before I left Shady Glenn, your father admitted he'd just told you that you were adopted. That must have been a shock. What will happen if you *are* the

prince?'' she asked, gazing down at her ring and looking back up at him. ''I know you don't want that. I
know—''

''The queen asked me what I'd do if I *wasn't* the
prince and you accepted my proposal. She wanted to
know if I expected you to turn your life upside down
for me. I don't have all the answers, Amira. I don't
know how I'll feel if I am the prince. But I do know
that I love you and that I want your happiness as
much as mine. I told her we'd work everything out
together.''

Amira's hand came up to his jaw then, and she
stroked it with her fingers. ''You're right. We'll work
everything out...together.''

Then, unmindful whether anyone else was watching or not, they kissed again. This time they weren't
interrupted by applause. This time the kiss went on
much longer until finally they both needed to come
up for air.

After their lips clung and they drew apart, Marcus
gave a wry shake of his head. ''How soon can we get
married?''

''A few weeks maybe?'' she asked.

''Is that enough time for you to plan a fairy-tale
wedding?'' He imagined that's what she would want,
and he could see from the light shining in her eyes
that he was right.

''My mother and the queen can do wonders. It will
be enough time.''

''Good. I don't think I could last more than a few
weeks without really making you mine.''

''You can do that tonight,'' she said from a new
boldness that came from a confidence in what they
were together.

But he shook his head. "No, I want to do this right. You'll be giving me a wonderful gift, and I want to give it the respect it deserves, the respect *you* deserve."

She threw her arms around his neck and tilted her forehead against his. "No matter what the DNA testing shows, you *are* a prince. You're my prince."

Marcus knew he would do everything in his power to live up to her faith in him. "I love you," he said again, wanting to make sure she knew it.

In a few weeks he would pledge his heart and soul and life to her and she to him. Whatever life brought, they'd face it together—hand in hand, heart in heart. They would love and cherish each other…forever.

* * * * *

THE ROYAL TREATMENT

by
Maureen Child

MAUREEN CHILD

is a California native who loves to travel. Every chance
they get, she and her husband are taking off on another
research trip. The author of more than sixty books,
Maureen loves a happy ending and still swears that she
has the best job in the world. She lives in Southern
California with her husband, two children and a golden
retriever who has delusions of grandeur.

Visit her website at www.maureenchild.com

To everyone at the ASPEN in Galveston conference.
It was a memorable week—you guys are the best.

One

Jeremy Wainwright checked his wristwatch, then lifted his gaze to sweep the exterior of the palace. The three-story structure looked like something out of a fairy tale. The gray limestone seemed to shimmer in the crisp, clear November air, and late afternoon sunlight dazzled the gleaming, mullioned window panes. He had a feeling that if he listened just right, he'd be able to hear the clang of long-silent swords and the proud blast of trumpets.

He felt a strong connection to this place and its history. For more than two hundred years, the Wainwrights had been here, on Penwyck, protecting the royal family, guarding the palace. They'd served with pride and honor, every last one of them, and he was proud to take his place among them.

The wind off the sea had a bite to it and made Jeremy grateful for the thick blue sweater he wore. The trees in the courtyard and those just outside the palace walls bore the bright stamp of autumn. Red, gold, yellow leaves rustled in the wind and floated down to litter the palace yard with bits of color.

But Jeremy didn't take time to appreciate the beauty of the place. Instead, his sharp-eyed gaze, alert for trouble, continued a thorough yet quick scan, noting that everything seemed to be as it should be. The Royal Guard walked the perimeter, rifles at their shoulders. The iron scroll-work gates, which had protected the palace for centuries, stood closed, locked, impenetrable. And the last of the tour groups were just leaving the public half of the palace.

Good. Jeremy never really relaxed until the gates were closed behind interlopers. Oh, he knew it was important for the citizens of Penwyck—not to mention international visitors—to be able to tour the palace. At least the rooms set aside for public viewing.

But tours were a security man's nightmare.

There were just too many things that could go wrong. One man getting past a checkpoint with a concealed weapon could turn into a hostage drama.

And then there was the headache of a tourist wandering away from the crowd and finding his or her way into the royal family's apartments. Not to mention the queen's habit of sometimes surprising the tours with a royal visit.

Shaking his head, Jeremy kept an eye on the chattering visitors leaving through the iron gates, and didn't stop watching until those gates were sealed again. Once they had been, he stepped into the tiny guard station to pour himself an end-of-shift cup of coffee.

Taking a sip of the strong, black liquid, he let the heat of it roll through him, and ignored the raised voices filtering to him from the gates. Whoever it was, his guards could handle it. Picked as the best of the best from the Royal Army, and trained by him, they could handle anything. Their duty was to protect the king and queen and the rest of the royal family. And there wasn't a one of them that Jeremy didn't trust to lay down his life for the royals.

And by the sound of things, he thought suddenly, that might just be on today's agenda. Setting his coffee cup down on the desk, he stepped out of the kiosk and listened more carefully to the raised voices.

"Damn it," Jeremy muttered. "Trouble couldn't wait five more minutes?" He checked that his pistol was discreetly tucked on his right hip, beneath the bulk of his sweater, and then headed for the gate.

Naturally, he heard the woman first. Not difficult, since she made no attempt to keep her voice down. He stopped midstep as he recognized that voice. It hit him hard. Just as it did every damn time he dreamed about her.

Jade Erickson.

Lover.

Ex-wife.

Pain in the neck.

"Not too late," he muttered. "Still time to get in your car and let the next poor fool on duty handle her." His shift was over. Let Lieutenant Gimble take care of this. "Hell," Jeremy grumbled with a disgusted snort, "that's like sending a kid with a pea-shooter up against an armed tank."

He just couldn't do it to Gimble.

Penwyck was too damn small, that's what the problem was. For three years, he'd managed to avoid a face-to-face confrontation with the woman he'd once promised to love, honor and cherish forever. But he saw plenty of her anyway. Every time he turned on the news.

Jade Erickson was PEN-TV's latest darling. Once upon a time, she'd been *his* darling. But those days, he reminded himself, were long gone.

She stood five-foot-five, and packed a lot of

curves onto that tiny frame. Curves he remembered all too well. Her shoulder-length auburn hair danced about her face in the sharp, cold wind. He could still recall the feel of that silken mass sliding across his skin, and his fingers itched to touch it again. In memory, he saw her sea-green eyes go smoky and soft with pleasure as he loved her. Now those eyes were narrowed and shooting daggers at the lieutenant.

Thinner than he remembered, she wore a black suit that clung to every curve, a white blouse and a diamond that flashed from her left lapel. When they were together, she hadn't had diamonds. Jeremy couldn't afford them. He'd bought her a small aquamarine—the color of her eyes—set in gold for an engagement ring. But that was gone now, too.

Her long fingers were curled around the scrolled emblem on the palace gates, and as he watched, she gave it a good shake. He laughed shortly. She hadn't changed *too* much, then. That temper of hers still simmered just below the surface. She made a helluva picture, and Jeremy was male enough to appreciate it even while already working on ways to get rid of her.

He caught the young soldier's glance and waved him off. "I'll take care of this," he said.

"Yes, sir." The lieutenant beat a hasty—and grateful—retreat.

Jeremy turned to face her then, and his breath actually caught in his throat. Staring into those sea-foam-colored eyes of hers he felt like he'd been hit over the head. Damn. She still packed a punch.

He had to force himself to speak after a few seconds of stiff silence. "Jade."

"J.T."

Jeremy Thomas. J.T. Only his family called him that. It sounded good hearing it from her again. Damn it.

She cleared her throat, and he wondered if she'd felt the slam of desire as hard as he had. Then he decided he was better off not knowing.

"What are you doing here, Jade?"

"You know why I'm here."

Yes, he did. Stubborn woman. "If it's about the interview, then you're wasting your time. And more importantly, *mine*."

"Blast it, J.T.," she said, and gave the gates another shake for good measure. "You should be helping me."

"Why would I do that?" he asked.

"For old times' sake?"

He glanced past her to the skinny, older man standing behind her with a camera perched on his bony shoulder. Lowering his voice, Jeremy shifted his gaze back to her and said, "Old times' sake? Are you nuts?"

She blew out a breath that ruffled the wisps of hair dusting her forehead. "Fine." She let go of the gates and lifted her gaze to glare at him. "No old times. But the least you could do is be civil."

"I was civil," he reminded her, "the first three times you requested this stupid interview."

"I thought if I came down here and we could talk, face-to-face, you'd change your mind."

"Wrong."

"The king is sick, J.T., and the queen—"

"The queen is attending her husband and doesn't want to do an interview."

"She has to say something."

"She will. When *she* decides to."

"I'm just trying to do my job," Jade said.

"So am I."

She tapped the toe of one high-heeled shoe against the pavement. "The people have a right to know."

"The people have a right to know about business. They don't have a right to invade the royal family's private life."

"The king is sick," she argued.

"And being cared for."

"By whom?"

"You know," he said, leaning in closer still, "if you had put half this determination into our marriage…"

She flushed. Good to know she could still do that.

Her cameraman moved closer, a small red light blinking at the base of the lens, and Jeremy lifted one hand, pointing at him. ''Turn that thing off.''

''Do it, Harry,'' Jade ordered without even looking at the man. The cameraman complied and moved off a few paces.

When they were alone again, she pushed her hair back out of her face, looked up at him and said, ''J.T., I only want five minutes of her time.''

''The queen is busy with her husband. She puts a high priority on caring for her family.''

Jade winced at the direct hit. ''Low blow, J.T.''

''Maybe,'' he acknowledged, and admitted silently that he'd be better off not stirring up old resentments. What good would it do, anyway? ''But you're still not getting through the gates.''

''This isn't the end of it, you know.''

''Yeah, I know.''

''This is important to me.''

''I can't help you.'' And that didn't make him as happy as he'd thought it would. She could still get to him. Just being this close to her, inhaling the scent of her flowery perfume, was enough to wipe the years away and take him back to that small apartment they'd shared. Back when they'd thought they had a future.

When they were young and naive.

Back when they'd thought love would be enough.

She looked past him, toward the castle doors and across the grounds, before shifting her gaze back to his. He could see the wheels turning in her brain and knew that she was far from finished with this. He'd never met a more hardheaded woman. Strange to think now that that was one of the first things he'd liked about her.

"So this means war?" she asked, and he recognized the tone. Whenever Jade got scared or felt pushed into a corner, she went stiff and snotty.

"If that's the way you want it," he said. Jeremy hid a smile of appreciation as he watched her fight down a wave of anger that was clearly clawing at her throat. But he had to give her credit. After a few seconds, she'd managed it. She hadn't always been able to put a lid on that temper. He still had the scar on his forehead from when she'd pitched a plate at him.

On their honeymoon, no less.

But along with that scar, he also had the memory of how they'd spent hours making up. It had been well worth that little scar.

Taking a deep breath, she said, "You need to put someone else on this gate. Your little soldier there is a moron."

One dark eyebrow lifted as the desire crouched inside him eased back a bit. "Is he?"

"He refused to let me inside," she snapped. "Refused to even answer my questions."

"Well then," Jeremy told her, "the lieutenant is clearly as bright as I'd thought him to be."

She sighed, tapped her shoe a little harder, then put both hands on those deliciously curved hips.

Jeremy chuckled, folded his arms across his chest and planted his feet wide apart. Comfortable in his fighting stance, he said, "You might as well go, Jade. You're not getting in."

"You know," she said, giving him a thoughtful, up and down look, "you really should work on your people skills, J.T. They never were your strong point."

"Oh, that's good, coming from you. Judging by the conversation you were having with Lieutenant Gimble, you're in no position to give lectures on winning friends and influencing people yourself."

She inhaled sharply and blew the air out in a rush. "All right, I'm sorry about that. I haven't lost my temper in a long time."

He fingered that old scar just above his eyebrow. "That's a shame. Fury does great things for your eyes."

She flicked him a warning look, but Jeremy knew those gates were strong enough to hold off a tank, so they'd probably be able to protect him from a single reporter.

Even Jade.

"Besides, my people skills are fine, babe," he assured her. "It's my 'reporter' skills you seem to be having trouble with. And frankly, if you don't like 'em, then I must be doing something right."

"As charming as ever, I see," Jade retorted.

"You used to think I was pretty damn charming."

"I used to believe in Santa Claus, too," Jade said tightly. "Then I grew up."

Frustration simmered just below the anger surging inside her. Out of all the men on this little island, why did it have to be her ex-husband standing between her and her goal?

She stared up—*way* up—into J.T.'s hard brown eyes and didn't see a glimmer of hope there. She did, however, feel that slow, sweet surge of want rise up inside her again. From the moment she'd locked eyes with him, she'd felt it. A heady rush of pulse-pounding desire that was so thick it nearly choked her. And she sensed he'd felt it, too.

It was as if the last three years hadn't happened. Three long years of not seeing him, not hearing his voice, not feeling his touch, and one look from him and she was going up like a skyrocket.

"Jade?" Her cameraman's voice cut into her thoughts and she sent the tall, thin, older man a quick look. "I'm heading back to the van."

She nodded, and thought she caught a wisp of a

satisfied smirk on J.T.'s face. Irritating, frustrating, completely sexy man.

Once Harry had moved off, she switched her attention back to the wall of muscle that stood between she and her destiny. She'd tried being nice. She'd tried being commanding. Nothing had worked.

"Look," she said, trying yet again, and this time using her patented let's-be-friends tone of voice, "there's no reason we can't come to a meeting of the minds."

A corner of his mouth twitched. She thought. It was there and gone so fast she couldn't really be sure. Still, she latched on to that one small hope and kept talking in the same, gentle tone. "We're adults. We're professionals. Surely there's a way we can solve this…difficulty."

He snorted and unfolded his arms, giving her a lovely view of a chest broad enough to star in dozens of female fantasies. As she knew all too well. "You're really something," he said, his gaze running up and down her body quickly and yet so thoroughly it was almost as if he'd touched her.

She squirmed a bit against the flash of heat that briefly dazzled her bloodstream, but held her ground. She hadn't been intimidated into leaving. She certainly wouldn't be *aroused* into leaving.

"Thank you," she said.

"Wasn't a compliment."

She inhaled sharply, deeply, then dug her manicured nails into her palms as she fisted her hands.

"Jade," he continued, before she could think of something suitably witty to say, "I've told you every day, you're not getting in here. So why don't you do us both a favor and go away?"

"I'm just trying to do my job," she repeated.

"So am I."

"Fine." She could be generous. Find some common ground. "I understand that."

"See," he said, planting his hands on his hips, "I don't think you do."

"Your job is to protect the royal family. But I'm not a threat."

"Not every threat is a physical one."

Jade felt the pulse of anger quicken inside her. "I only want to do an interview with *my* queen."

"And *my* queen," he countered, "isn't interested."

"She can't stay hidden away forever."

"She's the queen. She can pretty much do what she wants."

"This isn't the Middle Ages, you know," Jade snapped, giving in to the fury goading her into a fight with the bane of her existence. "We aren't simple crofters huddled around campfires."

"Too bad," J.T. said. "As I recall, you look

pretty good by firelight.'' Motioning to Lieutenant Gimble to come closer, he said, ''Good seeing you again, Jade.''

''This isn't over, J.T.''

''Sure it is.'' Then he flicked her a quick glance. ''You've still got great legs, babe.''

''You can't walk away from me like—'' She broke off. Pointless to keep arguing when the man whose neck you wanted to wring was already striding away from you.

The young lieutenant gave her a wary glance and a wide berth. Jade ignored him and stared after J.T., with a look cold and hard enough that, had he been the slightest bit more sensitive, would have sent him to his knees. As it was, he walked through the double doors to the palace and disappeared.

Disgusted, she gave in to the urge riding her and kicked the iron gate. All she accomplished with that smooth move was to darn near break her foot.

She limped down the drive to the sidewalk and the van waiting for her at the curb. Amazing. Five minutes with J.T. and her professionalism had dissolved into a sea of raging hormones and temper.

Sometimes ''ex'' didn't really mean a thing, did it?

Two

___

Jade walked into her apartment, tossed her purse and keys onto the narrow hall table and slammed the door behind her. Automatically, she snapped both locks, then slapped the chain into place. She took extra care in turning the new dead bolt.

Temper, she warned herself, then kicked off her shoes and limped across the room in her stocking feet. Her toes ached. ''Darn him, anyway. Why did it have to be *him?* Thousands of soldiers in the army, and J.T.'s the one I have to deal with.''

The plush, mauve carpet caressed the soles of her feet as she walked straight across the neat, uncluttered living room to the sliding glass doors. She flipped the lock, pushed the heavy panel open and stepped out onto her balcony.

The wind slapped at her, made her shiver, but she welcomed the cold, hoping it would put out the fire still burning in her blood. But the chances of that were pretty slim. Like it or not, J.T. could do things to her with a look that any other man wouldn't be able to accomplish with a touch.

Jade sighed, reached up and rubbed her eyes with her fingertips, as if by doing so she could wipe away the memory of J.T.'s penetrating gaze. Seeing him again shouldn't have been so hard. Three years had passed. Three long, busy, *lonely* years. It should have been more than enough time to get him out of her mind and heart.

But nothing about her relationship with J.T. had *ever* been easy. Jade closed her eyes and saw his face again. Those dark, chocolate eyes that seemed deep enough to hold the secrets of the universe.

She blew out a long, shaky breath. Her hair flew about her face and she reached up to scoop the long strands back. Tipping her face into the breeze, she inhaled the scent of the ocean and listened to the seabirds screeching as they wheeled and dipped in the gusts of wind.

Her pulse rate slowed and the knot in her stomach slowly dissolved. The sea-damp fall air was just what she had needed to cool off. Worked every time. Well, against her temper. The lust still humming in her veins was something else entirely. Usually, no matter what problem was bothering her, Jade could step out here, let the wind caress her, and she'd feel her troubles slide away. In fact, this wide, private balcony with a view of the bay was the reason she'd rented the apartment in the first place. Wouldn't you know that J.T. would be the one problem not so easily gotten rid of?

She leaned her forearms on the railing and stared down at the world below. From her home on the top floor of the three-story building, she felt as though she could see forever. The horizon stretched out before her, filled with possibilities. And from three stories up, she felt safe from...

"Don't go there," she told herself firmly. But it was too late. Her mind had already drifted into dangerous territory. It wasn't enough that work itself was becoming a problem. That J.T. had popped back into her life. No, she also had to worry about whoever it was sending her letters that were just creepy enough to make her install a new dead bolt on her apartment door.

The latest one had been delivered to her desk at work only yesterday, and she'd already memorized the contents.

My lovely Jade. Soon we will be together. Soon the world will know, as I do, that we were meant to be. Soon, my love, soon.

The police assured her she wasn't in serious danger. Most of these cases, they insisted, turned out to be nothing more than an enraptured fan who didn't have the courage to confront the object of his affection face-to-face. Still, that didn't make her feel any better about having an unknown admirer stalking her.

Wrapping her arms around her middle and leaning against the weathered stone balustrade, she forced her thoughts away from what she couldn't control and back to the problem at hand.

Getting into the palace.

Which would entail getting past her ex-husband. No small feat.

Just thinking about J.T. was enough to heat up her bloodstream again, and it wasn't all due to anger. Life would have been so much easier if it were.

With the king in a coma, the public wanted to know that their country, their interests, were being taken care of. And it was Jade's job to investigate that. At least, it was if she ever wanted to move away from fluff pieces to real news. If she ever wanted to prove to her father that— No, this wasn't about her father. Or the baggage she carried around with her. This was about her goals. Her plans. Her ambitions.

Something J.T. had never understood.

Now, once again, standing between her and accomplishing her task was that mountain of a man. "Nothing's changed there, has it?" she asked herself. Three years ago, he hadn't wanted her to work, either. He'd wanted a traditional wife. A woman who would have dinner on the table every night at six and be content with taking care of him and their future children.

On the surface, there was nothing at all wrong with that. But Jade wanted more. Always had. And when she couldn't get it through J.T.'s thick, chauvinistic skull that her ambitions were no less important than his, she'd stomped out of his life in a fit of righteous anger.

The only problem was, she'd left her heart behind.

Looking back now, she could see that she should have stayed and worked it out. Or at least tried. But she'd been so much younger then. So full of fire and impatience. And J.T., she conceded in her own defense, hadn't been much better.

Jade sighed heavily and faced reality. The plain fact was she'd left, determined to have a career. But now that she had it, the career she'd wanted so desperately wasn't making her happy. Maybe things would change if she actually managed to get the interview with the queen. But right now, Jade felt as though she'd made a stupid bargain when she'd given up her marriage for ambition.

Seeing him again hurt. The near electric shock of meeting his gaze was still buzzing through her brain. Almost as if she'd found something she hadn't known was lost.

"Oh, you're in sad shape," she muttered, turning away from the ocean view to go back inside. She left the glass door open, and the sheer white drapes billowed in the wind like a sail. Like her, they were anchored and going nowhere.

A knock sounded on the apartment door and she jumped. Unease skittered along her spine, but she went to answer it anyway. Any interruption at all was better than letting her brain focus on J.T. and what they'd both lost. But she froze with her hand on the knob. The days of just throwing her door open without thinking about it were over.

She peered through the peephole and sighed as she recognized her building's doorman.

"Charles?"

He stepped back and smiled, knowing that she was looking at him, then held up a manila envelope. "A package was delivered for you. From the television station. I'll just leave it outside your door."

"Thank you." Quickly, she disengaged the locks and opened the door.

Charles was already walking to the elevator.

Jade snatched up the envelope, stepped back inside and closed and locked the door again. She looked down at the envelope. From the feel of it, there was a video tape inside, and when she tore it open, she was proved right.

A piece of notepaper fell from the envelope and she bent over to pick it up. "Found this on your desk. Thought it might be important." It was signed by Janine, her secretary.

"On my desk?" Jade muttered as she walked back into the living room. There were no labels on the tape. Nothing to indicate what it might contain. But someone in the newsroom must have left it for her. Heading directly for the TV, she slipped the tape into the VCR, then turned on the set and hit Play.

An image of the palace appeared on the oversize television screen, and a chill crawled up her spine to lift the tiny hairs at the back of her neck. Traffic sounds, the call of birds and the sighing of the wind across the microphone were the only sounds. The unseen cameraman worked the zoom lens, and Jade was suddenly watching herself—with Harry, the station cameraman, right behind her—standing just outside the palace gates. She saw her own image argue with the guard, then grab the iron gate and shake it. She watched as she sent Harry back to the van, as she confronted J.T.

She relived the whole confrontation because she was simply too stunned to hit the stop button. In the video, she saw her hair ruffled by the wind. She felt the cameraman's obsession as he slowly tightened the zoom to pan in on her alone—in effect, cutting her off from J.T. and the rest of the world. Keeping her separate.

For him only.

Slowly, the camera panned from the top of her head to the sole of her tapping foot and back up again. Jade felt her stalker's obsession as if it were a living thing in the room with her. The shot tightened further, lingering on her eyes, her mouth. She could hear the cameraman's labored breathing as he watched her, and the sound nearly choked off her own air.

At last, when she was turned away from the palace gates, the tape ended, fading into a solid blue screen that finally woke her out of her stupor. She jabbed the stop button with one fingertip, then dropped the remote to the floor as if it were poisonous.

Silence crashed down around her. The drapes, still billowing in the wind, suddenly made her aware of an unsecured entry point, and Jade hurried across the room. Of course, to break into a third-story apartment through the balcony doors, her stalker would have to be Spider-Man. But it made her feel better to slam the glass door shut. She locked it, then bent down to drop the metal guard into the track behind it.

Alone and scared, she turned her back on the view and stared at her apartment. For the first time, she didn't see the comfortable, yet stylish furnishings. What she saw now was her sanctuary...*invaded* by a threat she couldn't identify.

And she wanted to call J.T. so badly, her heart ached.

There was too much going on for J.T.'s liking.

He sat in the single chair opposite his boss's desk and let his mind wander while Franklin Vancour was on the phone. In his fifties, Franklin was as fit as a man half his age. It came from years of military training, no doubt, and J.T. could appreciate that. The other man was as dedicated to duty as he was, and on that common ground, the two men understood each other.

Morning sunlight filtered in through the windows of the security office located on the ground floor of the palace. The wood-paneled walls gleamed richly from years of careful polishing. Framed certificates and royal proclamations hung on the walls, and their glass fronts winked when a stray sunbeam glanced off of them. A row of bookcases lined one wall, and hundreds of leather-bound, well-read volumes rested alongside mementos left behind by former heads of security.

The RII—Royal Intelligence Institute—was responsible for the safety and security of the royal family. The guards posted outside, as well as J.T. himself, had been plucked from the different branches of the Penwyck military and assigned to the palace. Every man here was the best of the best.

Next door was the king's office, and J.T. knew without having to be told that Sir Selwyn, the king's secretary, would be there, positioned to keep out all intruders. A thin, wiry man, he was dedicated to his employer. Even to the point of putting up with Broderick, the man who so wanted to be king of Penwyck, but never could.

But until Morgan, the rightful king, either recovered from his illness or was succeeded by one of his sons, Morgan's twin, Broderick, would remain temporarily in charge, reigning in his brother's stead.

J.T. could not understand how twin brothers could be as different from each other as the king and Broderick were. Morgan was fair-minded and loyal, with an innate sense of decency. Broderick, on the other hand, couldn't be trusted as far he could be thrown. But since it was J.T.'s sworn duty to protect the royals, he was bound to keep his opinions to himself and simply do his job.

As Franklin hung up the phone and leaned back in his black leather chair, J.T. turned to find the man studying him. "What's this I hear about you and a female reporter having a public argument at the gate yesterday?"

He shouldn't have been surprised. Not much got past Vancour. Which was why he was in charge of security around here.

"Not really an argument," J.T. countered, crossing his right foot atop his left knee. "She wanted in. I disagreed. I won."

Franklin's bushy gray eyebrows lifted slightly. "So I heard. But the point is, we can't afford to offend the press right now."

"Offend her?" J.T. almost chuckled, but he knew it wouldn't be appreciated. "With her attitude, she's lucky she didn't get shot. Lieutenant Gimble deserves a medal for putting up with her tirade."

Franklin sighed and shook his head. "Ms. Erickson is a popular personality these days."

J.T. shifted uncomfortably in his chair. He had the distinct feeling he wasn't going to like the direction this conversation was taking.

His boss continued. "The queen watches her *People in Penwyck* reports every day."

"Yeah," J.T. said. "Real in-depth reporting

there. What was her last bit? About the cats who've lived in the palace?''

"Doesn't matter," the other man countered. "The point is, your former wife's making a name for herself."

"I know." There were only a handful of people on this whole island who knew that he and Jade had once been married. They'd divorced long before she'd become an on-air personality. Vancour knew only because of the security check J.T. had had to pass before accepting the promotion to the palace guard.

But this was the first time in two years the other man had mentioned it.

"No way," J.T. muttered, suspicion crawling through him. He pushed himself out of the chair. "You're not suggesting we let her into the palace to do her interview, are you?"

"No." Franklin propped his fingertips together as he thought about it. "Not yet, anyway. Soon, though. Won't be able to avoid it much longer. What I'm suggesting is that you show her around the palace grounds for now." He shrugged. "Give her a little and maybe she'll be satisfied."

J.T. doubted that. "Not her. She wants an interview and she won't be satisfied until she gets it."

"No interviews. Yet."

There was something in his tone, an underlying edge of excitement, that caught J.T.'s attention.

"Is there news on the king?"

Franklin studied J.T. for a long minute, decided he had no qualms about telling him what he knew. Jeremy Wainwright was the most trustworthy man he'd ever known. The lad was headed for big things one day, Franklin mused. Maybe even this job.

And in this office, with the door closed, the two men could talk freely, without worrying about being overheard or quoted.

Nodding, he said, "The king's doctors seem to think there are encouraging signs. It seems he may be rousing from the coma."

"That is good news." Hell, it was great news. As a citizen of Penwyck, J.T. had been as worried about his king as anyone else. And being a member of the inner circle, he'd been a part of the coverup that had been so dangerous to his country. "So does this mean that Br—"

"No." Franklin stood up, too. "The king's brother will remain as temporary head of the country." Pacing, he seemed to be carefully considering something as he said, "And frankly, the easier we can make this on the queen, the better. Her Majesty is inundated with problems and trying to keep things running despite Broderick's interference."

J.T. nodded and waited for the man to continue. It didn't take long.

"The RET is doing what it can. But security here is up to us."

The Royal Elite Team was probably champing at the bit to do something—anything. But when it came to palace security, the RII was in charge. And J.T. was just competitive enough to enjoy knowing that the members of the RET were clearly unhappy with the situation.

"I understand," he said, though he wasn't entirely sure he knew where Franklin was going with this.

The older man laughed shortly and stopped his frenetic pacing to stare at him from across the room. "I don't think you do, or you wouldn't be so agreeable."

"What's going on, Franklin?"

"I need you to distract your ex-wife."

"That's going above and beyond the call of duty." Dumbfounded, J.T. swallowed back a rising tide of anger.

"You know her best. Know how to keep her off track. Keep her happy."

If he'd known how to keep her *happy,* J.T. thought, they'd still be married. This was a bad idea. Real bad. And he didn't mind saying so. "Won't work. Jade's not exactly my biggest fan."

"Just buy us a couple of days."

"And then what?"

"She'll get her interview and you won't have to deal with her again."

Now that should be good news. But the fact was, J.T. had done nothing but think about her since seeing her outside the gates. She'd haunted his every thought, stalked his dreams and filled his mind until he couldn't even draw a breath without imagining her scent.

Now that he'd seen her again after three long years, he wasn't exactly in a hurry to be rid of her. And that surprised him as much as it would have her.

Vancour walked across the room slowly, keeping his gaze locked with J.T.'s. "I need your cooperation in this, Wainwright. Your king needs it."

J.T. studied him. There was something in the other man's eyes that hinted at the seriousness of the situation. Well, hell, they'd all been living in a pressure cooker for weeks. Ever since the king had collapsed unexpectedly.

Placate Jade.

From a purely male standpoint, that wasn't such a tough assignment. There was so much history between them, though. So much hurt and pain and misery. Yet before the pain, there had also been...a *connection* between them that had been stronger and deeper than anything he'd ever experienced before or since.

But she also had an argumentative streak that would give the most patient man in the world the urge to throttle her. Just remembering how she'd stood up to him, shaken the iron gates and glared at him without an instant's hesitation was almost enough to make J.T. smile. A man his size didn't usually meet people who weren't instantly intimidated. Jade never had been, though, and he'd always admired her for it.

She wouldn't be an easy woman to manipulate. And if Franklin Vancour thought she could be bought off by a walk through the palace gardens, he was sadly mistaken.

Still…if all the palace required was a few more days' respite, maybe J.T. could pull it off. Maybe he could keep her busy enough that she wouldn't notice that she wasn't any closer to the interior of the palace than she'd been yesterday. And, if he spent enough time in her company, perhaps the attraction he felt for her would die a natural death. Maybe this was what they both needed to completely end what they'd finished three years ago. Maybe they needed to spend time together again to realize that it was all really gone.

And maybe he was a masochist.

At any rate, it'd certainly be the most interesting assignment he'd been given since joining the RII.

He looked at Franklin. "A few days?"

The man nodded slowly. "At the most."

"I'll do my best," J.T. told him.

"I knew I could count on you."

A few minutes later, Jeremy was letting himself out of the security office and heading back to the guardhouse. Autumn sunshine spilled out of a cloudy sky and he told himself that he should enjoy it while it lasted. He had a feeling he was headed into stormy weather.

Three

The next morning, J.T. sat through the security briefing, but his mind was several miles away. Five, to be exact. He imagined Jade in a plush office, snapping orders at a battalion of minions. Once she'd finished making heads roll, she would no doubt sit back in a comfortable chair, sip a morning cup of tea and plan how next she would try to ruin his life.

And she'd do it all with a smile curving that fabulous mouth of hers.

Around him, the other members of the RII shifted and muttered to one another, but as far as J.T. was concerned, they had the easy jobs. All they had to do was concern themselves with defense of the palace. Routine tasks, with only the occasional chance to jump in front of some crazed assassin. *He,* on the other hand, would soon be dealing with the only woman who'd ever been able to get to him.

His fingers tightened around the pen in his right hand. Just to torture himself, J.T. had started his day by watching her early morning report on PEN-TV. Real investigative stuff, he mused now, making a point of relaxing his hand. Jade Erickson had looked directly into the camera and, with a beaming smile on her face, reported a story on the old smugglers caves. Then she'd even launched into the local belief that ghosts of long-dead pirates still haunted the dank caverns.

His amusement had died quickly enough, though, when he reminded himself that she'd walked out on him and what they might have had together for the opportunity to smile into a camera.

Of course, he didn't want to think about just how good she'd looked, standing in the wind, with the roaring sea just behind her. How her auburn hair had flown about her face with abandon and how her sea-green eyes had seemed to stare directly into his.

All right, he thought, pushing her image out of his brain. He didn't need to think about her now. He'd be seeing her all too soon as it was.

*   *   *

After a sleepless night, Jade was in no mood to be stonewalled at the palace gates today. She'd thought about it long and hard during the hours she'd spent sitting straight up in bed, gripping her self-defense weapon—a golf club. For weeks now, she'd been receiving those vaguely threatening letters. Only recently had they begun to get a bit creepier. But the video stalking was definitely upping the ante.

Yet she couldn't allow this individual, whoever it was, to affect her work. If she crawled off into a hole and hid away, then the person trying to scare her would have won. Besides, there was no guarantee that hiding would protect her. Maybe it was safer to stay in the public eye. Certainly, it would be difficult, if not impossible, for someone to kidnap her out of the station. Or from in front of a news camera.

No, the thing to do was to go on with her everyday life as if nothing were wrong. To surrender was to lose power in this, and she wouldn't allow that to happen. She'd fought for a long time to have the kind of career she'd always dreamed of. She'd given up the man she loved. She'd made this choice and now she would find a way to make it work.

In fact, she hadn't even bothered to go into the station first this morning. Hadn't had to. They'd run one of her taped pieces on the morning news. She'd simply called in and had Harry meet her at her apartment. Might as well beard J.T. in his den as early as possible.

"You okay?" Harry asked as he steered the station van down the tree-lined street toward the palace.

"Dandy," she said, and tugged the hem of her camel-brown skirt over her knees.

"Well, you don't look okay."

"Gee thanks, Harry." Jade smiled at her cameraman. They'd been together for two years and Harry was her best friend at the station. "You're such a sweet-talker."

The older man grumbled unintelligibly for a minute or two, then sucked in a deep breath and blew it out again. "I only meant that you look tired."

So much for the miraculous properties of makeup. She flipped the visor down and peered at her own reflection in the small mirror. He was right. Jade sighed, flipped the visor back up and admitted, "I didn't get much sleep last night."

"Another letter?" he asked, his voice tight with worry.

"No," she said quickly, "no more letters." She'd already decided not to tell him about the videotape. The police and her bosses at the station weren't concerned about the letters she'd been receiving. But Harry, bless him, was. No point in telling him about the tape. Anyway, she had the video with her and planned to take it to the police station herself this afternoon.

Besides, it hadn't been worry keeping her up half the night. It had been dreams of J.T. Memories. His face floating through her mind and the recollection of his touch on her body... Nope. No sleep for Jade.

"That's good." Harry steered the van around a stalled car, pushed his way into the stream of traffic again, then asked, "So why are we hitting the palace bright and early? This could have waited until later."

"Maybe," she conceded, and stifled a yawn. "But why wait? If I catch him early enough in the morning, maybe he'll be off guard."

"Him?" Harry snorted a laugh and came to a stop as a gaggle of schoolchildren raced across the street, their laughter bubbling in their wake. Sliding a glance at her, the older man said, "I don't think that man's ever had his guard down."

"You don't know the half of it," she muttered, keeping her gaze fixed on the passing traffic. Anything to make her mind too busy to dredge up yet another image of J.T. "There's a first time for everything."

"Yeah," he muttered, stepping on the gas again, "and that goes for getting hit by lightning, run down by a car...."

"That's the spirit," she said with a laugh.

Harry shook his head as he parked the van. Throwing the gearshift into Park, he cut the engine and slanted her another look. "Spirit's not going to cut it in this one, Jade. If they don't want you in the palace, you're not going to be able to charm your way in."

She stared through the windshield at the palace gates fifty feet away. Uniformed guards were positioned just outside, and through the iron scrollwork, she saw more guards marching across the compound. None of them looked friendly. But then, they weren't supposed to, were they?

This was her country, though. As a citizen of Penwyck, she had every right to enter that compound. Heck, she could sign up for a tour and get farther inside than she had yesterday. As that thought occurred to her, Jade's brain raced with possibilities. It was as though she were in a cartoon and a light-bulb had just clicked on over her head. She could pay for a tour, and then somewhere along the route through the public rooms, she could simply...get lost. If she wandered away from her tour group and just happened to stumble into the royal family's private quarters, no one could really blame her, right? After all, they didn't behead people anymore. What did she have to lose?

"Oh," Harry said softly, "I don't think I like that look in your eyes."

"I'm going to get inside the palace today," she assured the man beside her. "By hook or by crook."

"And when they arrest us?" Harry asked, his normal gloomy tone even more morose than usual.

Jade turned to look at him. Reaching out, she patted his arm and said, "We'll ask for adjoining cells."

"Now that's real comforting, thanks."

"Relax, Harry," Jade said, a slow smile curving her mouth. "When have I ever gotten us in over our heads before?"

"Let's see…" Harry held up his right hand, ticking off items on his fingers one by one. "There was the time you wanted to do an exposé on the Royal Navy and we got stuck belowdecks of that carrier when she shipped out."

She waved one hand dismissively. "They found us within hours."

"Then there was the time you wanted to do an aerial report from a hot-air balloon and you accidentally pulled the string releasing the hot air and we—"

"Made it safely down to earth," she pointed out quickly. Besides, it had been a great report. She'd had to do outrageous stunts over the last couple of years. Anything to get herself noticed, to stand out from the crowd of pretty faces looking for a shot at success.

He sent her a look from beneath raised eyebrows. "Then there was—"

"Okay," she said, holding her hands up in mock surrender. There was definitely a downside to having the same cameraman over the years. Especially one with a memory like Harry's. "You made your point. So, there've been a few unfortunate incidents."

"Unfortunate?"

"We survived."

"They say God protects fools and drunks."

She smiled wryly. "Since I don't drink, I know which category you're filing me under."

"Me, too, Jade," he said. "Though after a shoot with you, I rarely say no to a good, stiff drink."

"We got the stories though, didn't we?"

"True."

"And now we've got a shot at the big time."

His fingers tightened around the steering wheel. "Why are you making such a big deal of this, Jade? Why push for the interview now? Once the king's better, the queen'll be more than happy to talk to anyone from the press."

"That's why, Harry." Jade shifted in her seat and leaned toward him. "I have to snag this interview. It's what I've been working toward, waiting for for three years." *This is the chance I gave up my mar-*

riage for, she thought, but managed to keep that to herself. "This is my shot at proving to the powers-that-be at the station that I'm more than a fluff reporter. It's my chance at a co-anchor job."

She'd served her time on the gossip circuit. She'd done the lost-dog and hero-fireman stories. She'd covered parades and fairs and the opening of supermarkets, all the while telling herself that her time would come. That eventually, she'd have the career that had always been so important to her.

If she didn't…then she'd failed.

And she'd walked away from J.T. for nothing.

That was something she couldn't live with.

She unbuckled her seat belt, opened the door and stepped out. Slamming the door behind her, she leaned in the open window.

"I'm going to stop at the gates first. So get the camera. If we can get past J.T., er, Jeremy Wainwright, we'll do it that way." She patted the door. "Otherwise, I'll be signing up for a tour this afternoon."

"A tour? Oh, I've got a bad feeling about this."

Reaching up, she straightened the lapels of her brown suede jacket, tossed her hair back from her face and gave him one last smile. "Ignore that bad feeling. I'll meet you at the gates."

"I'll be right behind you," he said, clearly unhappy about the whole thing.

Nodding, Jade walked off, her heels clicking loudly on the leaf-strewn sidewalk as she headed for the palace gates.

Harry looked after her for a long minute, then, shaking his head, moved to get his camera. There was no stopping her, he knew. The best he could do was be close by when the you-know-what hit the fan.

She looked amazing.

Even better than he remembered. And he would have been willing to bet that wasn't possible.

J.T. watched her approach, not surprised at all that she'd shown up first thing in the morning. The woman had a head like a rock. Of course, that was a personality trait he could appreciate, being fairly hardheaded himself. He'd known yesterday that Jade would be back. She'd never been a woman to give up easily—except, of course, when it came to their marriage.

What a package she made.

That body of hers was enough to tempt a saint right out of heaven. Her hair lifted off the collar of her brown suede jacket and blew softly in the wind. He'd never understood how women could stand wearing high heels, as they looked particularly un-comfortable. But as a man, he was incredibly grate-ful that women were willing to put up with the discomfort. His gaze swept up her legs, enjoying the view, and when that view ended at the hem of her skirt, he lifted his gaze to hers. Even from a distance, it wasn't hard to see the glitter of determination in her sea-foam-colored eyes.

Well, she wasn't the only one who had a job to do, he told himself as he started for the gate. Distracting his ex-wife might not seem like much of an assignment, but he had never been one to question orders, either. So he'd do what Vancour expected of him. After all, no one had to know that he was almost looking forward to butting heads with Jade.

J.T. waved aside the uniformed soldier standing guard and waited for her himself. It didn't take long.

In seconds, she was standing directly opposite him. Her gaze moved over the elaborate iron gate and paused on the lock before lifting to meet his.

"Morning, J.T."

He nodded. "Jade."

She waved one hand at the gate. "I see we're still at a stalemate."

"On the contrary," he said, and had the pleasure of seeing a spark of curiosity light her eyes.

"Really?" she countered. "Because from where I stand, I still seem to be on the wrong side of the gate."

"Opposite sides, huh? The story of our lives."

"J.T...."

"Today, at least, that's easily correctable," he said, enjoying the suspicion now written across her features. In a few quick moves, he had the gate unlocked and was pushing it open just wide enough for her to slip inside.

But she didn't.

Eyes wary, she looked from the opening to him and back again before asking, "What's going on?"

He drew his head back, a look of pure innocence on his face. "Why, Jade. Don't you trust me?"

"Said the spider to the fly."

J.T. laughed. God, he'd missed her. He'd missed it all. The fights, the loving, the laughter. It had been hard as hell to get to the point where he didn't miss her every damn minute. Now here he was—about to put himself through the misery all over again.

And he couldn't wait.

He slapped one hand to his chest. "Jade, honey, you wound me."

One of her auburn eyebrows lifted in a high arch. "Not without a flamethrower, I'm thinking."

He laughed again and paid no attention to the soldier standing nearby. Stepping through the gate to the sidewalk, J.T. stopped directly in front of her. In fact, he was so close to her he swore he could feel her heat shimmering around him. He could damn sure smell her perfume. The faint flowery scent surrounded him, slipping inside him to his weakest point and attacking.

She'd probably planned that.

Shrugging it off, he lifted his gaze past her to the older man hurrying up the sidewalk, video camera clutched in his arms like a child.

She followed his gaze. "That's Harry. My cameraman. You remember him from yesterday."

"Yeah, I do." But truth to tell, Jeremy hadn't really counted on having the cameraman following them around all day. So he'd just have to get rid of the guy. Shifting his gaze to hers, J.T. said, "Look, Jade. I've been instructed that I can allow you into the palace grounds. Give you a tour of the private gardens. Show you around a little. But no camera."

She looked up at him, and he enjoyed the fact that she had to tilt her head far back to do it. His size had always been handy when trying to intimidate. Although it had never bothered her any.

"Excuse me? A tour of the gardens?" she repeated. "What about my interview with Her Majesty? J.T., I did a story on the palace gardens just last month. The people really don't care all that much if the roses are still blooming."

"It's all you get."

"I nee—*want* a hard news piece, J.T. And if I don't get it, the station'll just send another reporter."

"Is that a threat?"

"It's a promise." She gritted her teeth as she added, "Probably Vince Battle."

"Barracuda Battle?" Oh, wouldn't the palace love that? The hard-edged reporter made every interview an exposé. He dug and dug until he uncovered every last bit of dirt there was to find, and what he couldn't find he invented.

"That's the one."

"Perfect."

"Well, we agree on something, anyway. We'd both rather have *me* do this."

"Unfortunately, it's not up to either one of us."

With her right hand, she flipped the edge of her jacket back and planted her fist on her hip. She was trying like hell to hold on to her temper, and J.T. sort of admired her for the attempt. Still, he saw the sparks in her eyes and knew his Jade was alive and well. His gaze dropped briefly to the curve of that hip, then lifted slowly to appreciate the way her peach silk blouse caressed her breasts. Damn.

Scraping one hand across his face as if to wake himself up from a lust-induced coma, J.T. looked into her eyes and said, "All right. I can't promise anything, but I think if you'll be patient for a couple days…"

"Patient." She said it as if it were a word foreign to her nature.

As he knew it was. "Give it a shot, Jade. It's my best offer."

She didn't want to be patient. He could see it in her eyes, which were snapping with electricity like a storm at sea. "J.T.," she said finally, "is this the real deal or did they just tell you to give me the runaround?"

Harry stepped up behind her, but she didn't turn to look at him. She couldn't take her eyes off J.T., once her husband, now the king's pit bull. She wanted to trust him.

"Tours of the palace grounds can be…interesting," he said, and his voice held a promise of more than just a tour.

But maybe, she told herself as she fought down an urge to fan herself, she was just reading more into his body language and that voice of his than was actually there. Was it all her? she wondered. Was she the only one experiencing flashbacks of better days, happier days? Did he ever remember their too brief but amazing time together?

"So," he was asking, "do we have a deal?"

"Deal?" Harry demanded. "What kind of deal?"

Jade didn't glance at him. "No camera?"

"No cameras?" Harry sounded outraged. "This is TV, not radio!"

"That stinks." Jade looked at J.T., silently daring him to make it stick.

"That's the deal," he said. "The private areas of the palace stay private. So what do you say?"

Jade didn't glance at Harry. She knew what he'd say. The man treated his camera like an appendage. He'd expect to go inside with her. And rightly so. They were a team. On the other hand, wouldn't it be wise for her to take whatever she could get, here?

She kept her gaze locked on J.T.'s brown eyes as they stared directly into hers. She felt a...*connection* humming between them, and she wasn't at all sure what to do about it. For so long she'd wondered what it would be like to meet up again with the man she'd loved so desperately. And now that it had finally happened, there was a cowardly part of her that wanted to run and hide. But she'd run three years ago, and that hadn't brought her any peace. So this time she'd stand her ground and never let him know that he could still turn her knees to jelly. Now if only she could keep her hormones from zinging to life whenever she was around the man.

But that, she thought with an inward sigh, was a faint hope.

Okay, she'd take his tour. She didn't have much choice, did she? It was take this deal or go pay her five pounds at the palace tour entrance. And at least with J.T. guiding her through the place, she'd see more than the public rooms and gardens. Plus, she considered, still meeting his gaze squarely, she could always slip away from him as easily as she could from a tour guide.

With that thought firmly in mind, she said, "Harry, go on back to the station. I'll grab a cab when I'm finished here."

Harry grumbled, but ambled off.

A moment later, Jade held out her right hand and said sweetly, "It's a deal, J.T."

Then his hand took hers and a burst of heat skittered along the length of her arm to shatter in her chest, splintering her veins with a liquid warmth that surprised her.

And by the look in his eyes—her touch had the same effect on him.

Four

J.T. felt the loss the instant Jade snatched her hand back. The heat on his fingers lingered, a warmth he hadn't known in three long years. Looking into her eyes, he saw that she'd felt it, too, but was just as determined as he to ignore it. Fine by him. She'd shot him out of the sky once—he wasn't about to let it happen again.

Strange that they'd come together again after all this time. And wouldn't you know that it would happen *because* of the choice she'd made years ago? She'd given him up for dreams of a career. Now that career had brought her into direct opposition with his.

"Jade?" the cameraman called to her, and when she turned to talk to the older man, J.T. kept his eyes on both of them.

"Look, Harry," she was saying, with a brief glimpse over her shoulder at J.T., "I'm going in to do the tour. See what I can find out."

"Without film to show, what good's the tour going to do us?"

Jade hooked her arm through Harry's and pulled him a bit farther away, to make sure they wouldn't be overheard. "I'll get something. Right now, I'm going to play the game. Don't worry about it. We'll get film before we're finished."

Harry glanced over her shoulder at the big man standing at the open palace gate, then shifted his gaze back to hers. "I don't think this one's going to be easy to get around, Jade."

J.T. never had been, she thought. Checking her watch, she said, "I'll see you back at the station in a couple of hours, okay?"

Harry agreed reluctantly, then turned and headed off toward the van. She watched him go and briefly wished she were going with him. Suddenly, the idea of sitting at the station planning next week's show sounded a lot better to her than spending the next couple of hours with J.T. Still, he was her way into the palace, and she needed that interview. Nodding to herself, Jade walked back to the gates and stopped directly in front of the man. "Are you ready?" she asked.

"As I'll ever be," he muttered, then took a step back and waved her through the gates.

An hour and a half later, Jade had seen enough rosebushes and statuary to last her a lifetime. Oh, the private gardens were beautiful. Every last blade of grass was trimmed neatly. No stray leaves were left to scatter color on the stone pathways. Each rose bloomed to perfection and even the sunlight seemed more polished in this sheltered enclosure. Marble statues, carved centuries before, stood as beautiful and pristine as the day the sculptor had completed his work. Water splashed in the fountains and a soft sea breeze slipped over the high stone walls surrounding the palace.

And she didn't care about any of it.

Her gaze slid to the glass walls fronting on the garden. Behind that painfully clean glass lay the private quarters of the royal family. The people she needed to reach.

So near and yet so far.

J.T. never left her side. Like the old days, a quiet voice in her mind insisted. She remembered so clearly the evening walks they used to take along the coast road. Knowing he was there, right beside her, had filled her with a sense of peace and safety and hunger that she hadn't known since. Now, though, it was different, just as they were different. There was no intimacy between them. Just hazy memories of a brief marriage that probably never should have happened in the first place.

"The marble used in the statues was quarried in the Aronleigh Mountains," he was saying, and Jade stopped in her tracks to look up at him. "What?" he asked.

"I already know about the sculptures."

"Sorry."

He didn't look sorry. He looked amused. As if he was enjoying her frustration at getting the run-around. So much for fond memories and songs of yesteryear.

"J.T...." She waved both arms toward the gardens and said, "This is all lovely. But every child in Penwyck learns about the palace in school."

"Ah, but not every schoolchild gets a tour of the private gardens, now do they?"

"A rose is a rose is a rose," Jade said.

Nodding, he shoved both hands into his pants pockets and inhaled deeply enough to swell his broad chest to immense proportions. "Yeah, I know. I'm bored, too."

"Then why are we doing this?"

"Because you won't go away," he said flatly,

giving her a look that told her he wished to hell she would.

There was a time when that would have been the last thing on his mind. Jade walked over to a nearby stone bench and took a seat beside the closest fountain, a marble dolphin spraying water from its mouth. Barely glancing at it, she lifted her gaze to J.T.'s and said, "I *can't* go."

"You didn't have this much trouble leaving three years ago."

"How long are you going to throw that in my face?"

"How much time do we have?"

"For God's sake, J.T." She crossed her legs, smoothed the hem of her skirt down over her knees and clasped her fingers there tightly, as if to keep herself from flinging her hem up over her head and begging him to take her. Now. *Oh, good God, where did that come from?* Pushing the thought out of her brain, she tightened the leash on her temper. Surely that was a better bet than slavering all over him. "We were kids."

"You were twenty-five," he countered. "I was twenty-nine. Too old to be kids."

"You were born old," she said.

"That's nice."

"You know what I mean." Jade waved his pretend hurt feelings aside. "You always knew where you were going. What you wanted. I'd just gotten out of college. I didn't know anything.''

It had taken her years longer to get her degree than most people. She'd taken classes in fits and starts, working to put herself through school. Then, just after graduation, she'd met J.T. and been swept up into a whirlwind of lust and love and promises of a future. Three months later, they were married. Four weeks after that, Jade had walked out, and nothing had ever been the same since.

''You knew you wanted to marry me,'' he muttered, and took a seat beside her.

She shook her head and slanted him a look. ''I knew I wanted you. More than my next breath. You sashayed me into marriage before I knew what hit me.''

''Ah,'' he said, leaning back and stretching incredibly long legs out in front of him. ''So this is my fault.''

''I didn't say that.''

''Sure you did. I tricked you into marrying me.''

''No, you just kissed me into it.'' Disgusted with herself, Jade shifted, leaned back against the bench and folded her arms over her chest.

He'd entranced her so completely, so thoroughly, she'd have moved to the moon if he'd said, ''Let's go.'' So what did that say about her? That she was weak? Well, maybe she was. At least where J.T. was concerned.

Or she *had* been.

She'd grown up since then.

Right?

"It wasn't anybody's fault," she finally said, her voice barely audible above the splashing water beside her. "It just didn't work out."

"Because you didn't try."

"Because I wasn't willing to do things *your* way."

"Really?" he challenged with a snort. "You consider a four-week marriage to be a real test of a relationship?"

"Come on, J.T., admit it. You wanted me to be a stay-at-home wife and mom, and you wouldn't listen when I told you I needed more."

"I wanted to take care of you."

"I can take care of myself."

"You didn't even try to compromise. Didn't give us a shot."

"J.T., you didn't know the meaning of the word *compromise*. It was your way or the highway. I chose the highway."

"I'm not the one who walked out, Jade."

Her temper soared to the surface and frothed in a wild tangle at the base of her throat. Jade clenched her teeth tightly to keep from spilling it out in a furious tirade. Damn it. How did he *do* it? How did he push her so far, so fast?

No one else had ever been able to push her buttons the way J.T. could. And it looked as if three long years hadn't lessened his abilities any. But even if he hadn't learned anything during their time apart, *she* had.

Shaking her head, she only looked at him and said, ''I'm not doing this with you, J.T. Not now.'' She stood up, preferring to fight on her feet. And the first order of business was to steer this conversation back onto safe territory.

''I'm here to do a job, J.T. Not fight with you.'' She inhaled slowly, deeply, and felt the cool, damp air fill her lungs and ease away the heat inside. ''This could all be very simple.''

He stood up, too, no doubt hoping to cow her with his size. Good luck with that, she thought.

''If we give you what you want.''

The rumble of his voice did some very weird things to the pit of her stomach, but she refused to think about that at the moment. ''Would that be so terrible?''

He threw both hands high, then let them drop down against his thighs again. ''Has it ever occurred to you that there might be reasons why the royals don't want to do interviews right now?''

''The public—''

"Has a right to know." He finished the statement for her and held up one hand to keep her from saying anything else. "Yeah, I know. You guys pull that line every time you're getting stonewalled."

"It's true," she said.

"Maybe," he acknowledged, then looked her directly in the eye. "But maybe people should be allowed some privacy, too."

Jade laughed shortly. "The royal family aren't 'people.' They're news."

"They're people first, lady."

Jade paced back and forth in front of him, listening to the click of her own heels on the paving stones beneath her feet. She and J.T. were rehashing an argument they'd already had. It was still safer than talking about their shared history and what a mess they'd made of everything. "It's not like I'm trying to do some tacky exposé," she said.

"Depends on your definition of 'tacky,' doesn't it?"

"What's so terrible about wanting to talk to *my* queen to find out how *my* king is? To make sure that my country is safe? To let my fellow citizens know that they don't have to worry?"

"Oh," J.T. said, moving to intercept her as she turned to backtrack. She almost smashed into his chest, but he reached up and caught her shoulders in his big hands. "So that's what this is about," he

said. "Altruistic, are you? You don't care about rat-
ings or getting your face in front of a camera.
You're just doing this for your fellow citizens?"

She felt the imprint of each of his fingers, right
through the fabric of her jacket, as if he was branding her with his own personal heat. Just as he'd
branded her before. It took her a second or two to
unscramble the wires in her brain long enough to
reply.

"You're right," she said. "It's not just because I
think the people should know what's going on. This
is my job. And my chance to build the career I—"
She broke off and let her gaze slide from his.

"—left me for?"

"J.T."

"Fine. Sorry. We won't go there right now." He
didn't let her go, and for some reason, Jade was in
no hurry to break the contact between them. She
stood, caught securely in his grasp, and even while
she talked, a part of her simply enjoyed the heat
flowing from his hands into her body.

God, it had been so long. Now, with tendrils of
warmth spiraling through her, she realized that it
was the first time in three long years she hadn't felt
cold to the bone. Her mouth went dry and her knees
trembled. Everything in her screamed at her to move
closer. To step into his embrace and feel his arms
slide around her, pressing her to him. She wanted to

lay her head on his chest and hear that steady beat of his heart. She wanted to recall what it had been like to fall asleep like that, secure in his arms.

And because she wanted it so badly, she fought the craving fiercely.

Shaking her hair back from her face, she looked up at him and said, ''Don't you think the people of Penwyck are curious about what's going on in here? Our king is in a coma and his brother is standing in for him. Prince Dylan just returned and Princess Megan is pregnant. This is *news*, J.T. The country's buzzing and no one will talk to the press.''

J.T. let her go and she staggered back a step or two before catching herself. Damn it, he couldn't do it. Couldn't touch her without wanting—needing— more. And he couldn't have it. She was lost to him. As surely as she had been the day she'd walked out of their tiny apartment with only one sad glance for a goodbye.

He reached up and shoved one hand through his hair. This was expecting too much. His boss should never have assigned him to Jade. This was going way above and beyond the call of duty.

She was right about one thing, though. Things were in a mess around here. And it was up to men like him to keep a lid on what could be Pandora's latest boxful of trouble. One more wild story coming out of the palace and there would be even more chaos.

"Let's go," he said suddenly, and reached for her. Grabbing her elbow in a tight grip, he practically dragged her in his wake.

"Go where?" she asked, even as she hurried to keep up with him.

"Somewhere we can talk without me worrying about you trying to sneak into the damn palace."

The look on her face told him he'd struck a nerve. He'd known from the moment she'd agreed to a no-camera tour that her plan would be to get away from him and wander around on her own. But J.T. had served his time in the military and had come up against foes tough enough to prepare him for time spent with a news-hungry reporter.

Even Jade.

Now he just had to figure out how much he could give her that would ease her appetite and still protect the people in his charge.

An hour later, they were still driving. The landscape whizzed past, and Jade's fingers curled around the armrest on the passenger side door. She slid a glance at the driver of the low-slung convertible sports car and felt her breath hitch in her chest. He still drove too fast. And it still made her blood pound to be beside him as he rocketed along the coast road.

Both hands on the wheel, he steered his car around the curves with a practiced ease that made her remember how good he'd been at steering her toward climaxes that shattered her soul. Her stomach skittered as the cold autumn wind rushed at them. She shouldn't be thinking like that. Shouldn't indulge herself with vivid recollections of his hands on her body.

Then he trailed his long fingers along the leather-wrapped steering wheel and she shivered, remembering the feel of his fingertips tracing her spine.

Oh, boy.

She was in big trouble.

If she had any sense at all, she'd throw the car door open and jump out. Then she glanced at the speedometer. Nearing ninety. Okay, maybe not.

Conversation was impossible over the roar of the engine, so she kept her mouth shut and her gaze fixed on the scenery whizzing past. It was far safer than looking at J.T., after all.

But then the car began to slow as he downshifted, and she shifted her gaze in time to watch J.T. pull the car off the main road and into a parking lot in front of a small, stone pub. Weatherbeaten ivy crawled up the side and front of the building, nearly obliterating the sign that read Lion Heart, and smoke poured from the chimney on the far wall. Alongside the pub stood a house where she knew the owner lived. Open land stretched out behind the pub, and before it lay the ribbon of road, and beyond that, the ocean.

When J.T. cut the engine and yanked on the brake, the silence was instant. Yet below the quiet was the murmur of the sea and the soft sigh of the wind.

She turned in her seat to face him. "Why here, J.T.?"

He reached up, pulled off his sunglasses and gave her a half smile. "Why not here, Jade? Worried?"

"No," she said, though it was a lie. She was worried. She was being sucked back into J.T.'s world and she knew that leaving it again would kill her.

He was out of the car in a second or two and around to her side before she'd had a chance to open her door. He held it for her as she swung her legs out. Her tight, straight skirt inched high on her thighs as she scooted forward, and she tugged at it before looking up into dark-brown eyes alight with appreciation.

A slow smile curved his lips. "You may be a pain, Jade, but you've still got great legs."

Oh, God.

He held out one hand to help her up, and when she took it, he curled his fingers around hers, rubbing his thumb across her knuckles until Jade's knees wobbled dangerously. With her brain dazzled, her hormones doing a happy dance, she stepped around the car door, and when he slammed it shut, she pulled her hand free of his and tried to smooth her hair down.

"This is a mistake, J.T."

He shrugged. "Wouldn't be the first I've made."

"Me, either." The wind gusted and she pulled the edges of her jacket together across her chest. With nothing to slow it down, the wind out here raced along like an invisible freight train.

Jade sighed, shot the pub a quick look, then turned her gaze back to him. "Why are we here?"

"To talk."

Uh-huh. "About what?"

"Why don't we just get started and see where we end up?"

A woman could take that statement a couple of different ways, Jade thought. Her stomach squirmed again and her mouth went dry as she stared into those brown eyes. They were deep and dark, and the glint of something just a little wicked was enough to start a flicker of warmth deep inside her.

Just like the old days.

Darn it.

Why couldn't the palace have assigned a short,

geeky, older guy to placate her? Why did it have to be him?

"So?" he challenged. "You up for it?"

She shifted her gaze from him to the pub's scarred oak door and back again. This was his home ground. And by association, it had once been hers.

Going inside would probably be a stupid move. But if she just stood here for another five minutes, she'd freeze to death. Then they could plant her in the private gardens as yet another sculpture....

Bottom line, she'd have to take her chances. She could handle herself. J.T. wasn't the first man to send her hormones nuts.

No, her brain warned, he's just the first one to make your blood boil with a look.

"What's wrong, Jade?" he asked. "Do I worry you?"

She swallowed hard and lifted her chin. "Do I look worried?"

His gaze swept her up and down. "You look..." he paused for a long minute, then said, "like trouble."

"Maybe you should keep that in mind."

One corner of his mouth twitched. "Trust me, honey," he said, "that's one thing I'm unlikely to forget."

They headed for the pub, and the instant the door swung open, Jade was enveloped in warmth and so many familiar scents and sounds it was like coming home. Across the room, a huge fire blazed on an open hearth. A few people were seated at the small, round tables scattered across the worn but polished wooden floor. Bench seats lined the smoke-darkened stone walls, and on the far side of the room, a waist-high bar opened into the kitchen beyond.

"Have a seat," J.T. said. "What would you like to drink?"

"White wine."

He nodded, walked to the bar and slapped one hand atop it. Leaning across, he shouted, "Michael! You've got customers."

None of the customers paid any attention to J.T., or to the shouted response that came from a distance. "Is that you, J.T., boy?"

Almost instantly, a short, chubby, balding man with round red cheeks and a grin that spread across his face appeared behind the counter. Reaching across it, he slapped J.T. on the shoulder.

"Good to see you, boy. You don't get out here much anymore."

"Busy," J.T. muttered, but his deep voice carried through the room with no trouble.

"Ah yes, life at the palace," the little man said, then pointed at one of his other customers. "See you, David? This is my brother's son, J.T. Works at the palace, he does. Keeping an eye on things."

"Is that right then?" the man asked. "And the king, how is he?"

J.T. frowned to himself. *The public has the right to know.* Maybe Jade was right. Maybe the people of Penwyck did deserve to know more than they were being told. But it wasn't up to him to make that decision.

"Well, he can't be talking to the likes of you and keep his job, now can he?" Michael Wainwright countered. Then, turning back to his nephew, he asked, "What can I get for you?"

"A pint for me and a glass of white wine for the lady." He nodded his head in Jade's direction, and she watched the older man's sly smile broaden.

"Jade! By thunder it's good to see you, darlin'."

"Hello, Michael," she said, and smiled at the man who had once been family. His features creased into a broader grin and she felt herself return it. How could she not?

For three years she'd tried to keep from looking back. And now she was right smack in the middle of her past. Her gaze slid to J.T., and the warmth in his eyes reached across the room, across the years, and dipped down deep inside her.

And she didn't know how she would ever survive the cold again.

Five

"Two out of three," J.T. said, and the scowl on his face told her he still couldn't believe she'd beaten him at darts.

"Well, I see you still haven't perfected your gracious-loser skills." Jade gave him a sweet smile, but didn't bother to hide the gleam of victory shining in her eyes.

He stomped across the room, snatched the metal-tipped darts out of the board and walked back to her. Handing over the blue ones, he tightened his grip on the red and said, "I don't like losing."

No, he never had. J.T. was more accustomed to

bending things—or people—to his will, than submitting himself. He'd always been larger than life. Filled with enough confidence for three healthy people, he crashed through life full speed ahead. He'd been a highly decorated soldier before being recruited for the RII. And his advancement within the institute's ranks was legendarily quick. He expected the best from himself and those around him, and he generally got it. J.T. was a man who knew what he wanted when he saw it—and then he went after it.

Just as he'd gone after her.

A flutter in her chest told Jade that her heartbeat was doing its weird little J.T. dance again, and she deliberately tried to bring it under control. Without much success. There was just something about him that sent her cells into overdrive. It was one of those pesky little facts of life—like gravity.

She took her darts from him and her fingertips brushed across the palm of his hand, igniting yet another series of small fires in her bloodstream. *Ignore it,* she told herself. Shouldn't be much more difficult than ignoring an avalanche.

Oh, boy.

She cleared her throat, took a deep breath and asked suddenly, ''Why should I give you two out of three? I've already won.''

''Could have been a fluke,'' he challenged.

''It wasn't.''

"Prove it."

Jade's gaze narrowed on him. "You know darn well I beat you fair and square, J.T."

He inhaled slowly, deeply, filling his lungs and swelling his broad chest once more.

Jade's heart did the flutter dance again.

"My concentration was off."

She laughed. "This is pitiful. You just can't admit that I won."

"I play better when there's a prize at stake."

Suspicion flooded her. "What kind of prize?"

He leaned in, looming over her until she was forced to tilt her head back to keep from clunking their foreheads together. Keeping his voice low and intimate, he said, "We could play for the same stakes we used to."

Heat.

Good God, she was burning up.

Jade dragged in a shaky breath but still managed to glare at him. "There is no way I'm going to do that."

"Scared?" His voice came lower, rough and hushed, a scrape of sound that skittered along her spine and then slipped deep inside her.

Swallowing hard, Jade shot a look over her shoulder at the other patrons in the pub. They were far enough away that she felt comfortable whispering, "I am *not* going to play for sex."

One dark eyebrow lifted and his mouth curved in a slow, sexy smirk. "Not just sex, babe. Hot, soul-stirring, mind-bending sex—any way the winner wants it for as long as he or she wants it."

Her body went into damp heat mode.

Her mouth went dry.

And everything inside her curled up and whimpered.

"Remember?" he whispered.

She'd have to be dead to *not* remember.

One time, she'd lost a bet purposely, just so she could enjoy pleasuring him all afternoon. Her mind filled with images of sun-spattered sheets and a soft wind caressing damp, naked flesh. She could almost feel his breath, warm on her cheek. Taste his mouth. Feel his skin beneath her palms.

"You do remember then," he said, moving in closer until she felt surrounded by him.

"Yeah." Somehow, she found the strength to squeeze that one word out of a tight throat.

"Then you probably remember what happened the last time you beat me at darts."

She swayed and closed her eyes, reliving that long summer night when J.T. had fulfilled her every wish by taking her with his mouth, over and over again. Until she lay exhausted and pleading with him to stop and let her catch her breath.

And still he hadn't stopped. He'd taken her higher

and faster and—*don't,* she told herself. Don't remember. Don't let the past overtake the present. What they'd had three years ago was gone.

"Don't do this, J.T."

His right hand curled around her upper arm, and Jade was grateful for the support even though his touch skittered through her like fireworks exploding in a night sky.

"What we had was good, Jade."

She lifted her gaze to his. "For a while."

"Why'd you leave? Why'd you give up on us?"

"You know why," she said, her voice strengthening with purpose and resolve. Pulling out of his grasp, she took a step back on shaky legs.

He shoved his free hand into his pocket, and with the other fingered the steel tips of the darts clenched in a tight fist. A muscle in his jaw twitched a couple of times and Jade knew he was fighting to maintain control. After a few seconds, he seemed to manage.

"So, we gonna play again?"

"I don't want to play games with you, J.T." A simple sentence that she knew could be taken two ways. That was fine with her. She meant it both ways.

"Maybe I let you win," he said.

"Hah!" She actually laughed out loud at the idea. "Not likely."

"How will you be sure if we don't play again?"

"If I do, and I win...*again*," she said, "what's my reward?"

He chuckled and shook his head. "Not a chance that you can beat me again."

"Uh-huh. But if I do?"

"Isn't winning its own reward?"

"Not necessarily," she said.

He folded his arms across his chest and looked down at her warily. "Fine. If you won't play for the old stakes, what've you got in mind?"

"My interview."

J.T. laughed outright then, and even though it irritated her, she had to admit that she liked the deep, booming sound. God, his laugh used to shake the windows in that rattletrap apartment they'd shared.

"You're not going to let go of this, are you?"

"Thought we'd covered that already."

"So we have," he said, the smile fading from his features slowly. "As to the interview, I'm not the one who can give you the okay on it."

"But you could put in a good word for me."

"I could."

"So then," Jade said, stroking one fingertip along the length of one of the darts, "I guess it all boils down to...are you game enough to make the bet? Or are you too worried that I'll beat the pants off— ah...win again?"

J.T.'s gaze dropped to her hands, and something

inside him tightened as he watched her slowly caress that dart. Images flashed through his mind, visions of the two of them lying upon tangled sheets, so tightly wrapped up in each other that hours passed without notice. He remembered exactly what her hands felt like on his skin and how the near electrical charge of touching her always hit him as hard as it had the first time.

His memory was good. Too good. He recalled everything. Her scent, her taste, the sweet soft sighs she made just as she peaked. And how her body welcomed his, taking him deep within her warmth and cradling him in a kind of love he'd never known before or since.

He sucked in air like a drowning man and banished those images as fast as he could.

Tearing his gaze from her hands, he looked up into those incredible eyes of hers and measured his chances. She was pretty good at this, but he'd had three long, lonely years in which to practice. He'd been working on his game, subconsciously trying to beat her even though she wasn't around anymore. Well, here was his chance to prove to himself—and to her—that he could.

J.T. had never turned down a challenge in his life. But at the same time, he had to wonder what would happen if the unthinkable did happen and she actually beat him again.

"Worried?" she asked, one corner of that delectable mouth curving into a half smile filled with confidence.

"No way." He dismissed the doubts racing through his mind.

"Then it's a bet."

He glanced from her to the dartboard and back again. "Oh yeah. It's a bet."

"Excellent," she said, grinning now like a child given the keys to a candy factory. "After our game, we can arrange a time for the interview."

"Don't sound so cocky, babe," he warned, and reached out to chuck her chin with his fingertips. "A lucky win doesn't make you a champion."

"Luck?" She shook her head and stepped back. "Luck doesn't have a thing to do with it."

"Uh-huh," J.T. said. "But about our bet. What do I get when *I* win?"

One russet eyebrow lifted slightly as she gave him a slow look. "I picked my prize…why don't you pick yours?"

Instantly, his gaze swept over her as all kinds of possibilities flashed through his mind. She seemed to have no trouble reading exactly where his thoughts were headed, since she cleared her throat and said, "Within reason, of course."

Nothing he wanted from her was reasonable, but

he heard himself say, "Dinner. My place. You cook."

She laughed, and the soft, musical sound settled over him like a promise.

"That's no prize, J.T. You remember what a terrible cook I am."

"I'll risk it."

"You like taking risks, don't you?"

"You never get anywhere without a risk or two."

"And if it blows up in your face?" she asked, suddenly wondering if they were still talking about that interview or not.

"Then at least you have the satisfaction of knowing you tried."

Satisfaction. That word hung in the still air between them and Jade shivered slightly as thoughts having nothing to do with darts filled her mind. The rest of the room seemed to drift away until it was only the two of them in that darkened, shadow-filled pub.

Oh, it had been a mistake coming here with him. She'd have done better if she'd stayed outside and frozen into statuary. At least then her heart wouldn't be twisting and her body wouldn't be going up in steam.

Seeing him again was hard. Seeing him again away from the palace was harder still. She'd been to this pub many times with J.T. She'd thought of

Michael as her own uncle. She'd worked the bar and helped serve drinks. She'd sat by the fire and dreamed silly dreams. Here, away from the palace, J.T. seemed more approachable—and that wasn't necessarily a good thing. But it was too late now to change anything. Their course was set.

So to avoid being dragged more fully into a reenactment of their past, she *had* to win their little tournament. It wasn't just to get the interview now. It was to keep J. T. Wainwright at as safe a distance as possible.

"Who goes first then?" she asked suddenly, tearing her concentration away from the thoughts careening wildly through her brain.

"Ladies, naturally," he said, and half bowed.

Nodding, she aimed and tossed her first dart. It hit the board with a solid thunk, just outside the bull's-eye.

Two hours later, he parked his car in front of the television station and switched off the engine. Turning in his seat, he glared at her. "Three out of five."

Jade laughed and shook her head. "No way. A deal's a deal, J.T."

"I still can't believe you beat me," he muttered with a shake of his head. "Nobody's beaten me in years."

"I was motivated." Whether she was more motivated to get the interview or to stay out of his apartment, she wasn't sure. But it didn't really matter, did it?

"So was I," he said, his voice a deep rumble of sound that snaked along her spine to settle low in the pit of her stomach.

Okay, she told herself, *outta the car.*

She opened the passenger door, stepped out and whipped her head to one side, snapping her windblown hair out of her eyes. "What about our deal, J.T.? Are you going to stick to it?"

His fingers tightened around the steering wheel. "I said I'd see what I could do."

"Then I'll see you tomorrow."

"Tomorrow?" He shot her a look through narrowed eyes. "I didn't say anything about tomorrow."

"Whether you come through or not, I'll be at the palace tomorrow. And every day after," she promised, leaning forward, "until I get that interview."

"And you called *me* a pit bull."

Jade laughed and eased back from the car. He looked totally disgruntled and she couldn't blame him. "See you then."

"Yeah," he muttered, then fired up the engine, threw the car into gear and swung back into the stream of traffic.

The sidewalks were crowded. People bustled past, and slowly, Jade turned to join the flow. She hadn't taken more than a step or two toward the building before she felt the hair at the back of her neck prickle.

A bone-deep chill started at the back of her shoulders and went straight down her spine. Her stomach flip-flopped. Her mouth went dry and breath staggered in and out of her lungs. *He* was there. Her stalker. He was there. In the crowd.

Somewhere.

Close by.

And he was watching her.

Spinning around quickly, Jade held her breath and scanned the faces of the people pushing past her. But there were just too many of them. And she didn't know who she was looking for. It could be anyone, from the old man on the bus bench to the young guy with long hair leaning against a phone booth.

Tears burned the backs of her eyes. Whether they were from fear or anger or both, she wasn't sure. Her stomach pitched and rolled and even her knees went wobbly. Who was it? she wondered. Which one of these people was responsible for the letters? The tape?

Suddenly feeling much too vulnerable, Jade

turned her back on all of them and hurried across the sidewalk, escaping into the safety of the Penwyck TV building.

"She's not going to give up, Franklin," J.T. said, pacing the floor in his boss's office. He'd come right back to the palace after dropping Jade at the station. But distancing himself physically from her hadn't wiped her from his mind. In fact, he could still smell her perfume, as if it was clinging to his clothes, reminding him of the hours spent in her company.

As if he needed reminding.

"I didn't expect she would," his boss said, pouring himself a cup of coffee from the insulated carafe on the corner of his desk. "Coffee?"

J.T. stopped, shook his head and said, "No, thanks."

"Suit yourself." Franklin Vancour leaned back in his maroon leather chair and studied the man opposite him.

"She wants an interview, and maybe the best thing to do here would just be to give it to her so she'll ease up."

"That's quite a turnaround," Franklin said.

"Yeah, well..." J.T. stopped in front of the desk. "She's stubborn. And smart." And a dart hustler, he told himself silently. But that didn't have anything to do with this. Sure, he'd lost a bet. But if he didn't think it was in the best interests of his country, he wouldn't be speaking up on her behalf.

Much as he hated to admit it, Jade had made some good points. The rumors flying about the king were only going to get worse if somebody didn't address them. And if she was serious about the station sending that Barracuda in if she failed, then it was in everyone's best interests to oblige Jade.

She might be a reporter, but she had scruples.

"Everyone knows the king is sick. We're only feeding the rumor mills by shutting the press out entirely."

"True." Franklin sat forward and set his coffee cup down precisely in the middle of his desk blotter. "We'd hoped to give it a few more days. But frankly, the longer we wait, the worse it looks."

"Exactly." J.T. pushed one hand through his hair. Rumors were flying and had been for weeks. Not only outside the palace, either. The guards, the soldiers, even a few members of the royal family were still in the dark as to the king's condition. "You said the queen likes Jade's reports."

"Yes, the queen enjoys her work."

"So who better to do the first interview?"

"I spoke to Her Majesty this morning, as a matter of fact," Franklin said. "And she agrees with you."

"You don't?"

"Not entirely," Franklin admitted. "I have a

healthy aversion to members of the press. Good news seldom follows a press conference or an interview session. But my opinion doesn't matter in this. The queen has decided to grant a brief interview in the hopes of easing the fears of our citizens."

"When?"

"Tomorrow morning," he said, reaching for his coffee cup again and pausing to take a deep drink. "Have your ex-wife here by nine."

J.T. looked at him long and hard for a minute. "I hope you know my opinion isn't based on the fact of my past relationship to Jade."

"I know." Vancour looked tired. He eased back in his chair again and cradled that coffee cup as if needing its heat. "But it doesn't hurt, either. At least there's one reporter we can count on to do an honest job of it."

As J.T. left the office and walked down the long hall leading to the front of the palace, he thought about his boss's words. Yeah, she was honest. Painfully so. Three years ago, she'd looked him dead in the eye and told him love wasn't enough.

Six

"**Y**ou're here early."

Startled out of her daydreams, Jade jumped and half turned in her chair. "Janine." She slapped one hand to her chest and felt the thundering beat of her own heart. "Geez, you scared me half to death."

Her assistant laughed and plopped down onto the chair opposite Jade's desk. "Sorry. Didn't mean to. You must have really been concentrating."

Hmm. Concentrating? No. Completely focusing on the mental image of being naked in J.T.'s bed? Yes.

Oh, boy.

It was a good thing Janine was efficient, capable and unable to read minds. How embarrassing was this? Behaving like some love-struck teenager. It had been a long time since Jade's hormones had been this stirred up. Actually, it had been since the last time she saw J.T. What was it about that man that could get to her so completely? So quickly?

"Hey!"

Jade blinked and realized that her assistant was waving a hand in front of her eyes. "What are you doing?"

"Just what I was going to ask you." Janine sat back in her chair and folded her arms across her chest. "You zoned out on me there."

"Sorry." Jade pushed her hair back from her face, then reached for her cup of coffee. She took a sip, shuddered and nearly gagged.

"Cold, is it?"

"Beyond cold," Jade assured her. "It's moved into the frigid and truly terrifying world."

"Want more?"

"A barrelful ought to do it." Jade looked at the woman opposite her. They'd worked together for two years now, and in that time they'd become friends. Janine was every bit as ambitious as Jade had been when she started. She saw herself in the slightly younger woman. Not just her attitude and her drive. But there was even a strong resemblance between the two of them. Janine's shoulder-length hair was almost the same color as Jade's, and they were built alike, as well. Like sisters separated at birth, Jade had often thought. And as the thought came again, she wondered if her life would have been different, easier, if she'd had a sister.

Another female in the house of testosterone.

When Jade was eight, her mother had died, and Jade's father, never very comfortable around his only daughter, had distanced himself even further. It wasn't as though he hated her or anything. It was simply that Bill Erickson didn't have a clue as to how to raise a girl. Instead, he'd focused on his four sons, and Jade had spent the rest of her life trying to be enough like her older brothers that her father would notice her, too.

Naturally, it hadn't worked.

"Hello?" Janine called, and it was clear from her tone it wasn't the first time.

"Huh?" Shaking her head, Jade said, "Wow. I really need more coffee, huh? I just seem to be wandering today."

"No problem." Janine stood up, smoothed the skirt of her navy-blue suit and asked, "How about if I sneak out and run over to the latte shop around the corner?"

"Oh God," Jade said, leaning her forearms on

her cluttered desk. "For a steaming hot mocha, you can name your price."

Janine grinned. "The chance to help edit when you get the interview with the queen?"

There was that ambition again. "You're on."

"Great." Janine turned and started for the door. After a few steps, she stopped and looked back over her shoulder. "Hey, is it okay if I borrow your coat? I left mine in my car and it's freezing out there."

"Sure, go ahead. And thanks again. But for the use of my coat, I demand at least a grande."

"No biggie," Janine assured her. "Back in a flash."

Alone again, Jade turned to her pile of notes. Picking up a pen, she made a couple of notations on the page of questions she had for the queen. There wasn't a doubt in Jade's mind that she'd get the interview. It was just a matter of time.

Her cell phone rang and before she answered it, she glanced at the incoming phone number, but didn't recognize it. Intrigued, she pushed the send button and said, "Hello?"

"Jade."

The sound of J.T.'s voice sent a conga line of goose bumps rippling along her spine. She shivered, swallowed hard and demanded, "How did you get this number? It's unlisted. Private."

"Remember where I work?"

"Oh." The palace. So what? Did that give the palace security men the right to track down private citizens at will?

Apparently.

"Well, what do you want, J.T.?" That's the way, Jade, she told herself. Attack. That'll help.

"Still charming in the morning, huh?"

She closed her eyes and took a long, deep breath. She would *not* let him get to her. She would not be drawn down memory lane one more time. Hell, she'd spent most of last night tossing and turning, her body on fire for a touch it hadn't felt in three long years. She wasn't going to do it again today.

But she also couldn't afford to tick him off. At least not until she'd gotten inside the palace. Forcing a smile, she choked out, "Good morning, J.T."

"See? Was that so hard?"

Her fingers curled tightly around the slender silver phone until she thought it just might shatter. Deliberately, she relaxed her grip while fighting down the urge to reach through the receiver and grab J.T.

"So, to what do I owe the dubious pleasure of having you track down my cell number?"

There was a long pause, and she'd almost convinced herself he'd hung up when he blurted, "Be at the palace by nine."

"What?" Her heartbeat skittered and she jumped to her feet, suddenly unable to sit still. Irritation forgotten in the swell of excitement peaking inside her, she waited, wanting him to repeat what he'd just said.

"I know you heard me."

Yes, she had. She just didn't quite believe it yet.

"I have the interview?"

"Ten minutes."

"*Ten* minutes?" It hadn't taken long to pop her balloon. She grabbed up her list of questions and knew it would take her longer than that just to read them aloud to herself. "It's not enough time."

"Nine minutes."

"J.T...."

"Eight."

"Fine," she snapped. "I'll take ten minutes."

"Good." He sighed into the phone, and Jade knew he wasn't happy about this. "Get here a little early. I can walk you through the protocol."

"I think I can handle it." As long as there wasn't a lot of curtsying involved. She did a lousy curtsy. Always had. Even in ballet class when she was a kid. At the end of a performance, she'd just bow along with the boys, rather than humiliate herself by getting her legs all tangled up.

"Probably," he agreed. "I'd still like to talk to you before you see Her Majesty."

That was reasonable, she thought. And hey, in

victory she could be gracious. "I'll be there at eight-thirty."

"See you then."

"J.T.—"

He hung up and a dial tone hummed in her ear.

Jade wasn't at all sure what she'd been about to say. She only knew that the abrupt conversation stung more than their arguments had.

"Cut it out, Jade," she muttered, and pushed the end button on her phone before tossing it back into her purse.

She sat down behind her desk again and told herself it didn't matter if J.T. was happy about this or not. It was her job. Her career. Her choice. She'd left J.T. for this world, so she had to succeed at it.

Otherwise, all that pain would have been for nothing.

Deliberately, she picked up her sheet of questions again and, forgetting all about her need for coffee, settled down to work.

She stepped out of the cab, and J.T.'s blood ran hot and thick in his veins.

Simple as that.

Jade Erickson stirred something inside him that had never eased up. He'd managed, for the last three years, to bury the passion and the need and the hunger for her. He'd told himself that he didn't care.

That he was over her. But it had taken only a day or two in her presence to bring it all back. Hard for a man to admit, even to himself, that he could be brought to his knees by a woman who'd already made it clear she didn't want him.

But as long as he kept that thought firmly in mind, he should be able to survive being with Jade—yet not being with her.

"Good morning." She looked at him and gave him a thousand-watt smile.

"You're pretty chipper," he noted, when he finally found his voice. "Nothing like getting your way to cheer you right up, huh?"

She actually winced, and he felt like an ass. Hell, it wasn't her fault his body was on full alert. Well, actually it was, but it wasn't like she was trying to do it.

Jade adjusted the strap of her black leather shoulder bag, then swung her hair back from her face. The wind had its own ideas, however, and twisted her soft, auburn hair into a wild halo that made his hands itch to touch it. Her forest-green jacket made her eyes glitter like emeralds. But unlike those cold, green stones, her eyes damn near glowed with an inner fire that warmed him even as it threatened to consume him.

But though she had him heated through, she

looked half-frozen. "In such a hurry you forgot your coat?"

"No, my assistant borrowed it and..." Her voice trailed off and a thoughtful expression flashed across her features.

"She didn't give it back?"

"I didn't even think about it until now, but no. Huh. She never brought me my coffee, either. That's strange."

"Yeah, a real mystery."

"So," Jade asked, shaking off her confusion. "Do I get to come inside, or will you be bringing the queen out here?"

"Right." He unlocked the iron gate that stood like a wall between them, and pulled it open, ushering her in. She smiled at the young soldier standing guard nearby, and J.T. noted the kid's near dumbstruck look. She carried quite a punch when she turned on the charm. J.T. almost felt sorry for the soldier. Almost.

"Come on, Jade," he said. "I'll get you some coffee."

She stopped and looked up at him. "As long as you didn't make it."

One dark eyebrow lifted. "I make good coffee."

"Yeah, if you're tarring a roof."

"Ouch." He'd argue the point, but why bother?

No one in the security office let him make coffee, either. "You're safe. Trust me."

He laid his hand at the small of her back and steered her toward the palace. Barely touching her, just the slightest brush of her jacket against his fingertips, he could still feel the electrical jolt of her nearness. But he cleared his mind of it. He wouldn't go back down that road.

They walked through the wide double doors and Jade stopped dead. Acres of marble stretched out in front of her and on either side. A wide, imposing staircase swung elegantly from the ground floor up to the second story. On the walls hung portraits of generations of kings and queens. A massive crystal chandelier dropped from the ceiling in the center of the entryway, and in the morning sunlight, hundreds of prism rainbows danced around the cavernous room.

She took a single step forward and did a slow, appreciative turn before letting her gaze drift back to J.T. "It's…"

"Big?" J.T. shoved both hands into his pockets to keep from reaching for her.

"Beautiful. And very fairy-taleish."

He smiled. "I don't think that's a word."

"It should be." She walked farther into the reception area and her high heels clicked against the gleaming marble floor. "I feel like I should be whispering or something."

"Not necessary," he said, though his own gaze did a quick sweep of the area. He worked here. He tended to take for granted the splendor that surrounded him every day. Not that he had the run of the place or anything, but even the public rooms in the palace were pretty damn impressive.

When he shifted his gaze back to Jade, he found her staring at him thoughtfully. "What?"

"Nothing." Jade couldn't have told him what she was thinking because she wasn't sure herself. All she knew was that he was even more stirring than this place. The grandeur of it all was enough to take anyone's breath away. But it had been too late in her case.

Just walking alongside J.T. was enough to do that.

"Okay then," he said, moving toward her. He caught her elbow in a firm grip and guided her across the floor toward a narrow hallway. "Let's get started."

Way ahead of you, she thought, and fought to ignore the heat streaming from the point of his touch right down to the soles of her feet.

Jade's stomach did a series of roller-coaster moves while her palms grew damp and her mouth went dry. She glanced at the clock on the wall of the security office where she sat waiting for J.T. He'd gone over protocol with her—no curtsying, thank God—and now she was just waiting for the go-ahead.

She was minutes from interviewing the queen of Penwyck.

"I think I'm gonna be sick," she muttered, then swallowed hard, hoping her stomach would cooperate and stay where it was supposed to.

What had she been thinking? Why had she pressed so hard for this? Who the hell was she to be interviewing a queen, for heaven's sake?

Jumping up from her chair, Jade paced to the window on the far wall. She looked out at yet another section of the gardens and wished she was out there, sprinting for the main gate and the street beyond. She'd been working toward this moment for three years. This one interview would push her over the top. Put her in a position to move forward in the career that had always meant so much to her. Now that the moment was here, she was terrified. And she wasn't sure what terrified her more, the idea of screwing it up or of succeeding.

"You ready?"

J.T.'s voice sounded behind her, and she turned to look at him. Those dark-brown eyes of his locked onto her and she felt the warmth of his stare ease away the last of the nerves rattling her insides.

"As I'll ever be." She stopped long enough to snatch up her purse from the corner of a desk, then walked out of the office, J.T. at her side.

"We'll have to take the service elevator," he was saying, and it took a moment or two for his words to register.

"But the stairs. The marble staircase—"

"Being polished as we speak." He guided her farther down the hallway. "No sweat, though. The service elevator's small, but it'll get us upstairs."

"Small." Jade's stomach did another weird dive, but she held it together. How bad could it be? One short elevator ride. No problem.

He came to a stop and punched a button. As a motor whirred, Jade tightened her grip on her purse, digging her fingernails into the pliable leather.

The door slid open, J.T. followed her inside and she turned around in time to watch the door slide closed again. Small, she thought. Too darn small. What's the matter with this place? They couldn't afford a bigger elevator for the employees? What was this, the Middle Ages?

Her heartbeat sounded like a bass drum.

The elevator shimmied, shuddered, then stopped with a jerk.

She stared at the closed door, willing it to open. One second passed. Then another.

"Why isn't the door opening?" A reasonable question, she told herself.

"I don't know." J.T. punched a couple of the buttons, and when nothing happened, he opened a panel on the wall and plucked a phone from its cradle.

His conversation was pitched low enough that Jade missed most of it, but chances were even if he'd been speaking in a normal voice, she wouldn't have heard him over the wild hammering of her heart. At last he hung up the phone and turned to look at her.

"Get comfortable," he said, clearly disgusted. "Power's out. Looks like we're stuck for a while."

"What?" She grabbed two fistfuls of his sweater. "Get me out of here, J.T. Now!"

Seven

"**W**e can't be stuck." She released her grip on his sweater, then pushed past him and pressed first one then another of the buttons on the narrow panel. "How can the power be out?" she mumbled, her fingers flying over the numbered buttons. "We can't be out of power. We're in the palace. They *own* the power." She shook her head, refusing to believe. "Palaces don't run out of power."

"The power's not off for the whole palace. Just the back end here. Somebody crossed a couple of wires that shouldn't have been crossed and…" He shrugged. No point in going into the clumsy details.

"Wires?" Stunned, she spared him a glance. "Well, why can't they uncross the stupid wires?"

"They blew something. Relax, Jade." J.T. watched her for a long minute and frowned as she repeatedly hit button after button, each stab stronger than the last. What the hell was going on here?

"I'm relaxed," she assured him, tossing him another quick look over her shoulder. "I'm just trying to fix this, that's all."

"We can't fix it from in here, babe." He lowered his voice instinctively. He'd never seen her like this before. The Jade he knew just wasn't the type to get frantic over a glitch.

Reaching out, J.T. caught her hands in his and turned her around to face him. Her green eyes looked wide and scared, and that hit him hard. He'd seen her furious and passionate and tender and hurt and even worried. But he'd never seen her scared before. So he did what came naturally to him. He pulled her up close and wrapped his arms around her. Smoothing his palms up and down her back, he felt the tension inside her coil even tighter as the seconds ticked past.

"Hey," he said, keeping his voice hushed and comforting, "what's the deal? There's nothing to worry about, Jade. We'll be out of here soon."

She buried her face in his chest, pressing her cheek against his thick, navy-blue sweater. She sucked in a deep breath and blew it out again. "How soon?"

"Maintenance says a couple hours, tops."

"Hours?" She drew her head back and stared up at him, clearly appalled. "Hours? For a couple of wires? No way. Uh-uh. I can't do it, J.T. I can't stay in here for two hours."

J.T. stroked her hair back from her face, and though he was trying to soothe her, he couldn't help enjoying the soft, silky feel of the strands brushing across his fingers. Her eyes, those cool, sea-green depths, looked stormy now, wild with a need that he couldn't ease and didn't understand. "What's going on, Jade? Talk to me."

"It's…" She broke free of his embrace and took a half step back. Her gaze shot around the enclosed space, darting over every inch of the richly paneled elevator as if searching for an escape route. When she didn't find one, she turned her gaze back to him. "I'm just a little…*claustrophobic.*"

Now it was his turn to be surprised.

"You never said—"

"It never came up."

"We were married," he said, torn between sympathy for her and irritation that she'd hidden this from him.

"We had a ground-floor apartment. It didn't seem important."

"Looks pretty important right now," he said, and reached for her again.

She forced a smile that didn't go anywhere near her eyes. "I'm okay. Usually. I mean, I can stand it for a quick ride if I have to."

"You should have told me before we got into the elevator."

"I said I'm okay for short rides." She laughed and the sound was high and unnatural. "It's hours in a tight space I'm not so good at."

"All of this for an interview."

Her eyes went even wider. "The interview. It's ruined. I don't believe this." Shaking her head, she shot an angry glare at the ceiling, but aimed her barb a lot higher. "Does somebody up there hate me or something?"

"Will you relax about the damn interview?" J.T.'s temper flared. He pushed both hands through his hair, telling himself to calm down. To remember she was scared. All she ever thought about was her job. Even in a panic, the first thing that came to her was worrying about the blasted interview.

Her eyes flashed and he saw the same anger churning inside him reflected there. J.T. remembered her temper well, and idly, he reached up and fingered the scar she'd given him on their honeymoon. She noted the action and ground her teeth together.

Claustrophobic panic forgotten in the surge of anger, she faced him down like an amazon. Swinging her hair back, she tossed her purse to the floor. Brushing the edges of her jacket back, she planted both hands on her hips and glared at him.

"Easy for you to say 'oh relax, Jade.' *You* didn't want me to succeed at this, anyway."

"I never said that."

"You didn't have to."

"Ahh…so you're a mind reader, too." J.T. nodded sagely and folded his arms across his chest. "Hell, no wonder the station wanted to send you for this job."

"That's very funny," she snapped. "But inaccurate. I didn't have to read your mind to know what you thought of my working, J.T. Don't you remember? You made yourself perfectly clear."

He *did* remember. All too well. Their fights, the arguments. She'd wanted a career, he'd wanted a wife. And they hadn't been able to compromise enough to see that maybe both were possible. He guessed that was what happened when two hard-headed people came together. No one wanted to give an inch.

"Fine. So shoot me. I loved you. I wanted to take care of you."

"You wanted to keep me quietly at home."

"Well, there's a crime."

"I didn't *say* it was a crime," she retorted with

a frustrated groan. "I only said it wasn't for me." Jade walked the three steps to the opposite wall, then came back again. "God, you never listen. Not then. Not now."

That stung. "I listened plenty." He grabbed her and yanked her close up against him until he could have sworn he felt her heart beating against his chest. She tipped her head back to stare up at him, and he damn near drowned in the sea of her eyes. Her scent invaded him, surrounded him, flooding him with sensations, memories, until he was choking with them. He forced himself to shove his reactions aside and say what he'd wanted to say for so long.

"That last morning. You said you couldn't be happy without a career. Said that marriage to me wasn't enough. That our family wouldn't be enough."

Her eyes filled, but she blinked back the tears, and he couldn't be sure if they were tears of frustration or anger or just plain misery.

"You said you needed to find your own way," he added. "To make your own choices and forge a career that would mean as much to you as mine did to me." He pulled her even tighter to him. "Remember?"

"Yes," she whispered, and her mouth worked as her teeth bit into her bottom lip.

"So now I want to know. You walked away. Was it worth it? Are you happy, Jade?"

Happy?

Right now, the only thing making Jade happy was his nearness. She felt the heat pouring from him and the brush of his breath across her cheeks. She stared up into the dark-brown eyes she'd been dreaming of for three long years and knew that she'd still be seeing them in her sleep if she lived to be ninety.

Happy?

Without J.T.?

Impossible.

But she couldn't tell him that. Couldn't tell him that so far, her career hadn't been enough to fill the emptiness he'd left behind. Couldn't admit that maybe, just maybe she'd been wrong to walk out.

"I have a good job."

"Are you happy?"

"I have a good life."

"Are you *happy?*"

His voice was a low growl of need, demanding an answer.

"Yes." She lied. Looked right at him and lied through her teeth. Because anything else would just be too hard. Telling the truth would only toss a sackful of salt into a wound that was still obviously gaping open, unhealed.

Three years apart and neither one of them had

moved on. And there was a small voice inside her whispering that she was glad. Glad he still cared. Glad he missed her as much as she missed him.

"You're lying," he said tightly, pulling her even closer and wrapping his arms around her with a vise-like strength that threatened to snuff out her breath. "I could always tell when you were lying, babe."

"You're wrong."

"You miss me."

"No."

"You want me."

"J.T.—"

"As much as I want you."

Her knees quivered, and deep down inside, she went damp and hot and needy. Breath shuddering from her lungs, she licked her lips and watched his gaze lock on her tongue. "J.T. don't do this.…"

"I've never stopped wanting you," he said, clearly not listening again. "I dream about you, then wake up, hard for you."

Desire coiled low in her belly and sprang loose, sending shards of excitement spiraling throughout her body.

"I know those dreams," she whispered, and just admitting it out loud was a sort of freedom. She moved her hands up his arms, letting her fingers explore the muscles hidden beneath the bulky sweater he wore. Her breasts flattened against his chest, her nipples aching for his touch. She shifted slightly, pushing herself against his body, and felt the thick, hard strength of him.

Instantly, her blood boiled. Heat poured through her, swamping her in a sea of need so vast, so deep, there was no escape but through him.

"No more talking." A low, tight moan pushed through his lips as his right hand swept up her spine to the back of her neck. He held her, fingers spearing through her hair, as he lowered his head and took her mouth in a kiss so wild, so fierce, he stole her breath along with any reservations she might have had left.

He parted her lips and let his tongue seduce her. At the first wet, warm stroke, Jade gave herself up to the reality of the moment. If she didn't have him *now,* it'd kill her.

J.T. backed her up against the wall, his hands moving over her body, ripping her jacket off and tossing it aside. As his mouth taunted her, teased her, stoked her inner fire, his fingers moved clumsily, eagerly to the buttons of her pale-yellow silk shirt. She pushed her hands between their bodies to help him, and in seconds, that, too, hit the floor. She didn't care. Didn't care about anything but his touch. His fingers moving now over her skin. His callused palms scraping along her rib cage to cup her breasts, still trapped in her lacy bra. J.T.'s thumb and forefinger tweaked at her nipples, pulling, teasing, and her knees turned to butter. She couldn't stand up, but again he was there, bracing her with the solid strength of his body.

She reached for the hem of his sweater and scooped her hands beneath it, yanking his shirttail free of his khaki slacks. Then she was touching him, feeling the hard, muscled planes of his abdomen, his chest. She ran her palms across his flat nipples and felt him shudder. Power scuttled through her and she gloried in the knowledge that she alone could bring such a big man to his knees.

Sliding up, up, she dragged his sweater and the plain white T-shirt beneath it up and off, tearing it from him and throwing it in a heap atop her own clothes. His upper body bared to her, she ran her fingers over his tanned, well-defined chest, relishing the feel of him.

J.T. reached behind her back, quickly worked open the clasp of her bra, and when she let the lacy straps slide off her shoulders, he cupped her breasts again, scraping his thumbs across the rigid peaks of her nipples. Jade moaned and tipped her head back with a thunk against the oak paneling. When he bent to take first one nipple, then the other into his mouth, she groaned louder, barely able to muffle the sound of the pleasure roaring through her.

His tongue and teeth did magical things to her

body and she trembled with the force of need rippling through her. It had been so long. So terribly long since she'd felt such wonders.

"I need you, baby," he muttered against her skin, and goose bumps raced along her spine at the brush of his breath.

"Yes, J.T. Now. Please now."

He swept one hand down the length of her, grabbed a fistful of her skirt and yanked it up around her waist. Then with his left arm he lifted her, bracing her back against the wall as she wrapped her legs around his middle.

J.T.'s heartbeat thundered in his ears. Somewhere deep inside him there was a small, logical voice whispering that he was nuts. That they were in a palace elevator. That he could lose his job for this. Hell, he could probably be *shot* for this.

And he knew it would be worth it.

He ignored that voice and cupped her center. Even through the fragile silk of her panties, he felt her damp heat waiting for him, and nearly came undone. Her lips were puffy from his kiss. Her nipples poked at his chest, and every time she breathed, they rubbed against him, pushing him onward. As if he needed the encouragement.

Watching her, he kept his gaze locked with hers as he slipped his hand beneath the thin elastic at her upper thigh and slid one finger into her depths. She sighed and arched into his touch, moving against his hand, rocking her hips and pulling him closer, deeper. Which was just where he wanted to be. One finger moved within her, slowly, deeply, and then it was two fingers exploring her inner heat, diving deep, as his thumb worked the tiny bead of flesh at her core.

She trembled in his arms and tightened her legs around him. "Fill me, J.T.," she whispered brokenly. "I need to feel you inside me."

Throat tight, breathing labored, he pulled his hand free, then with a snap, broke the elastic on her panties. She sighed heavily and moved even closer to him, scraping her hands up and down his chest, over his shoulders, to score her fingernails along his back. He felt every touch, every caress, like a branding iron. She marked him, inside and out, staking her claim to his body, even if she didn't want his heart.

But for now, this was enough.

This was all.

Quickly, he freed himself and pushed himself home. Her eyes went wide and glazed with a heat and passion that fed his own until he felt as if he was burning up from within.

Her tight, damp heat surrounded him, welcomed him and held him where he belonged. J.T. rocked his hips and pushed her higher against the wall. Her slim, elegant legs locked around his middle and pulled him tighter, closer. Her head tipped back and he buried his mouth in the curve of her neck. Inhaling her scent, tasting her, he fed on the pulse point hammering against his lips, and gave himself over to the crashing need racing through him.

Again and again he pulled free and slammed home, and each time it was like the first time. The same magic, the same heat, the same need. Building, firing up until he was blind with the urgency of desire and deaf to anything outside the tiny world created in the circle of her arms.

Jade held on for dear life. Her short, trim nails dug into the flesh of his back. Her legs tightened around his hips. Her back ached each time he pushed himself higher, deeper, but she wouldn't—*couldn't*—stop him. It was as if they'd been building to this climax for years. Everything in her life came down to these stolen moments in a stalled elevator, and nothing else in the world mattered but what J.T. was doing to her body.

Blood blistering in her veins, her heartbeat pounding in her ears, she forced herself to keep her eyes open, to keep them locked on J.T.'s. She needed to see him when she reached her peak. And as they climbed, as the tension grew and tightened and coiled within, her breath shortened and the low, familiar tingling erupted.

''J.T.'' She choked out his name.

"That's it, baby," he urged, his hands gripping her hips, his fingers digging into her flesh. "Give it to me, honey. Give it all to me."

She shook her head, swallowed hard. Fighting desperately to keep satisfaction at bay, she muttered, "Not without you. This time, we have to find it together."

"Together," he said with a groan, and leaned in for a kiss. One brief touch of his lips to hers and he reared back, saying, "Now, babe."

She felt his surrender and let go of her own quickly shredding control. As he pulsed within her body, Jade rode the crest of a tidal wave of sensation that took her higher and higher until at last it exploded onto the shore and left her mind and heart and soul splintered in its wake.

Eight

In the basement, two men huddled around a mass of wires spilling from behind the wall. The tall man in uniform standing behind them glowered. "Well?" he demanded. "Can you fix it or not?"

One of the workmen chanced a quick scowl at their observer. "'Course we can fix it. Just take some time, is all."

"How much time?" the soldier asked.

A loud snap, followed by a series of blue-white sparks shooting into the air, interrupted them. When the scent of burned rubber filled the air, the work-man sighed, knowing that a few more insulated wires had just bitten the dust. "Gonna be a while yet."

Disgusted, the soldier stomped off to make his report. Man. He didn't want to be around when J. T. Wainwright finally got out of that elevator. The man would be pissed off enough to shoot first and ask questions later.

"Hope they don't fix this thing anytime soon," J.T. murmured, his voice muffled against the base of her throat. "If the door opened this minute and the king was standing there, I don't think I'd have the strength to care."

Jade clung limply to him, knowing he was absolutely the only thing holding her onto the planet. Without his heavy body pressed to hers, she'd probably float, weightless, right up through the roof of the elevator and out into the open sky.

She'd never experienced anything like that. Not even when she and J.T. were together. Oh, the sex had always been fabulous for them. But today was in a category all by itself.

"I don't think I can move," she said softly.

"No problem. I like you just where you are."

So did she. With his body still locked within hers, she felt...complete, for the first time in three years. For the first time since leaving him.

He lifted his head and smiled at her. "How's your claustrophobia?"

She laughed shortly. "I think I'm cured."

"Just think of me as your friendly neighborhood doctor."

"You give great prescriptions."

He shifted slightly and she moaned, feeling him fill her again as his body thickened.

"I don't think we're finished with your cure."

"There's more?"

"Oh yeah," he said, and brought his mouth down to cover hers. There would always be more, he thought wildly as he took her mouth in a deep, fierce kiss that demanded as much as it took. For her, there would never be enough. She was as she'd always been—the one woman for him. It didn't seem to matter that what they'd once shared was gone.

All that mattered was now.

And right now, she was naked and ready for him.

He moved, rocking his hips, pushing himself deeper, higher within her, until he wouldn't have been surprised to touch her heart. And still he wanted, needed more. He wanted to be so deeply imbedded in her that they would never be able to be separated again. And though his logical mind told him that was impossible, that there were too many obstacles still standing in their way, his heart didn't listen.

And his body didn't care.

As he took her mouth, his tongue exploring, caressing, he slipped one hand between their bodies until he'd found the juncture of her thighs. She gasped into his mouth when his thumb found that one most sensitive spot. Her hips lifted and she opened herself further, inviting him to touch, to stroke.

His fingers worked her and he felt each ripple of excitement, each purr of satisfaction as it hummed through her. She fed him. Fed his need, fed his hunger and fired his blood until he looked at her through a red haze that wouldn't lift. Tearing his mouth from hers, he watched as clouds settled over the sea green of her eyes. Clouds of passion that only he could create. She trembled again in his arms and whimpered desperately as the first of the tremors began to course through her.

"J.T.—J.T.—"

"It's okay, babe," he murmured. "Feel it. Just feel it, Jade. Let me take you there again."

"Only you, J.T." She moved against him, tipped her head back and moaned through gritted teeth as her climax slapped her hard. Her body shook with the force of it, and J.T. indulged himself, watching her eyes glaze, seeing her skin flush, feeling her body contract and pulse.

And as the last of it passed over her, he moved

within her, in a slow, erotic dance that kept her dangling from the precipice. He teased them both with long, languid strokes, feeling every inch of her as she took him inside.

"Again," she told him breathlessly. Wrapping her arms around his shoulders, she hung on and hitched her legs higher around his waist. "Take me again, J.T. Take me even higher."

A low growl erupted from his throat and he gave her what she wanted, what they both wanted. Rocking his body into and out of hers, he took them both on a wild, dizzying ride of sensation, and this time when they fell, he held her closely and cushioned her fall.

Passion was a great equalizer.

Two people wrapped up in each other saw nothing, heard nothing, felt nothing of the outside world. But once that passion was sated, everything came rushing back. Jade closed her eyes briefly and rested her forehead on his shoulder. Despite what they'd just shared, despite the amazing "rightness" of being with J.T., absolutely nothing had really changed.

"You okay?" he whispered, and his voice was a low rumble of sound in her ear.

"Yeah," she said, because it was easier than the truth.

He eased back from her and set her gently onto

her feet. Turning around, Jade bent down to scoop up her blouse. When she straightened, her gaze landed on something she hadn't noticed earlier.

"Oh, God."

"What?" He reached for her, one big hand coming down on her shoulder.

"Is that what I think it is?" she asked, lifting one hand to point.

He followed her gaze. His hand tightened, fingers digging into her shoulder. "Damn."

"I'll take that as a yes," she said, still staring at the security camera tucked discreetly into a corner of the ceiling. Quickly, Jade turned her back on the blasted thing and slipped into her bra, then her blouse, in record time. *Talk about locking the barn door after the horse is halfway to town.* She was worried about getting dressed in front of the camera when she'd already...oh, God.

Her fingers flew over the bone-colored buttons, but she still managed to shoot J.T. a quick look. "Please tell me that if the power to the elevator is out, the power to that camera is out, too."

He scowled thoughtfully as he pulled his T-shirt and sweater down over his head. Why was it that men could get put back together again so quickly? It didn't seem fair.

While she kept her back turned to the glass lens pointed at her, J.T. moved in for a closer look. A minute passed. She knew, because she was counting the seconds.

"It's okay," he said finally. "I mean, we're okay."

"How do you know?"

"Look."

Oh, she didn't want to turn around. Didn't want to look at the stupid camera and think about what exactly could be on a security tape. Would they show the thing at parties?

"Jade, will you just look?"

She whipped around to face him, still keeping her gaze from the camera.

"It's as dead as the elevator," he said. "No red light."

"You're sure?" *Please* be sure.

"I'm sure." He shoved one hand through his hair and, clearly disgusted, said, "But if it had been working, I wouldn't have noticed."

"Me, neither," she pointed out.

"Yeah, but then it's not your job to notice things, is it?"

"Not your fault. We were a little…distracted."

That one simple word hit him like a bullet. He snapped her a look that froze her to the bone. All trace of softness in his face was gone as if it had never been, and in its place, his features took on the hard, distant look of the professional soldier.

"Distracted?" he repeated. "Is that all we were?"

"J.T.—"

"I don't believe this. You're doing it again."

"I'm not *doing* anything."

"Yeah, you are. Hell, you're backing up so fast, I can almost see smoke lifting off your heels."

He could read her better than anyone ever had. Though at the moment, Jade thought, that fact was far from a comfort. She *was* backing up. Distancing herself. For both their sakes.

"This isn't the time to talk—"

"It's never the time, is it, Jade?"

"That's not fair."

"But it's accurate."

"Come on, J.T.—"

He shook his head in silent amazement. "I should have seen this coming."

"You're impossible."

"And you're a liar." He stepped up so close, so fast, he stole her breath and gave her just a half second of worry before she remembered that this was J.T. and he'd kill himself before ever hurting her. "This was more than a distraction. More than just sex, and you damn well know it, Jade."

His eyes blazed with a dark fire that sizzled her skin. She watched a muscle in his jaw twitch and knew he was grinding his back teeth together. Just as he had every time they'd had a fight. She threw things and he ground his teeth into powder. Theirs had been a brief, but colorful, marriage. And even after all these years, he still knew her better than anyone else in the world.

Yes, making love here with him was more. It had been everything. Everything she'd dreamed of and thought about for three long years. Her body was still humming, every nerve ending on red alert, and if he looked the slightest bit interested, she had no doubt that she'd slip right out of her clothes again for another go-round.

And the moment that dangerous thought scuttled through her mind, she pushed it right back out again.

"What do you want me to say?" she demanded, deciding quickly to fight fire with fire. Planting both hands in the center of his chest, she gave a shove, and though it was like trying to move a mountain on a skateboard, she made her point and he quit looming. "What is it you want to hear, J.T.? That I saw stars? Well, I did. That it was great? Of course it was." She paused. "But it doesn't change anything."

"Well, you haven't changed any either, babe."

Prickly now, she snapped, "What's that supposed to mean?"

"You're the same Jade you were three years ago." He moved in again with a quiet, stealthy grace that threatened even as it excited her. "You're not only lying to yourself about us, you're too big a coward to stick around long enough to find out if things could be different."

So much for excitement.

Instinctively, she struck out. Drawing her right foot back, she swung out and kicked him dead in the shin. He winced, but gave no other sign that she'd hurt him. And damn it, she wanted to hurt him as badly as his words had cut at her.

"I'm not a coward."

"You ran away from me—from us—three years ago."

"I left, I didn't run. There's a difference."

"Not much. Just speed."

Exasperated, she demanded, "You think I wanted to leave?"

"Jade, I learned a long time ago you don't do anything you don't want to do."

"You didn't give me a choice."

"There's always a choice, babe."

"And stop calling me babe."

"Changing the subject?" he asked, and though he drawled the words out slowly, casually, his rigid posture and fierce expression told her how he was really feeling. "Getting a little too close to home, am I?"

"You're such a jerk, J.T."

"Name calling." He clucked his tongue at her. "And not very inventive name calling for Ms. Penwyck TV."

She fumed silently and he read her correctly again.

Both eyebrows lifted and he glanced around the floor of the elevator. "Sorry, no dishes for you to pitch at me. But I'm sure if you kick me again, I might forget about the whole coward thing."

"I'm not a coward and you know it. I wasn't afraid of you, J.T."

"No, you were afraid to stay and give our marriage a shot."

"It wouldn't have worked."

"We'll never know, will we?"

"Yeah, we do. You wanted a wife. A mother for your kids."

"Well hell, shoot me now for being an insensitive toad!"

She stalked forward, forcing him to back up in the too-small elevator. Funny, the tiny space didn't seem to be bothering her at all anymore. Poking him in the chest with her index finger, she went on. "You wanted dinner on the table at six. You wanted me to be happy staying at home, and you couldn't understand when I said I wanted more."

"What is so wrong with a man wanting to take care of his wife? His family?"

"Nothing's wrong with it, J.T. What's so wrong about a wife wanting to help out? Take part in her family's future?"

He sucked in a gulp of air, then clamped his lips together. Again she watched him grind his teeth together, and while he was silent, she said, "What's the matter, J.T.? No smart comeback? No witty rejoinder?"

"Fine. I was hardheaded. Stubborn. So were you."

"And butting our heads together was getting us nowhere."

"We might have found a way," he said, and once again his voice was pitched to a low rumble that seemed to scrape along her spine, leaving a trail of goose bumps in its wake.

"And we might have just gone on hurting each other." Jade swallowed hard and took a step back from him. "I didn't want that anymore. For either of us."

J.T. pushed one hand through his hair and took a long moment to get control of a temper that was still too close to the surface. He hadn't meant to open up that old can of worms. But being with her again, feeling her pressed to him…listening to her hushed sighs…he hadn't been able to stop himself.

"This really is just like old times, isn't it?" he

asked with a harsh, brief laugh. "Mind-blowing sex and then a big fight."

"I don't want to fight with you anymore, J.T."

He looked at her then and temper faded to a pang of regret that seemed to ricochet around his chest, leaving him bruised and battered. Reaching out, he stroked his fingertips along her cheek before letting his hand fall back to his side.

Then he bent down, picked up her jacket and held it out to her. She took it, shoving her arms into the sleeves as if she were putting on a suit of armor. But she didn't need it. Old hurts, old pain had risen up between them and stood there, strong as a brick wall.

"Sex was never the problem with us, was it, babe?" he asked, bending down one more time to snatch up her torn panties from the floor. "It was the whole pesky problem of trying to live together that did us in, wasn't it?"

She looked up at him and he saw pain shimmering in her eyes. "I've missed you, J.T."

"Ah, baby, I've missed you, too." He pulled her close for a hug that felt too much like goodbye for him to be able to enjoy it. "That's the hell of it, Jade. I'll always miss you."

Whatever she might have said was lost as the elevator jerked, the motor hummed and they started moving again.

"Looks like they fixed the problem," he said unnecessarily.

Jade grabbed her panties from him and shoved them into her jacket pocket. Smoothing back her hair, she picked up her purse, slung the strap over her shoulder and looked up at J.T. "Do I look okay?"

"Beautiful. As always." But his eyes were shuttered now. The J.T. she'd been with just moments ago was gone again, leaving her with the security expert who didn't like reporters.

And Jade's heart ached.

Nine

When the door slid open, J.T. knew instantly that something was up. The young soldier waiting opposite the elevator looked up at him and snapped to attention.

"Sir. Mr. Vancour would like to see you in the queen's reception room, sir."

"Now?" J.T. took a grip on Jade's upper arm and held her in place when she would have moved away from him.

"Right away, sir." The soldier nodded at Jade. "Ms. Erickson is to come along."

This didn't make sense. J.T. checked his watch

and realized they'd been trapped inside the elevator for a little more than an hour. *Time flies when you're havin' fun.* The queen, like every other royal, spent most of her days keeping to a tight schedule. Though the public no doubt thought of the royal life as an indolent one, there were any number of demands on their time, from charitable events to political meetings. And that wasn't even including the everyday things involved in trying to have a family life.

Taking all of that into account, J.T. knew there was no way the queen would simply be sitting in her reception room waiting for Jade to be released from a stuck elevator. The interview would no doubt be rescheduled. The fact that they were being hurried along to a meeting that wouldn't take place told J.T. that something was definitely up.

"What's happening?" Jade asked as they started off down the richly carpeted hall.

"Not sure," J.T. admitted, but he kept a tight hold on her arm and wasn't entirely certain whether it was for her benefit or his own.

Their steps were muffled and yet seemed to echo along the hall. As she walked beside him, J.T. felt Jade's fascination with the private area of the palace very few people ever saw. Landscape paintings, portraits and the occasional tapestry dotted the cream-colored walls. Chairs and desks lined the hall, antiques of staggering age, yet they looked almost new, a mark of the centuries of care given them here in the palace. Soft pools of ivory light spilled from golden wall sconces and created pale puddles of brightness on the dark-red carpet. Heavy velvet drapes were pulled across windows, keeping the morning sun from damaging fragile fabrics.

The beauty surrounding him was something he took for granted. After three years of duty at the palace, he'd long since ceased to be impressed with the casual elegance of the place. To him, it was simply the royals' home. The home he'd sworn to defend. But now, seeing it through Jade's eyes, J.T. felt a swell of patriotic pride in his country's seat of power.

"It's beautiful," she whispered. He kept her moving, but she turned her head from side to side, taking it all in.

"Uh-huh. It's right down here. Second door."

Jade suddenly stopped beside him and brought him up short.

"What's wrong?"

She swallowed hard and gave him a sheepish look. "I just wanted a second to sort of catch my breath."

"Gonna run?" he asked, and regretted it the minute the words left his mouth. Nothing like beating a dead horse right into the ground.

"No." Jade straightened up and took a calming breath. She'd have a breakdown later. Right now, in front of J.T., she sure as heck wasn't going to appear nervous.

Nervous.

A weak word for what was whipping around inside her at the moment. She'd come to the palace to do an interview with her queen. Scary on its own. Then she'd been trapped in an elevator and had made wild crazy love with her ex-husband. Just your average day.

She glanced at the open doorway. Just beyond the threshold was everything she'd been working for, striving toward for three long years. And now a part of her didn't want to go in. How logical was that?

It had all come down to the next few minutes. Did she have what it took to make it?

She'd reached her point of no return.

"Let's go," he said, and extended his arm in an invitation for her to precede him.

"Right." Lifting her chin, she walked stiffly toward the open doorway on her left and tried not to think about the fact that she was about to meet the queen—while carrying her torn panties in her jacket pocket.

Oh, God.

The reception room, unlike the dimly lit hall, was bright and airy. Sheer linen drapes were pulled aside, allowing sunshine to pour through glistening window panes that overlooked the rose garden. Directly in front of the floor to ceiling windows sat two Queen Ann style chairs with a small round table between them. Atop the table was an ivory porcelain vase filled to bursting with roses of every possible color. Red, yellow, ivory, lavender, they spilled from the vase with an artful ease and filled the room with their sweet scent. A lovely, inlaid writing desk was on the right, its surface dotted with neat stacks of papers. Bookcases lined two of the walls and a marble hearth boasted a cheery and welcome fire.

Beauty surrounded her.

But the queen wasn't there.

Jade buried a sharp stab of disappointment and glanced at the older man walking toward them.

"Ms. Erickson, I'm Franklin Vancour, head of—"

"The RII," she finished for him. "Yes, I know."

He nodded.

Why was the head of palace security waiting to see her?

"Problem?" J.T. asked.

The older man sent him a quick look before turning his gaze back to Jade. "Her Majesty understands why you were unable to keep your appointment, Ms. Erickson—"

"Jade, please."

"Very well. And she's offered to reschedule."

"Thank you. But that doesn't explain what's going on. Why was I brought in here when the interview has been postponed?"

"It'll be easier to show you." With that, he walked across the room to a hand-carved teak cabinet and opened the doors, to reveal a wide-screen television. He pushed the power button.

Instantly, Vince Battle's face appeared on the screen. Holding a microphone, he gave his audience the "sincere" look he was so well known for and started talking. "The young woman, Janine Glass, was abducted this morning...."

Jade gasped and took a step closer. J.T. moved up close behind her.

Janine's photo appeared in the upper left corner of the screen as Battle kept talking.

"So far, the police have no leads in the mysterious disappearance of the woman, who is employed by PEN-TV as an editorial assistant to our own Jade Erickson. Ms. Erickson has recently been the recipient of several threatening letters. We will be covering this story as the investigation continues...."

Vince's face disappeared and an ad for dishwashing soap bounced across the screen. Franklin Vancour shut the set off midjingle and Jade was grateful. Her nerves were suddenly stretched to the breaking point and one bottle of dancing soap might be all that was required to send her screaming down the halls.

"The police would like you to go in and answer a few questions."

"Of course."

Janine. Missing.

Instantly, memories rushed through Jade's mind. Only that morning, Janine had borrowed her coat to make a coffee run. And Jade had been so distracted by her own problems, her own coming interview, she hadn't noticed that Janine had never returned.

"How could I not notice?" she muttered.

"Jade." J.T.'s voice sounded low, reassuring, worried. His hand came down on her shoulder and she instinctively turned toward him, lifting her gaze to his.

"It's my fault," she confessed.

"What are you talking about?"

"Janine. She—" Jade shook her head and pointed at the now dark television "—went out this morning for coffee. I wanted a mocha. She volunteered to go, but it was cold, so she wore my coat. That's why I didn't have it when I came here and—"

"I'll leave you two alone," Franklin said softly, and he left the room. Neither of them paid him the slightest attention.

"So stupid," she continued, moving out from under J.T.'s grasp and striding to the wide windows.

Once there, she stared out at the tranquil beauty below and knew it couldn't help the racing thoughts pushing through her mind. "I forgot all about the mocha. I talked to you and found out about the interview and everything else went right out of my mind. God, I was in such a hurry to get here, I left the station without my coat. Never even thought about it. Should have noticed that Janine didn't come back. Why didn't I *notice?*"

"You didn't do anything wrong, Jade."

She whirled around to face him. Her heart thudding against her rib cage, she fought the wild sense of panic skittering through her. "Of course I did. I was so wrapped up in my own stuff, so full of myself and my precious 'career' that Janine wasn't even a blip on my radar. I just never gave her another thought." Tears shimmered in her eyes and she brushed them away impatiently. "J.T., what kind of person does that make me?"

"Human," he insisted, and closed the distance between them in a few long strides. Grasping her shoulders firmly, he gave her a little shake, more to get her attention than anything else, and said, "Jade, there's no way you could expect this woman would be kidnapped."

"No, but she didn't come back. She should have, but she didn't." Jade lifted a shaky hand and scooped her hair out of her eyes. "She was wearing my coat—'' Her eyes went wide and scared. She sucked in a gulp of air that tasted cold and bitter. ''It was a mistake. God. Janine was a mistake. Whoever took her probably thought they were grabbing *me*.''

His heart twisted in his chest and the pain staggered him. J.T. tightened his grip on her, as if to prove to himself that she was here, with him and safe. *Threatening letters.* The reporter's voice echoed in his mind as he realized that she was right. Jade probably had been the target. It was just bad luck for her assistant that whoever grabbed her had been sucked in by a slight resemblance and a borrowed coat.

''What the hell is going on, Jade? What's this about threatening letters? How long have you been receiving them?''

''A few weeks…'' She shook her head and sighed with a weariness that seemed to come from her soul.

''Weeks? What did the police say about them?'' His voice deepened into the one he used to command troops and get instant acquiescence. ''You *did* go to the police with them?''

''Of course I went,'' she snapped. ''They said it was probably nothing. That this kind of person is usually too cowardly to actually approach the object of his…*affection*.'' She groaned tightly. ''But they were wrong, weren't they?''

He looked down at Jade and everything in him went still as stone. She was in danger. She'd been receiving threatening letters. Some nameless bastard had focused on Jade and only a borrowed coat had kept her safe.

Helplessness, an emotion he rarely experienced, roared to life inside him, and J.T.'s instinctive reaction was to go out and pummel something. There had to be a target for this anger, this frustration at knowing that she'd been in trouble and he hadn't known a thing about it.

Three years ago, he'd promised to love, to honor, to cherish her. Now she was on her own, with a major threat hovering over her. Damn it. How was a man supposed to live with that?

Staring down into her eyes, he saw worry and misery there, and anger churned inside him at the man who'd caused it. "We'll get to the bottom of this. I swear it. He won't bother you again."

"You don't know that."

"Oh yeah, I do." Carefully banked fury crackled inside him, and J.T. vowed silently to do whatever he had to do to make sure she was safe.

"I'm not worried about me, J.T. Janine's gone. How can we fix that?"

"Trust me," he muttered. Dropping one arm around her shoulders, he pulled her close. "Trust me."

* * *

After two hours at the police station, they grabbed a cab and went to Jade's apartment. J.T. refused to leave her side and Jade didn't ask him to. Fear curled in the pit of her stomach and sent out tiny flickers of awareness every few seconds. Her mouth dry, palms damp, she tried to tell herself that everything would work out. But even she didn't believe that.

She stared out the cab window at the passing cars, the pedestrians strolling along busy sidewalks. The sun darted in and out of steel-gray clouds, in between fitful spatters of rain.

Janine was out there…somewhere. Fear curled up in the pit of Jade's stomach and formed a heavy knot that felt as though it was weighing her whole body down. She slumped back against the worn, green vinyl seat, then braced herself as the cabbie took a hard right.

She fell against J.T. and he caught her to him before she could pull away. He felt big, strong…*safe*. And everything in her wanted to fold up against him. Because she wanted it so desperately and didn't have the right to expect that kind of comfort from him, she straightened up.

"How long have you been getting the letters?"

"A few weeks."

"And the video?"

Jade closed her eyes and pictured his face as he'd watched the video tape she'd given to the police only a few days ago. Pure, raw fury had chiseled J.T.'s familiar features into a mask of rage that had convinced more than one of the police officers to lecture J.T. not to take matters into his own hands.

"It was delivered to my apartment just the other day."

"Delivered."

"Yes."

"So this guy—whoever—knows where you live."

She drew in a long, shuddering breath and struggled to fight off a new set of chills snaking along her spine. "Yes."

"You're not staying there alone."

"J.T.—"

"I mean it, Jade." He wrapped both arms around her as if she were trying to escape him.

That so wasn't her plan. She didn't want to be alone any more than he wanted her to be. Alone, she'd have too much time to think. To worry about Janine. To wonder where she herself would be now if she'd gone for her own coffee.

Oh, God.

"Where'm I supposed to go? A hotel?" Where she didn't know anyone? At least at her apartment, she knew her neighbors. There was a doorman she could call on for help.

"Home with me."

She looked up at him and saw that he meant it. Those dark-brown eyes of his locked on to her with an intensity that stole what little breath she had left. Oh, she wanted to go with him so badly she ached with it. She wanted to wrap herself up in his strength and let the world slide away. At least for a while.

But going with him now would only complicate a mess they'd pushed way out of shape with that incident in the elevator. And it wouldn't be an answer to her problem, because it would be only temporary.

"J.T., that wouldn't solve anything."

"Maybe it doesn't have to." He squeezed her tightly, briefly. "Maybe I just need to have you where I know you're safe. I need to *keep* you safe."

And for tonight, she thought, that was enough.

Ten

The vultures were gathered outside her apartment building, despite the now heavy rain.

As the cab pulled up to the curb, dozens of reporters rushed forward. Cameras snapped, flashes popped like tiny lightning bolts, and radio, TV and tape recorder microphones jutted from the crowd like quills on a porcupine.

J.T. tossed a handful of bills at the driver, grabbed Jade's left arm and pushed the cab door open, taking out an overeager reporter. The man stumbled back, wincing, but someone else jumped into the fray, more than willing to take his fallen comrade's prime spot.

"Ms. Erickson, is it true—"

"How do you feel about your assistant—"

"Do you *know* your stalker?"

Rain plopped onto umbrellas and spattered on the sidewalk. Thunder rolled across the sky, drowning out most of the voices. But the rabid eyes, the eager curiosity came through loud and clear.

"Get out of the way," J.T. ordered, half dragging Jade from the cab. Pulling her in close to his side, he strong-armed the foolish few who didn't step aside.

"A comment, Ms. Erickson—"

"The public has a right to know—"

J.T. kept stalking forward and the fury on his face kept most of the reporters at a discreet distance. The doorman hustled forward and opened the door just before they reached it, and once they were inside, the uniformed man tugged it shut again. The noise level dropped abruptly and J.T. gave him a grateful nod.

"Thank you, Charles."

"Of course, Ms. Erickson. If there's anything you need…"

But J.T. was already moving.

"I live on the third floor," Jade muttered, automatically heading for the stairs.

"I know," he said, and countered her move by steering her toward the elevator. He stabbed the up button, and while they waited, looked down at her. Her beautiful eyes looked bruised, shadowed with a kind of misery he'd never seen there before, and his heart ached to ease it.

"Elevator," she mused. "I've lived here two years and I've never used it."

He forced a smile, because she looked as if she could use one. "I figure after today, elevators would be no problem."

"Or the least of my problems." Her eyes closed and she leaned toward him, resting her forehead on his chest. "Gosh, J.T. What are we going to do?"

We. One little word. And it had such an impact.

He glanced over her head toward Charles, who kept his back turned, offering them a bit of privacy. Beyond him, though, were the reporters, clamoring at the glass doors, focusing their cameras, hoping for a good shot that would feed their afternoon news programs—or grace the front page of their newspaper.

Behind J.T. the elevator door slid open with a soft sigh, and he steered her inside, punched the third-floor button and kept her hidden from view with his own body until the door closed again.

Alone, he tipped her chin up with his fingers and looked directly into her eyes. "What we're going to do is keep you safe and wait...while the cops do their job."

"Wait?" She took a half step back, sucked in a greedy gulp of air and let it out again in a shaky rush. "Waiting is the hard part. The I'm-useless-and-twiddling-my-thumbs part."

"It's called patience."

"Never one of my virtues."

"I remember."

The elevator door opened onto her floor and she stepped out, J.T. right behind her. She heard his footsteps and counted each one as a blessing. God, how had she lived for three years without being able to turn to him?

Rifling through her purse, she came up with her key ring and quickly opened all three locks. Locks? Oh, they'd been very useful. But for a borrowed coat, she would have been kidnapped off the street by the man she'd feared would break into her apartment.... Thoughts tumbled over each other in her mind, each demanding her attention, until her head pounded with a pain that nearly blinded her.

Pain, guilt, fear, fury all swirled inside her until she was a bubbling froth of emotions demanding to be released. She stumbled into the room, threw her purse at the sofa and watched as its contents spilled onto the cushions, then rolled to the floor. Burying her face in her hands, she felt the tears come, and couldn't stem them. She hadn't cried in so long it was as though a dam had burst somewhere inside her, and now that the floodgates had opened, there would be no stopping the deluge.

"I can't believe this," she sobbed.

"It wasn't your fault."

"I hate this, J.T."

"I know. I'd like to be out there, doing something. Tracking down the creep who's been sending you letters." He shoved one hand through his hair with a vicious swipe. "Letters. A stalker."

She shivered.

"A career, Jade. This career you wanted so badly is what got you this nutcase."

She shot him a searing look through narrowed eyes. "I don't need this right now, J.T."

"Yeah, I know. But here it is." He scraped one hand across his face and tried to wipe away the image of some faceless creep following Jade, peeping at her from the shadows, threatening her. Scaring her. And it burned him up so much, he just had to say it. "This damn career of yours—putting you out in the spotlight for every head case in the world to see—that's the problem here. If we'd stayed married…"

"What?" she demanded. "Crazies only go after famous people, J.T.? Is that it? Well, turn the news on once in a while and watch more than the sports scores. It's not just celebrities being hounded." Marching up to him, she jabbed her index finger at his chest. "If we'd stayed married and had kids and I'd stayed home just like you wanted me to, I could have picked up a stalker in the grocery store."

"Chances are less likely than—"

"It's all chance, isn't it?" Looking up at him, she silently dared him to argue. "This could have happened anytime, anywhere. Unless you were planning on locking me up in a closet and never letting me out of your sight."

"I never intended anything like that and you damn well know it, Jade."

"How do I know?" she asked, and gave him a shove that didn't make her feel any better when he didn't so much as budge. "All you could talk about was what it would be like—you going off to work, me waiting for you with a kiss when you came home."

"Is that so bad?"

"For some people, no," she darn near shouted, hoping to get through to him, finally. "For me, *yes.*"

He looked down at her and read the fierceness in her eyes. "Fine. Maybe I was stupid and stubborn."

"A breakthrough."

"I didn't mean to chase you off, Jade."

"And I didn't want to run," she muttered, turning away.

"But the point is, you *did*. You left rather than try to make it work."

"Oh, J.T. Do we really have to go through all of this again? Haven't we beaten this dead horse enough?"

The cold knot in his chest dissolved slightly. "Yeah. We have."

"For what it's worth," she said, turning her gaze on him and heating him through, "I'm glad you're here today."

"Good. Get used to me, because I'm not going anywhere."

It almost sounded like a threat. But Jade chose to take it as a promise. One for which she was immensely grateful. No matter what had happened between them three years ago, there wasn't a man alive she felt safer with than J.T.

She didn't know what she would have done without him the last few hours. A deep, bone-chilling cold had settled on her the moment she'd seen Janine's face on the television report, and it hadn't left her since. She couldn't get warm. No matter how long she rubbed her hands or leaned into J.T.'s bulk, the cold remained.

Janine had been kidnapped in *her* place. There was no getting around it. Even the police were convinced that Jade's stalker had finally come out of the woodwork only to make a mistake by grabbing the wrong woman. *She must be so scared. So frightened. And she, unlike Jade, was alone.*

"The police have some leads," J.T. reminded her. "Witnesses who saw a van idling in front of the station."

"Good," she said, and heard her voice break. "Can't be more than a few thousand vans on the island."

"They'll find her."

"In time? Will they find her in time? What is this guy gonna do when he realizes he grabbed the wrong woman?"

"I don't know. And neither do you, so stop imagining the worst."

"The worst is all I can think of, J.T."

She sensed more than heard him come up behind her. And when he turned her in his arms and pulled her close, Jade gave in to the need to cling. She wrapped her arms around his middle and hung on as if he was the last stable point in a whirling universe. And he was.

Everything that had been true and right in her life a few days ago no longer existed. Her comfort zone had been eradicated and there was no way to get it back. She'd fooled herself for three long years. She'd taught herself to believe that she didn't need J.T. Didn't want him. Didn't love him. She'd schooled herself in the belief that a career she'd built and forged for herself out of nothing would be enough to ease the loneliness that crawled through her during the long hours of the night. She'd fought her way nearly to the top of the heap, and now found it didn't mean anything. She'd worked hard, slept little and thought about nothing but her work for so long that only now was she realizing how small and insular her world had become.

Then, with a solid thump, reality had crashed down on her, slamming her back with a force that still staggered her hours later.

Facing those reporters, mirror images of herself, had hit her like a hard fist to the midsection. Their single-minded pursuit of the all-important "story" made them look like a pack of hungry wild dogs. They'd practically slavered over the chance to be the one to get her to speak.

They didn't care that her heart was wounded, that her mind was tortured by what-ifs. They didn't care that she was a real person, with wants and needs and fears. To them, she was only a story. A short piece on the evening news. Two columns in tomorrow's paper.

And Jade was suddenly sickened by the realization that she'd been doing everything in her power to become one of them.

"Oh, J.T.," she muttered thickly, tightening her grip on him until her arms ached nearly as much as her heart. "What was I thinking? How could I be like them? How can I keep on being like them?"

"You're not," he assured her, but she knew he was wrong. Felt it deep inside. And as if he sensed her doubts, he held her back from him so that he could look down into her eyes, convince her with the steely confidence gleaming in his own. "You're not like them, Jade. Yeah, you're a reporter. A good one, though it pains me to admit it." He smiled, and she wished to hell she could smile back. "But you still have a soul. A heart."

"Do I?" She pulled free and shoved both hands through her hair. "I'm not so sure."

"I am."

"How can you be?" She whirled around to challenge him. "I've badgered you for days just to get into the palace."

"Doing your job."

She laughed shortly, a harsh bark of disbelief. "Listen to you! How can you stand there and defend me when you've been doing everything you can to keep me out of the palace?"

"*My* job."

"This all went so wrong," she said, her voice reflecting the confusion blistering her mind. "I don't know how. But somehow, somewhere, I lost it."

"It?"

"My reason," she said, trying to explain something she still didn't quite get. "My reason for doing this. For starting this whole mess in the first place."

"Jade…"

"No." She shook her head fiercely, sending her hair into a flying wedge of auburn. "I have to figure it out. Have to know. Then I'll know how to fix it." She paced, her steps fast and muffled against the plush carpet. "My dad, but that's so politically correct. Blame it on your parents if you screw up your life."

"Jade, stop it."

"But you knew him. You saw how he was with me and my brothers. I wanted to prove to him that I was as good as the guys. Wanted him to look at me and know that I'd done something. Something well." She laughed again and the sound tore at J.T.

He'd watched her try to please her father, but even back then, he'd known it was useless. The old man would never be the kind of father she'd wanted, needed. Not because he didn't love her, but because he just couldn't understand her. Give him a rugby match or a night in a pub, and he was an affable man. Put him in a room with his daughter and he couldn't think of a thing to talk about.

"But it was more than that," she was saying, and J.T. paid attention, following her herky-jerky movements as she walked back and forth across the apartment. "I wanted it for myself." She looked up at him, and even across the short distance he saw guilt and remorse well in her eyes. "I wanted to prove to myself that I could make it to the top. And when I fell in love with you, I couldn't let you get in the way of that."

"I know." Old anger rose up inside him, but he tamped it back down. Hell, she was already being torn in two. He wouldn't add his pain to the burden staggering her. He took a step forward, but she stepped back, maintaining the distance and holding him at bay with one raised hand.

"I loved you, J.T. More than I've ever loved anyone or anything. But you scared the hell out of me."

"What?" Apparently, they were going to beat that dead horse just a little longer.

"You wanted me to be what I don't know how to be. What the heck do I know about being a mother, for God's sake?" She threw her hands wide and let them slap down against her thighs. Her bottom lip trembled, and he watched her deliberately calm herself. "And a wife? I don't remember much about my mother, but I do remember seeing her jumping up and waiting on my father like he was a king. She did what he asked, when he asked, to keep him from shouting, and as far as I know, she never had much of a life herself."

Damn it. Between the two of them, they'd managed to make a mess of things. Of course Jade had left him. Why would she stay when he seemed to be saying and doing all the things her father had?

J.T. had had three long years to regret past mistakes. Now he wondered if she, too, regretted what they'd lost. What they might have had. What they might have found, together.

"I got scared and I ran. From you. From *us*."

"Yeah, well, I made plenty of mistakes, too," he said softly, soothingly. He spoke as if he were trying to coax a frightened wild animal closer. "But it was a long time ago."

"Yeah," she agreed. "But here we are again. And I don't know what to do about that."

He took a step toward her and celebrated internally when she didn't back up. "Maybe we shouldn't worry about it right now."

She shuddered, a violent trembling that started at the top of her head and wracked her body all the way down to her feet. "J.T., I'm so tired of being alone. I—"

He reached her then and pulled her close, his heartbeat pounding in a rhythm to match hers. It killed him to watch such a strong woman torturing herself. To see tears in her eyes. To hear the shaking in her voice that she couldn't quite disguise.

"You're not alone, babe. Not now."

Reaching up, she cupped his face in her hands

and drew him down to her. "Don't leave me, J.T. Stay. Stay with me."

"I'm not goin' anywhere." Hell, he couldn't have been blasted from her side by mortar fire.

He kissed her, pouring his love, his fear, his worry into the act and nearly sending them both toppling to the carpet. But he caught himself in time.

Scooping her up into his arms, he muttered, "Bedroom?"

"There." She pointed and he started walking.

They were barely through the door when J.T. was setting her on her feet and helping her lose the clothes that were now so clearly in their way. Within seconds they were naked on the bed, and he rolled her onto her side, stroking her skin, relishing the feel of her smooth body beneath his hands. His insides lit up like a damn Christmas tree just to be holding her again, touching her again, and when he looked into her eyes, he saw the same desperate pleasure staring back at him.

He took her mouth in a deep, soul-satisfying kiss, and while he teased her lips, her tongue, he stroked her long, lean body until she trembled beneath him. Want and need and pain and love shimmered in the air around them.

Rain slashed at the window panes, beating out a rhythm designed for lovers. Wrapped in the warm cocoon of soft quilts, fresh sheets and the heat of dazzled flesh, they found each other again. Tomorrow or the next day, things might be different. Might change.

But for now, J.T. thought as he slid into her damp heat, this was all that mattered. She was all he'd ever really needed.

She arched into him, breathing his name. Her hands moved down his back, her fingernails scraping at his skin. He bent his head to kiss her as their bodies moved in an ancient dance, and with the first brush of her lips, he knew he'd found his home. The home he'd lost three years ago.

The home he might never find again.

The crashing pleasure of being a part of her and feeling her slip into his soul overwhelmed him, tearing at him. He linked his hands with hers, their fingers entwined, squeezing tightly. He moved and she shifted with him, silently urging him on, wanting him to take her higher and higher.

And when they took the plunge into oblivion, they made the leap together.

Eleven

A few hours later, Jade was settled in J.T.'s apartment on the palace grounds. While she napped, J.T. flopped onto the couch, picked up the television remote and stabbed the power button.

He flicked the channel to PEN-TV, turned the volume down and watched Barracuda Battle do a live report from outside the palace.

"Police are saying very little about today's abduction of Janine Glass, editorial assistant to our own Jade Erickson. Ms. Erickson has been unavailable for comment, but PEN-TV has discovered that she is now staying with Jeremy Wainwright, a high-ranking member of the RII.'' He waved a hand at the closed and locked palace gates behind him. ''Could this mean the palace has information about the abduction of Ms. Glass? For the moment, no one is saying.''

''My God.''

Jade's voice from behind him had J.T. shutting the TV off and tossing the remote onto the table in front of him. ''I didn't know you were awake.''

''Can't sleep.'' She rubbed her hands up and down her arms as if trying to ward off a chill. ''Did you hear him? Now he's making it sound like a national conspiracy.''

J.T. shrugged. ''He's a reporter.''

She looked at him. ''Don't think much of us, do you?''

''Necessary evil, I guess,'' he said.

''Like taxes?''

He gave her a half smile, but Jade hardly noticed. She started pacing, moving about his small living room, running the tips of her fingers across the glass fronts of the framed commendations lining the walls. J.T. just watched her. He'd tried to imagine her here before, but somehow he'd never been able to pull it off. He had one of the smallest of the bachelor quarters, but it suited his needs. If he and Jade had stayed married, they'd be living in one of the huge apartments set aside for high-ranking married officers.

Here, there was a tiny living room, a bedroom, a bath and a closet-size kitchen—not much to show for a man's life. The awards he'd received for doing his job were gathering dust, and when he went to bed at night, he went alone. He had a few close friends, but no family, except for his uncle Mike.

J.T. had expected his life to be different. He'd expected Jade to be in it. And seeing her here now, he tortured himself with thoughts of what might have been. But a few minutes of that were all he could take. Pushing himself up from the couch, he asked, "Want a drink?"

"What?" She half turned and looked at him blankly for a long second or two. "Oh. Okay."

He walked into the kitchen and felt more than heard her follow him. The room got smaller with every passing second and he told himself to ignore it. When this crisis was over, she'd go back to her world and leave him to his.

Reaching into the fridge, he pulled out two bottles of beer, twisted off the caps and handed her one. Then he shut the refrigerator and leaned back against it.

"Thanks." She took a drink, then studied the bottle between her cupped palms as if the label held the secrets of the universe.

J.T. took a couple of long swallows and waited. It didn't take long.

"You know," she said, keeping her gaze fixed on the damn beer bottle, "I never really thought about what it was like for the person on the other end of the story."

"Didn't you?"

"I know now what it's like to be the target of a hundred microphones. To have cameras pointed at you and questions shouted at you until you just want to scream." She set the beer down on the small table and dropped onto one of the two chairs. "What if the police don't catch this guy? What if they never find Janine? Then what?"

J.T. took a drink of his beer. "It's a small island, babe. They'll find her."

"Alive? Unhurt?" She leaned forward and cupped her face in her hands. "Either way, the world will go on, and the only people who'll remember will be me and Janine's family. To everyone else, this is just the latest story. The biggest splash. By next week, there'll be something different. Something fresh. Something new. And nothing will have changed."

But she had.

Jade felt the change right down to her soul. She'd worked so hard, planned so long to get to just this point in her life. Yet what did she have now that she'd reached it? She was suddenly the quarry rather than the reporter. A stalker was after her. Her assistant was missing. She couldn't stay in her own apartment because it wasn't safe.

So what was the point of any of it?

She'd gained a career that was suddenly becoming less and less important as the seconds ticked past—and in the process, she'd lost J.T. Being with him, making love with him again, had only served to remind her of just how much she'd given up when she'd walked out of his life.

And she wasn't sure she'd be able to walk away again. Even if she wanted to.

The next couple of days, J.T. kept Jade close by. Until the police found the man they were looking for, he wanted Jade where he could protect her. And the palace was the one place he knew was secure. No one would be getting to her here.

Of course, living with her again wiped away the misery of the last three lonely years. It all came back, what they'd had together, and he nearly choked with the sweetness of being able to reach out for her in the middle of the night. He held her while she slept, made love with her every chance he got, and called himself all kinds of a fool in his more lucid moments.

He was kidding himself.

He knew damn well this was temporary. Jade would no more stay with him when this was over than she had three years ago. In a crisis situation, people clung together. Once the crisis was past, they drifted apart again.

It tore at him, knowing that soon she'd be gone and his apartment would once again only echo with memories. But at the same time, he told himself it was better this way. Better to lose her outright than to let her all the way back into his heart, only to have her walk out again when things got tough.

Right now, she was torturing herself with guilt and misery over Janine. But when the woman was found, when this was all done and finished, then what? Jade hadn't been the homebody sort three years ago, and that hadn't changed.

"Anything from the police?" Franklin Vancour stepped up behind him as J.T. kept a wary eye on the reporters still camped outside the palace gates.

"Nothing," he said without turning around. "They're still saying they're following leads. But it's been nearly three days."

"Yeah, and the sharks are still circling."

J.T. nodded. Even as he stood there and watched, a couple of reporters tried to interview the gate guards. Naturally, the professional soldiers wouldn't even look at them.

"On the bright side..."

J.T. snorted. "There's a bright side?"

"With every reporter in the country focusing on

your ex-wife and the missing woman, no one's asking questions about the king.''

Well, that wasn't completely true. At this very moment, one reporter was finally getting that interview she'd wanted so badly.

J.T. turned and glanced at the palace. ''*Almost* no one.''

Jade sat stiffly on the edge of a Louis XVI chair and tried not to let her nerves show. Strange, all she'd been thinking about for a week was getting this interview. And now that it was here, it was almost anticlimactic. And so unimportant in the grand scheme of things.

With Janine still missing, Jade could hardly bring herself to care about something as trivial as a royal interview.

She jumped to her feet at the thought and walked toward the wall of windows overlooking the rose garden. From the vase on the table came the combined scents of fresh roses, perfuming the air until it was almost too thick to breathe. The sweetness seemed cloying, and Jade wished to heaven she could just open one of the windows. Take a deep breath. Clear her head. Try to remember why it had been so damned important to get to this one moment in time.

A scuffling sound beyond the nearly closed door

on her right caught her attention, and she moved a little closer. Frowning to herself, she heard a woman speaking, and in the next instant recognized that voice as the queen's.

"I assure you I've investigated the facts myself," the queen was saying—to whom, Jade had no idea. "There is no mistake. My brother was involved with the Black Knights and part of their plan to kidnap my husband."

A moment later, the queen lowered her voice. There was a hushed response and then a second or two of silence. Jade used that extra moment to slip quietly away from the door and retake her seat on the uncomfortable, but beautiful, chair.

Her brain spun with the impact of what she'd overheard. The king? A kidnapping plot? Had his illness all been a ploy to throw reporters and the public off the real story? And what was she supposed to do about this now that she knew?

That decision was postponed when the queen entered the room. Instantly, Jade rose, forced a smile and did a quick dip of her knee. "Your Majesty."

"Good afternoon, Ms. Erickson," the other woman said, as she stepped forward with her hand outstretched. "How lovely that we finally have the opportunity to talk." She checked a slim, gold watch on her left wrist. "I'm afraid I can only spare you five minutes, though. There are a few pressing matters...."

"I understand," Jade said, wondering exactly what those "pressing matters" might be. "And I appreciate your time." She waited until the queen was seated before taking a chair close by—and she couldn't help wishing her cameraman was here. An extra pair of eyes would have been helpful right now.

"Your Majesty, everyone has been concerned with the king's health."

The queen straightened her shoulders, lifted her chin slightly and said, "The king is doing well. He's being cared for by excellent doctors and has received a fine prognosis. There is no reason for concern."

Then why, Jade wondered, was there a flash of worry in the queen's eyes?

"Can you tell me why there's been a virtual blackout of the press? The palace has been refusing to speak with us for weeks now."

"I'm sure you understand that with the king ill, other matters have taken precedence over interviews."

It all sounded completely rational. And yet, as the minutes flew past, Jade was more convinced than ever that there was more to this situation than met the eye. The queen was nervous. Though she was gracious as always, her eyes shifted uneasily, and she seemed to consider every word before she spoke it.

Every instinct Jade possessed demanded that she tell the queen what she'd overheard, and ask for an explanation. But at the same time, she hesitated. Was it right to use something she hadn't been meant to hear? A corner of her brain scoffed at her for that. Of course it wasn't right, but it was what reporters did. They dug for dirt. Poked around until they found a weak spot and then reported it, not caring whether it did further damage or not.

And that, she thought, as the interview wound to its conclusion, was what separated her from the rest of the people in her profession.

She just didn't have that sharklike nature.

The question was…did she want to develop it?

A few minutes later, Jade left the queen's reception room with a notepad filled with quotes and a heart filled with confusion. She'd finally done it. She had the interview she'd been striving for, and now she stood in the empty hall and waited for the feeling of triumph to hit her.

But it didn't come.

This was the one thing she'd wanted, needed, to make the career she'd worked so hard for everything she'd planned it to be. There should be a sense of celebration. Victory. *Something.*

"But no—all I have is more questions." The interview was one thing. What she'd overheard was something else again.

She didn't know what to do. As a reporter, this might be the lead of a lifetime. The queen's own brother involved in a plot against the king? It sounded like a bad eighteenth-century novel. Every reporter clustered around the palace gate would sell their own mother to have this little nugget of information.

Yet Jade's indecision deepened by the minute. Her reporter's instincts told her to find a way to get this news out. To make a call to the station. Or at the very least, get access to a computer and start doing research on the queen's brother, the Black Knights and anything else she could find to add color to an already incredible story.

Walking down the long hall toward the marble stairs leading to the lower reception area, Jade's gaze passed over the portraits lining the walls. Centuries of Penwyck rulers glared down at her as if trying to intimidate her. And damn it, she did feel intimidated. She'd happened onto a private conversation. Did that give her the right to exploit what was obviously a painful family situation?

Her heels smacked against the marble steps as she

took them slowly, thoughtfully. Her right hand resting on the polished walnut banister, she let it glide along the cool, intricately carved wood and tried to imagine herself as one of the royals. They lived here. This was their home. In which she was a guest.

Here behind these walls, they strived to remain a family despite the pressure brought to bear on them by a country that demanded to know their every little secret. Triumphs and tragedies were reported and splashed across newspaper pages. Television cameras caught every misstep. And still there were the small secrets that every family had. Jealousies, heartbreak, celebration. These belonged here, in the palace. These were things that no one had the right to intrude on.

At the bottom of the stairs, Jade paused just long enough to glance out the front windows at the mob of reporters still clustered just beyond the gates. If she stepped outside, the shouts would begin and cameras would flash. Gritting her teeth, she turned her back on the others of her kind and hurried along the passage to the back of the palace, where she could escape into J.T.'s apartment.

''Ma'am.'' One of the soldiers posted in the reception area nodded to her as she passed.

How did they do it? she wondered. How did the royals put up with every little privacy being infringed upon? How did they smile when they wanted to scream?

And how could she be a part of causing the royals even more misery at a time when they surely didn't need it?

A brisk, cold wind lifted Jade's hair and sent a shiver along her spine as she left the palace and hurried across the open yard toward the apartment. Autumn leaves swirled and danced along her path, keeping time with her as she all but ran to the safety and warmth she'd found in J.T.'s place.

Stepping inside, she walked directly to the small, banked fire on the hearth and stood in front of it, letting the heat stretch out long fingers toward her. Then, leaning forward, she rested both hands on the narrow mantel and stared into the small, oval mirror above it.

Cheeks rosy from the wind, hair tousled and eyes troubled, she stared at her reflection and said, "A week ago, you wouldn't have hesitated. You'd have run to the station with this." And it shamed her a little to admit it.

But now there was so much more to consider. She wasn't just a reporter. She was also a citizen of Penwyck. And she certainly didn't want to report anything that might endanger the king's life. But that wasn't all. There was J.T. to consider, too.

She drew back and stared around the room at the

citations for valor and loyalty lining the walls. He'd brought her here to protect her. To care for her. He'd trusted her. And if she used information that she'd picked up because J.T. had given her a safe haven, what would that make her?

The front door opened and J.T. walked in as if Jade thinking about him had conjured him out of thin air. She turned to face him, and read questions in his eyes.

"So you got your interview at last."

"Yeah." And so much more, she thought. Too much more.

One corner of his mouth lifted briefly. "I would have thought you'd be happier. You've been aimed at this for days."

"I know...." Jade pushed one hand through her hair and wondered how to tell him. She had to tell him. Right?

"Get everything you needed?"

"Oh, you could say that." God, maybe she shouldn't say anything, should keep it to herself. But then, not talking to each other was what had broken them up three years ago. Hadn't she learned anything?

He stepped into the room, closing the door behind him. "What's going on, Jade? What aren't you saying?"

Before she could answer, the phone rang, and

Jade wasn't sure if she was grateful or upset by the interruption.

J.T. walked to the phone and snatched up the receiver. "Wainwright."

She moved away from him, not even listening to his half of the conversation. Her head hurt with the thoughts rushing through it, and all she wanted to do now was talk to him about everything. Silently, she willed him to get off the darn phone.

A minute or two later, he hung up, and Jade turned to look at him.

"That was the police."

Police. Good God. What kind of person was she to have forgotten, even for a few minutes, about the woman who'd been kidnapped in her place? Jade took a step closer and held her breath. "Janine?"

"She's safe."

That breath rushed out of her in a sigh of relief.

He shoved his hands into his pockets. "Your stalker turned her loose about two hours ago. Seems she talked her way into his good graces. Convinced him to let her go."

Jade's heartbeat quickened and her knees felt weak. "That's Janine," she said with a shaky smile.

"Thanks to her description of where she was held, the police picked the guy up just a few minutes ago." J.T. stepped up close, dropped both hands on her shoulders and said, "It's over. You're safe."

"Safe." A good word, she thought. A wonderful word.

"Yeah. So, I guess you'll be going back to your own place now. Going home."

Home.

Great idea. The only problem was, she didn't know anymore exactly where home was.

Twelve

Relieved the Glass woman had been released unharmed, and more especially that Jade was no longer in danger, J.T. felt his chest tighten. With the threat to her over, he knew she'd be leaving. Going back to the world she usually lived in. The world that didn't include him. It was time to say goodbye to Jade again. And this time, ''goodbye'' was going to kill him.

Three years ago, his pride had been kicked, and when he'd lost her, he'd told himself that it was for the best. That they hadn't been in tune with each other's wants or needs. He'd tried to ease the misery by telling himself that he'd find someone else.

But he'd learned the hard way that there was no one for him but Jade. That was the simple truth. He wouldn't settle for second-best, and if he couldn't have the woman he loved, then he was looking at another thirty or forty years of loneliness.

And damned if he'd give in to that without a fight.

He wanted to grab her and hold on tight. To avoid doing so, he jammed his hands into his pockets. "Look, Jade," he began.

"J.T., I have to tell you—" she said at the same time.

Confusion and worry glittered in her eyes, and something cold and hard settled in the pit of J.T.'s stomach. No, damn it. He wouldn't give in this time. Not without a fight.

"You're not saying goodbye to me."

"I—" She cocked her head and stared up at him. "What?"

"Goodbye," he repeated, jerking his hands from his pockets to rake viciously through his hair. "We're not doing this again."

"This isn't about goodbye, J.T."

A brief reprieve. Fine. He'd take it. But they would talk about this. He wouldn't watch her walk out of his life again. "Then what?"

She lifted one hand to her mouth, nibbled gently at her thumbnail, then caught herself and stopped.

She gave him a brief glance, then deliberately shifted her gaze to one side.

Jade pulled in a long, deep breath and blew it out in a rush before saying, ''Just before my interview with the queen…I, uh, overheard something at the palace I wasn't supposed to.''

All right. This, he hadn't been expecting. And the fact that she wouldn't look at him wasn't a good sign. Instantly, his security instincts went on full alert. He folded his arms across his chest and waited. ''Go on.''

''The door to the reception room was partially open. The queen was talking to someone.'' She shook her head. ''I couldn't see who. Guess it doesn't really matter *who,* does it? I mean, the point is really what I heard, not who she was talking to and—''

''Jade…''

''Right.'' Another deep breath. ''She was whispering, really, in a hurried sort of way, and she said her brother had been involved in a plot with the Black Knights to kidnap the king.''

There. It was out. Jade felt better already. At least now everything was out in the open.

Then she looked up at him.

His features had turned to stone. But his eyes flashed with a dark fire that reached across the room to singe her. If she didn't know him better, she'd already be backing up. Geez. As a professional soldier, he wouldn't even need a weapon to attack the enemy. Just that glare would be enough.

He tore his gaze from hers, shot a quick glance at the telephone, then turned that steel-melting stare back on her. ''Who've you told? Who'd you call before I came in?''

''Oh, that's very nice.''

''*Who?*''

Insulted, she straightened up and lifted her chin. ''No one.''

''Right.'' He snorted a harsh, mocking laugh as he stalked toward her. ''You expect me to believe that you didn't jump on the biggest story of the year?''

He grabbed the phone, punched in two numbers and practically snarled, ''Security.''

''What're you going to do?'' she demanded. ''Arrest me?''

J.T. spared her another quick, disgusted glance, accompanied by the closest thing to a growl she'd heard in a long time. ''Not hardly. But I am going to alert the palace press corps. Their spin guys can handle whatever you set in motion.''

Stung to her heart, she simply watched him for a long minute. How could he think that of her? After what they'd been to each other, didn't he know her better than that? Didn't he trust her at all? And if he didn't, could there ever be anything between them?

"You really think I'd do that?" She walked around him until she was looking directly into his eyes. What she read in his dark-brown gaze didn't make her feel any better. He stared at her as if she was some sort of bug under a microscope. Fascinating, but just gross enough to demand squishing.

Jade reached out, grabbed the receiver from him and slammed it down into its cradle. "I didn't tell *anyone,*" she said, willing him to believe her.

He looked at her, studying her eyes, but at least he didn't grab the phone again. "Fine. You didn't tell anyone. Yet, you mean."

Fury pounded through J.T. Fury directed at himself, not Jade. He'd known it was risky, having her stay here at the palace with him. There were too many secrets flying around the place. She was bound to stumble across one or two of them. And now that she had, he didn't know what to do about it.

God, what an idiot he was. He'd thought they'd reconnected over the last week. He'd been about to ask her to stay with him. To marry him again.

Idiot.

He glanced at her. Sometime during the last few minutes, she'd snatched up her purse and slung it over her shoulder. Ready to walk.

Perfect.

''I can't believe you don't trust me,'' she said.

''Why the hell should I?'' He waved one hand at her. ''Look at you. You're ready to hustle out the door already. Besides, all you've been talking about is getting a scoop. Now you stumble onto the best-kept secret in the palace and I'm supposed to just trust you not to say anything?''

She took off her purse and threw it onto the sofa behind her. ''Yes.'' She planted both hands on her hips and glared at him.

''Right.'' Damn it, he wanted to trust her. Wanted to believe her.

''I could have reported it,'' she was saying, and threw both hands into the air as if reaching for the reason she hadn't. ''God knows I thought about it. For a couple of seconds there, I imagined making the call, writing the story up and delivering it on camera. But I didn't—couldn't do it.''

''Why?'' He grabbed her upper arms and dragged her close. He studied her eyes, looking for the truth. And he found it. He knew those eyes too well for her to fool him. She hadn't told anyone, but that didn't explain anything. He had to know what was behind the change of heart. Why she'd turned her back on the very thing she'd left him for three years ago. ''Why wouldn't you tell, when this is the one thing that could have cemented the damn career you wanted so badly?''

"Maybe...I've changed."

"Changed. After hustling me for a week trying to get a story."

"Is it so hard to believe?"

"Yeah." It was, though a part of him wanted more than anything to believe.

She actually winced. "Well, that's honest."

"Why?" One word, pushed past the strangled feeling in his throat. He pulled her even closer, until her breasts pushed against his chest. Until every breath he took drew her light flowery scent deep inside him. Until he felt the pounding of her heart and knew the quick, staccato beat matched his own. And still she wasn't close enough. "Why would you change now? What makes today different than a week ago?"

Her breath came fast and hard. Her pulse beat pounded at the base of her throat. J.T. buried the impulse to taste her there, and held his breath when she started talking. "Three years ago, I walked out when things got tough. Rather than stay and fight for us, I ran. But I'm not that girl anymore, J.T. I grew up—a lot of it this past week. And I finally know that there are some things more important than a story. Than my career."

"Like what?" He wanted—needed—to hear what he hoped she was about to say. His fingers tightened.

She yanked free of his grip, gave his chest a shove

that didn't budge him an inch, then snapped, "Like you, you big jerk."

Pacing wildly, Jade muttered to herself as she walked, shaking her head, swinging her arms high and letting them slap against her sides. "Unbelievable. He doesn't get it. He's never gotten it and nothing's changed. I love him, and still he doesn't believe me. I can't do this anymore, I swear. It's ridiculous to keep going over the same territory again and again and getting nowhere."

"Can I say something or is this a private moment?" J.T. asked.

"I wasn't talking to you," she snapped.

"You said you love me."

"I'm a slow learner."

"I love you back."

She stopped dead and glared at him.

"How can you love me and think I'd do something like betray your trust?"

"Three years ago, you walked away from us to have the career that story would have skyrocketed."

"Three years ago, you let me leave." Jade stared at him as she remembered. "Fear drove me then, J.T. Fear of the future, fear of the unknown and my own doubts. Yes, I ran. But you let me go, J.T."

He reached up and rubbed the back of his neck viciously. "I know."

"I thought you didn't care. Certainly not enough

to come after me.'' She shook her head, paying no attention to the tears beginning to course down her cheeks. ''So I couldn't go home again—even when, later, a huge part of me wanted nothing more than that.''

God, the time they'd lost, he thought, and all through stubbornness.

''You're right,'' he said, each word bitten off as if it carried a bitter taste. ''I pushed you away, and when you finally took off, I let you go because my pride was hurt. Hell, Jade, it was all I had left, so I clung to it rather than go chasing after you.''

''And now?'' she asked, needing to know.

''Now, there's only you.'' He looked into her eyes and wondered how he'd survived the last three years without being able to lose himself in those depths. ''Pride doesn't mean squat if I lose you again. There's no way I'm letting you walk away from me this time, Jade.''

That voice of his scraped along her nerve endings and she shivered. But he wasn't finished.

''Three years ago, I let my pride do my thinking.'' He walked across the room toward her, one slow, deliberate step at a time. ''When you left, it damn near killed me, but I didn't want you to know it. So I buried the hurt and told myself to get over it.''

''Did you get over it?''

He shook his head. "Nope." Another long step, and she swore she could almost feel the heat of him drawing closer. "There's no getting over you, Jade."

Her breath caught and her heart gave a quick flutter.

"And I'm through trying."

She inhaled sharply, deeply.

"If you run again, I'll be right on your heels."

"I won't run," she promised, looking up into those dark-brown eyes where she could suddenly see her future shining brightly. "I'm not a kid anymore, J.T. I'm willing to fight for what I want."

"And what do you want, Jade?" He stopped right in front of her, lifted one hand and trailed his fingertips along her jaw. Heat erupted between them.

"You, J.T. It's always been you."

He smiled, a slow, wicked smile that quickened a flame of expectation deep within her. Curling his fingers beneath her chin, he tilted her head back until their gazes were locked.

"Marry me again, Jade."

"When?"

"Now."

She laughed. "Now?"

"Okay," he hedged. "Honeymoon now. Wedding tomorrow."

"Now that sounds like a plan!"

She went up on her toes, wrapped her arms around his neck and hung on. J.T.'s arms came around her and lifted her right off her feet. He bent his head to kiss her, and when his lips came down on hers, Jade gave herself up to the sensation of sliding into the heaven only she and J.T. together could create.

* * * * *

Don't forget to look out for the next exciting stories in the CROWN AND GLORY *series—* Taming the Prince *by Elizabeth Bevarly and* Royally Pregnant *by Barbara McCauley will be on the shelves in November 2003. Only from Silhouette Desire.*

0903/51a

❤ SILHOUETTE®
DESIRE™ 2-IN-1

AVAILABLE FROM 19TH SEPTEMBER 2003

RIDE THE THUNDER Lindsay McKenna

Morgan's Mercenaries

Beautiful Lieutenant Rhona McGregor was *dangerous*, but from their first death-defying flight together, Lieutenant Nolan Galway realised they shared something more powerful than passion...

PLAIN JANE MACALLISTER Joan Elliott Pickart

The Baby Bet: MacAllister's Gifts

Emily MacAllister thought she had no chance with her childhood sweetheart, gorgeous Dr Mark Maxwell—until he melted her doubts with kisses. But how would he react when he discovered her secret?

THE SECRET BABY BOND Cindy Gerard

Dynasties: The Connellys

For two years Michael Paige had been missing, presumed dead. But now his memory had returned—could he convince his wife Tara to give their love another chance?

CINDERELLA'S CONVENIENT HUSBAND
Katherine Garbera

Dynasties: The Connellys

Wealthy lawyer Seth Connelly told himself he'd only married Lynn McCoy to help save her home—but then he kissed her...

THE SECRET PRINCE Kathryn Jensen

Elly Anderson turned Dan Eastwood's orderly existence upside down when she told him he was the son of a king. But the unlikely prince had more important things on his mind—like a certain hazel-eyed siren...

THE RAVEN'S ASSIGNMENT Kasey Michaels

The Coltons

Samantha wished someone had warned her that the Special Agent who would be posing as her boyfriend was handsome Jesse Colton. For his 'pretend' kisses were inflaming very real desires...

SILHOUETTE

WITH A

*Southern
Touch*

HEATHER GRAHAM

DIANA PALMER

JENNIFER BLAKE

Three new stories from international bestselling authors

On sale 19th September 2003

*Available at most branches of WHSmith,
Tesco, Martins, Borders, Eason, Sainsbury's
and all good paperback bookshops.*

1003/009/SH61

Maitland Maternity

Where the luckiest babies are born!

The Detective's Dilemma
by Arlene James

A murder charge… A Maitland suspect!
A detective's temptation…

Beth Maitland is not sure she will be able to trust a
man again. After all, her ex-fiancé is trying to frame
her for murder!

Ty Redstone knows his chief
suspect is one of the Maitland
clan. But Beth is nothing like
the pampered princess he
expects...

Vincent Eckart: Why does
this angry stranger accuse
Jake Maitland of stealing
his wife?

Maitland Maternity

Where the luckiest babies are born!

Formula: Father
by Karen Hughes

A long-ago teenage crush… An unexpected reunion… A baby on the way?

Mitchell Maitland: Since his wife died, Mitch has concentrated solely on his career. So it's a good thing the woman of his dreams walks right into his office…

Darcy Taylor: She's got the looks, the fame and the fortune; the one thing she wants is a child—with or without a husband!

Harrison Smith: Another stranger arrives at the clinic, but why is he asking so many questions about the Maitlands?

0203/SH/LC54

SILHOUETTE®
DESIRE™

is proud to introduce

DYNASTIES:
THE CONNELLYS

**Meet the royal Connellys—wealthy,
powerful and rocked by scandal,
betrayal...and passion!**

TWELVE GLAMOROUS STORIES IN SIX 2-IN-1 VOLUMES: